The Concordia Deception

Space Colony One
Book 1

J.J. GREEN

J.J. GREEN

Copyright © 2018 J.J. Green

All rights reserved.

ISBN- 978-1-913476-00-7

Cover Design: Vivid Covers
Editing: L.M. Lengel

Sign up to my reader group for a free ecopy of
Night of Flames, the prequel to Space Colony One,
and for more free books, discounts on new
releases, Review Crew invitations and other
interesting stuff:

https://jjgreenauthor.com/free-books/

(I won't send spam or pass on your details to a
third party.)

CONTENTS

CHAPTER ONE

Their planet had no name, but they were about to fix that. Cariad sat on the stadium bench, a little bored, waiting for the Leader to get to the point. The votes had been cast. All the woman needed to do was make the announcement of the most popular choice, then the job would be done and everyone could party. But like the natural politician she was, the Leader wasn't going to miss out on an opportunity to speechify.

The colonists had been using the dry scientific designation or calling the planet their "new home" for long enough. It was time to finally settle the question of its name and get on with the colonization. Cariad stifled a yawn, conscious that, sitting in the box with the Leader, she was under everyone's gaze. Ethan caught her eye and winked at her. He had to find the experience as tedious as she did.

The other members of the audience were tiring of the Leader's drawn-out address too. The assembled Gens and Woken were restless and a low chatter had started up. Even the few Guardians present, stiff in their uniforms, appeared to be struggling to maintain their attention.

At last! The Leader was winding down her speech. She was consulting the interface in her podium. She placed a fingertip on the screen. "I am pleased to announce the winning name is—"

A massive explosion roared. Cariad was flung from her seat and through the air. She landed heavily, striking her head against something hard. Debris rained down, trapping her. She heard a crunch that sounded terrifyingly like a bone breaking.

As Cariad lay in the darkness, she found that she couldn't move. Her ears were ringing. Dizzy and faint, she pushed against the wreckage that held her down, but it was too heavy for her to lift. And one of her arms didn't seem to be working.

She was losing consciousness. Cariad fought to remain awake. She had to get out. She mustn't pass out. She mustn't. She hadn't come all that way and broken the hearts of everyone who loved her just to die within weeks of Arrival.

Her confused mind drifted over the events of the day, trying to make sense of what had happened.

***

Cariad's shift was over, but she wanted to check on the final batch of fetuses before she left for the Naming Ceremony down on the surface. She had time to catch the last shuttle planetside if she didn't take too long.

Planetside. Cariad smiled as she repeated the word in her mind. She was picking up the Gens' vernacular. Their English wasn't very different from hers and the rest of the Wokens', despite the one hundred and eighty-four Earth years that separated them, but the Gens had invented new words. She admired their creativity, though other Woken made a point of not adopting the new terminology. Quite a few Woken stubbornly insisted on calling themselves the "previously cryo preserved" or "project scientists" and using the Nova Fortuna Project's official designation for the Gens, referring to them as the Generational Colonists. Still, the Gens' words accurately described the new way of living. Why shouldn't Cariad use them? In time, a blending of Woken and Gen language was inevitable.

She thumbed in the code at the Gestation Room door and exhaled into the breath-reader. The lock gave out its familiar metallic whir and clunk. Cariad eased the heavy door open and stepped into the dim red light of the room.

Fifty thick-walled, transparent gestation bags hung in rows from the ceiling. Some of the bags were motionless, others gently swayed or jiggled as the human infants inside squirmed or kicked, their tiny limbs testing the constraints of the artificial wombs.

As she walked the aisles, Cariad checked the bag monitors. She could have checked the growing babies' vitals on her personal interface, but she liked to get a visual. She liked to see the little faces, slightly distorted by the pressure of the bag and the fluid that surrounded them. The babies would grimace and smile and yawn and suck their thumbs and sometimes even open their unfocused eyes. It was a pleasure to watch their personalities and habits developing even before they were decanted.

Her comm chirped, and she lifted her lapel button to check it. Ethan was calling. She opened the channel.

"Hi," she said. "You're still aboard the ship too? I thought you would have left by now."

"Yeah. I was packing the last of my stuff. I transfer planetside today. Do you want to meet at the shuttle bay?"

"Sure. I'll be there in around twenty minutes."

"I'll meet you at the entrance," said Ethan. "Don't be late. I'm not waiting for you."

Cariad chuckled as she closed the connection. Ethan *would* wait for her even if it meant he might miss the shuttle and the ceremony. That was the kind of person he was.

Taking a final look at the last generation of colonists that would ever be decanted aboard *Nova Fortuna*, Cariad left the Gestation Room, passed through the Fertilization Lab, and walked to the nearest transit bay. Her footsteps echoed faintly in the empty corridors. All but a skeleton crew would remain aboard for the duration of the Naming Ceremony. Afterward, most of the Gens wouldn't return to the ship unless for a special reason.

Cariad, as a Woken, would be able to come and go as the shuttle schedule allowed. For the time being, she was needed aboard ship. She would assist in the final decanting and wrapping things up in the reproductive facilities—shutting everything down properly was essential. If things didn't go according to plan, they might need to start up the processes again.

What she would do after she'd finished her work aboard the Nova Fortuna, Cariad hadn't yet decided. She would think about it during the Naming Ceremony, when she was planetside.

The transit car drew up and Cariad boarded the predictably vacant carriage. Without any more passengers to stop the car, she was whisked six klicks around the outer circumference of *Nova Fortuna's* gigantic spoked wheel in less than ten minutes, arriving at the shuttle bay ahead of Ethan.

A few more last-minute passengers passed her at the entrance while she waited for her friend. By the time she finally spotted him approaching, she was beginning to wonder if she would be the one who would miss the Naming Ceremony due to his delay.

Ethan jogged closer, a large bag over his shoulder.

"Sorry," he panted when he was within speaking distance. "Took longer than I thought."

"That's okay, but we'd better run. The shuttle's leaving in one minute."

They sped through the entrance and across the wide

shuttle bay to the station at the very end, where a single shuttle stood, its ramp down. An attendant appeared as they approached and took Ethan's case to stow it in the hold. The passenger cabin was nearly full but they managed to find two seats together, where they sat and caught their breath as the pilot made the final checks and sealed the hatch.

"I can't believe I almost missed the ceremony," said Ethan when his breathing had returned to normal and the shuttle was maneuvering from the bay. "What would I have told my grandkids when I'm old and gray? I'd have to make something up. *Oh yes, grandpa had a front row seat and saw everything. The Leader forgot her words three times!* No, that's no good. I'd have to think up something more interesting than that."

"Whatever you made up," Cariad replied, "it would likely be more interesting than the actual ceremony. I know it's a momentous occasion and all, but I'm not looking forward to it. Our new Leader's capacity for monotonous droning has to be some kind of record."

"Didn't you know that's an essential requirement?" Ethan asked, straight-faced. "The candidates take a test after nomination. If they can't drone monotonously for at least four hours straight, they're not allowed to stand for election."

Cariad chuckled, but when her laughter subsided she said in a serious tone, "I still think it should be you up there speaking today. It's what most people want. They look up to you. You would make a great Leader."

"Uh, no, I wouldn't. And I don't want that anyway."

Her friend began to look uncomfortable as he always did when she mentioned the issue, so Cariad let it slide. She would only be stating the obvious. The facts were plain: Ethan had saved hundreds of colonists' lives practically single-handed during the First Night Attack, when a sabotage on the planet surface had led to an invasion of predatory native wildlife. Everyone knew of

Ethan's heroism, though the man's role had never been formally acknowledged. The Gens and even some of the Woken would have felt safer with Ethan in charge, but his self-effacement wouldn't allow him to even contemplate the notion.

"It's a pity *you* can't be Leader," said Ethan. "You would be perfect for the job. Plenty of people would vote for you."

"No," Cariad replied. "It's right that none of the Woken can stand for election. We're from the old world. The new world belongs to you Gens. We're only here to help with the transition."

Ethan tutted and shook his head. "But if it weren't for you—"

Cariad placed a hand on his arm. "We've talked about this often enough already. Let's not go over it again, huh?"

He was referring to her actions that terrible night of the attack. She'd figured out how to repel the predatory organisms, but he always overstated her role. It wasn't *her* who nearly died saving others. What was more, Ethan was wrong to think that the Gens would countenance a Woken as Leader. Gens viewed the Woken with a mixture of suspicion, envy, and animosity. The friendship between her and Ethan was rare.

The window covers around the passenger cabin opened and retracted. The shuttle had entered the atmosphere of the planet and would be landing soon. Cariad looked out at the view of the blue and green dome beneath them and wondered what the planet would be called.

They dropped lower. The settlement was coming into view. At the center of the small town of prefabricated houses Cariad could see the open-air stadium. Within it, she could make out the tiny moving figures of what had to be more than two thousand people. The surrounding streets were empty.

Beyond the town, a low jungle of vegetation spread out. The life forms that had attacked the first night's camp had come from among the plants, and now a well-maintained electric fence and regular patrols protected against a reenactment of that terrible event. Cariad recalled the digging of the first cemetery afterward with sorrow.

To one side of the settlement the rest of *Nova Fortuna's* shuttles stood in short, neat rows, and standing out among them was the sleek, shiny shuttle that belonged to the Guardians, the most recent arrivals at the planet. Their ship, *Mistral*, humanity's first faster-than-light starship, hung in orbit above the new world like *Nova Fortuna* did, though Cariad had never been to it. The Guardians hadn't invited any of the Woken or Gens aboard. It was odd, but no one dared to challenge them on the subject.

The shuttle was making its final descent, and Cariad realized that the normally talkative Ethan hadn't spoken for most of the flight. He looked pensive as he gazed out at the rapidly approaching shuttle pad.

"Thinking about your new life?" she asked. "Have you received your allotment yet?"

"I haven't, no," he replied. "That's tomorrow, I think. All the farmers have a meeting in the morning. I expect they'll tell us then."

"Is there any area you'd prefer? The lake area looks pretty."

He shrugged. "I don't really mind what they give me. The work will be the same. Clear the land, plow, sow, reap, just as people always did on Earth."

"You don't seem too happy about it."

The cabin intercom chimed. "We have safely touched down," said the pilot. "Welcome to your new home and new life."

His announcement was met with cheers and applause. For some of the passengers, it was their first time on the planet. If they worked in a profession that had kept them aboard *Nova Fortuna*, they might not have had the opportunity to go down to the surface up until then, but everyone was invited to the Naming Ceremony.

"Disembark from the rear," the pilot instructed them. "That's the cool zone. And no pushing. You have plenty of time to get to the stadium before the ceremony begins."

In spite of his words, the rising excitement in the cabin did result in a mild scuffle among the passengers in their eagerness to leave the vessel. Cariad and Ethan waited for the aisles to clear. When they finally arrived at the bottom of the ramp, a Guardian called Strongquist was waiting for them. He had never told Cariad his first name.

Like all of the Guardians, Strongquist was tall and he wore the Guardian uniform: a tunic of dark gray with thin white stripes, close-fitting and neat from his gaiters to the collar. His hair was drawn into a neat top knot and not a trace of stubble was visible on his face. He nodded in greeting as they reached him.

"Ethan, Cariad," he said. "It's a pleasure to see you again. I was becoming concerned that neither of you would make it to the ceremony. None of the shuttles were posting manifests, and I believe this is the last one."

"You've been waiting for us all morning?" Cariad asked.

"I have, but that's no matter. It's been interesting to meet more colonists. Would you care to accompany me to the stadium?"

Cariad exchanged a subtle look with Ethan. Like her, he seemed uneasy about the invitation but she couldn't think of a reasonable excuse to refuse.

Everyone Cariad had spoken to about the Guardians seemed to share her unease regarding the newcomers.

They had set out in humanity's first faster-than-light starship centuries after *Nova Fortuna* had departed, to warn the colonists of the plot to sabotage the colony, which they had uncovered in historical documents. And they had been the colonists' ultimate saviors during the First Night Attack—no one could deny it.

"I have to collect my luggage," Ethan said, and walked around to the hold.

Strongquist was watching Cariad expectantly, waiting for her reply.

"Sure, we can go together," Cariad said. "Why not?"

Ethan reappeared with his bag. He looked hopefully at Cariad, but his expression fell when it became clear she hadn't thought of a way to turn Strongquist down.

The Guardian positioned himself in the middle as they left the shuttle pad and crossed the open area that led into the settlement. The passage of many feet had already worn paths through the rubbery, moss-like ground cover.

"You must both be very excited to be present at the naming of not only a new world," said Strongquist, "but also humanity's first deep space colony. I know I am. It's quite something, don't you think? The names of every person present today will go down in history."

"Are we still the first, then?" Cariad asked, seizing the opportunity to probe the man for information. The Guardians were always coy giving news about Earth. "No colony ships left after ours? I've always wondered about that."

Strongquist looked like he'd swallowed a fly. "Er, no, none did." He paused. "As you know, the Natural Movement was growing very powerful at the time *Nova Fortuna* departed, and soon afterward it entered its heyday. The Movement's influence continued for centuries." He brightened his tone. "But that's all in the past. Today we should be thinking about the future. And what a future it will be. *Nova Fortuna* colonists will thrive and spread across the planet. I'm sure of it. And, who knows, one day another colony ship may launch and humanity will take a step farther out into the galaxy."

"That's a long way ahead," Ethan said, "if we ever get there. I'll be happy if we make the first target of sustainability within five years. That's what we should be thinking about right now. Not what our descendants might achieve. We'll all be dust by then."

"Practical as always, Ethan," said Strongquist. "I can always rely on you to bring me back down to Earth, or rather, I wonder what name I should use? What did you vote for?" He addressed the question to Cariad.

"I didn't vote."

"You didn't?" said Strongquist. "Why not?"

"A: I really don't mind what we call it, and B: I don't feel I have the right."

"Don't have the right?" Strongquist's tone was surprised. He turned to Ethan. "What about you? Don't tell me you didn't vote either."

"I did vote. I voted for—"

A klaxon sounded within the stadium. The ceremony was about to begin.

"Hurry up," Strongquist said. "We don't want to miss the opening." He grabbed Cariad's and Ethan's upper arms and urged them forward.

Cariad squirmed free. "Ease up. It won't matter if we miss the first few minutes. The Leader's going to speak for at least an hour before she gets to the point."

"Oh yes, it will matter," Strongquist said. "Come on. They're all waiting for you."

Cariad and Ethan stopped in their tracks. Strongquist turned to face them then swept his arm in a wide curve, inviting them to lead the way. They shared a worried look. There seemed no other option than to do as Strongquist suggested, however. Together, the three went through the wide, open doors that led into the stadium.

A deafening cheer erupted from the assembled Gens, Woken, and Guardians. It was so loud and unexpected, Cariad's first impulse was to run, but Strongquist was right behind her, lightly pushing her forward.

Along with her friend, she walked into the open area at the center of the stadium, entirely bemused. She stood side by side with Ethan in the strong afternoon sunlight while the crowd cheered and clapped.

Eventually, the noise began to die down, and the Leader brought it down further by beginning to speak over the broadcast system. At first, Cariad couldn't make out what she was saying, but as the cheering subsided, it became clear that the woman was speaking about the First Night Attack, and the roles Cariad and Ethan had played in it.

At last, it all began to make sense to Cariad. The Leader was well aware that the Gens would rather have had Ethan in her position. By orchestrating this show of appreciation, she was piggybacking onto his popularity with the Gens and, to a lesser extent, Cariad's with the Woken. The Leader would be perceived as gracious, humble, and generous. She was an intelligent woman.

There was nothing Cariad could do except smile and bow to show her thanks.

The Leader talked on for an excruciating ten minutes or so, while Cariad and Ethan stood and waited for it all to be over. When she had finally, mercifully, finished, and the audience had given another round of applause, they walked toward the seats that had been reserved for them in the Leader's box.

As they reached the stadium steps, the Leader started up on another monologue that promised to eventually lead to the announcement of the winning vote on the name for their new home. A drop of water hit Cariad on the nose. She paused at the bottom of the steps and held out a hand, looking up at the sky. Gray clouds had blown in. The stadium roof would protect the seating areas, but it looked like the ceremony would be slightly spoiled by rain.

Cariad began to climb the stairs but she halted when she realized that Ethan wasn't with her. He was standing at the edge of the field, holding out both his hands and looking up in wonder at the sky. Gasps and murmurs were running through the crowd, and people were leaving their seats to run down to the stadium's center.

Rain had begun to fall, softening the light and dimming the view. *Of course.* Cariad laughed. It was the first time any of the Gens had experienced rainfall. They had grown up aboard the *Nova Fortuna*, where water had been a precious commodity. Each drop had been carefully dispensed, collected, and recycled. No Gen had ever felt the rain on his or her face or listened to a thunderstorm at night.

Nearly all of the two thousand Gens were wandering about the field, getting wet, grinning and whooping. Some of them were dancing. Cariad watched, her heart warmed by their enjoyment of the simple pleasure. Their lives on the new planet promised to be an amazing adventure.

CHAPTER TWO

Something was lying across Ethan's chest, pinning him down, and it was covering his face so all he could see was darkness. His legs were free, however, and he didn't seem to be badly hurt. The only discomfort he could feel was an ache where he'd hit his head and the crushing pressure on his rib cage.

All around him he heard sobs, screams, and cries of pain. The memory of where he was flashed back into his mind. There had been an explosion. He began to struggle. He had to find Cariad. She could be seriously hurt. He had to help the others.

Ethan pushed against the thing that was trapping him. He felt it shift, and he pushed harder, grimacing with the effort. The object seemed to move toward his head, so he concentrated his efforts in that direction. The pressure on his chest began to lift. He pushed harder, drew up his knees, and used his legs to drag himself downward.

As he eased out from the confined space, his chin caught on a metal corner. He twisted his head away, but he couldn't escape the sharp edge. He was panting with the effort of holding up the object that pressed down on him, but he couldn't let it go. If he did that, the corner would descend into his neck.

There was nothing for it. If he wanted to get out, he would have to drag his face down the corner. He took a deep breath, pushed upward as hard as he could. He lifted the trapping object another few millimeters and pulled with his legs. As he slid along, the corner bit into his skin at his jawline. He winced. A cut tore up his face to his cheekbone. He gasped in pain, and paused for a fraction of a second before making a final effort. The corner grazed his eyelashes and hit his eyebrow. It drew another cut up to his forehead.

With a yell of effort, Ethan pulled himself the last few centimeters. He was finally free.

His left eye immediately filled with blood from his cut and more ran down his face and dripped from his chin. He sat up and looked about him with his one good eye, wiping the blood from the other. Before the explosion, he'd been seated in the Leader's box roughly midway up the tiers in the audience section of the stadium. Now, he was nearly at ground level, and the seating were in broken chaos all around him. A section of seating had fallen onto him, and he realized he was lucky to have survived relatively unscathed.

People from other parts of the stadium were running over to help. Some were already lifting the wreckage left by the explosion, desperately trying to free trapped victims.

Still wiping the blood from his eye, Ethan leapt up. He had to find Cariad. She'd been sitting right next to him. She couldn't be far away. He scanned around and spotted a single white shoe. It was one of hers. Then he caught another glimpse of white deep within the jumbled remains of the seating. It was the other shoe. He was sure of it.

He scrambled over shards of broken plastic and metal and put his face to the opening where the shoe was visible. He could see a glimpse of her ankle.

"Cariad," he shouted. He repeated her name twice but heard no reply, and the shoe didn't move. He pulled at the ruins that were trapping her, removing the mangled pieces one by one.

"Have you found her?"

Strongquist had appeared by Ethan's side.

"Let me help you," the Guardian said.

Ethan briefly wondered where the man had been seated that had allowed him to survive the blast. He'd thought Strongquist had been sitting close by. But his fears about Cariad soon drove the thought from his mind. He could now see her leg. Blood was spattered across her dark skin.

Together, Ethan and Strongquist removed the remaining pieces that covered her. They each grabbed one end of a large section of seating and lifted it up. Beneath it, Cariad lay on her side. One of her legs was folded up but looked okay. However, one of her arms was bent at an unnatural angle. Her clothes were stained red and her eyes were closed.

Ethan crouched down beside her and gently touched her shoulder. "Cariad."

"Don't move her," said Strongquist. "Her neck could be broken. Is she breathing?"

Ethan watched her chest, which rose and fell slowly. "Yes."

"Good. Stay with her. If she wakes up, keep her still and calm. I'll be back as soon as I can."

The Guardian stepped down over the seating and ran across the stadium field, heading for the exit that led to the shuttles.

Other Guardians were working through the wreckage from the explosion, but many Gens were standing around in shock, simply watching what was going on or wandering around the muddy ground aimlessly. Rain had begun to fall again, but this time hardly anyone seemed to notice. Ethan remained with Cariad, his hand resting lightly on her shoulder. The fact that she didn't seem to be bleeding heavily reassured him a little, but he wished that she would wake up.

What had caused the explosion? There was nothing explosive in the stadium. No fuels or anything under pressure. It had to be a bomb. But who would want to set off a bomb during the Naming Ceremony? He didn't have to think hard to answer that question: it had to be a member of the Natural Movement.

After the sabotage on the First Night Attack, the perpetrator had been caught and executed, but now it was clear there was more than one of them. Natural Movement fanatics were living among the colonists, determined to prevent the expansion of humanity into the galaxy.

Memories of Lauren flooded his mind. He would never forget seeing her fall beneath one of the predatory native life forms on that fateful night. He couldn't erase the image of her remains from his memory. His feelings of loss were still raw. He couldn't face losing someone else he cared about.

Cariad's eyes were moving beneath their lids. They flickered, then opened wide in alarm. She tried to rise, but Ethan gently restrained her. "You're okay, but don't move. You've been hurt. Strongquist has gone for help. You're going to be all right, but you need to stay still."

She seemed to hear him because she stopped struggling. Her gaze sought out his. When their eyes met, he managed a small smile to try to reassure her, but he imagined the sight of his bloody face was less than reassuring. She struggled to speak but he couldn't make out the words.

"Don't worry. We'll get you fixed up. Everything's going to be okay."

Strongquist was back. He'd brought two of his Guardian buddies with him, and they were carrying a board somewhat like a stretcher and other items Ethan didn't recognize. A flitter hovered nearby, and more were spread across the field. Guardians were loading the injured onto them.

Ethan stepped back to give Strongquist and the other Guardians room to work. First, they pressed a jet injector against Cariad's neck. Immediately, her body relaxed and her eyes half closed. Then they carefully turned her onto her back while one of them held her head, keeping her as straight as was possible on the uneven surface. They slipped some kind of collar around her head, neck, and back, and lifted her onto the board.

Ethan helped the Guardians carry Cariad down to the flitter.

"Where are you taking her?" he asked.

"Back to the *Nova Fortuna*," Strongquist replied. "Her back or neck may be broken, and the settlement's medical facilities aren't yet equipped to deal with an injury of that severity. We can assist with her treatment best aboard the ship."

Ethan wanted to go with Cariad but he also wanted to remain to help search for more survivors. The scene was still in chaos. The Leader was nowhere to be seen and no one else seemed to be organizing a response to the emergency.

"Can you please send me word as soon as you know anything about her condition?" he asked Strongquist.

"Of course," the Guardian replied. "Don't forget to have someone check you over and fix that cut."

With those words, the Guardians sped away on the flitter with Cariad. Ethan turned to face the pandemonium. He went to the nearest group of bystanders who seemed to have been frozen to immobility and gave them instructions for organizing others who were also doing nothing, forming them into rescue teams. He also told them to find people with medical experience and send them to him.

They needed to divide the destroyed portion of seating into sections, and they could take it apart, piece by piece, shoring up unstable parts. They would find everyone who was trapped.

Ethan realized he was still using only one eye because the other was covered in blood. He took off his shirt and ripped off the sleeve. He tried to wipe the blood from his eye so that he could see out of it, but it was too crusted up. Instead, he cleaned his face as well as he could, though his cut continued to weep fresh blood, then he tied his shirt sleeve over his eye.

A Gen ran up to him, panting. "I'm a medic. Where should I go first?"

It was going to be a long, hard, heart-breaking afternoon.

***

When Ethan woke up the next morning, the whole left side of his face ached. He reached up to touch the gauze that covered his cut and the healing gel the settlement doctor had applied. He seemed to be the first to wake in the dorm of twenty men. Instinctively, he lifted his lapel to check his comm button for messages, then remembered that he was planetside and that the comm network wasn't set up yet.

The colonists were using stationary interfaces. Ethan remembered there was one in the dorm, and that the previous evening when he'd checked it, there hadn't been any messages from Strongquist about Cariad. He got up and weaved through the sleeping men to check the screen by the door again. A message had finally come. It was short. Strongquist only stated that Cariad had a broken arm and was heavily concussed. She should make a full recovery in three or four days.

Ethan exhaled in relief and rested his forehead on the wall beside the screen. After a moment, he lifted his head again to check the general news. Fourteen people had died in the explosion: thirteen Gens, including the

Leader, and one Woken. Thirty-two people had been injured. No one had claimed responsibility for the bomb but the Natural Movement was suspected. The Guardians were investigating the cause of the explosion and hoped to find evidence that would lead them to the bomber.

The Guardians were coming to their rescue again. Ethan couldn't imagine what they would do without these people and their advanced technology. He hoped they would catch the saboteurs before they killed or hurt anyone else.

The other men in the dorm had begun to stir and wake. Like Ethan, they were all farmers, or rather, they were all going to be farmers. Ethan hadn't had much success at school so not many professions in the colony were open to him. Farming had seemed as good as anything else when the time came to choose but he'd never been content with his decision. He would be confined to his farm for most of the time. His crops would need a watchful eye to guard against pests, disease, drought, and any of the other hundreds of things that could affect them. On the other hand, the colony needed farmers. The colonists were relying on the success of the farms to survive. If their buildings leaked or their children didn't learn much from their teachers, they could live with it, but they couldn't live without food.

Yet for as long as he could remember, from when he'd first understood the purpose for which he'd been born, Ethan had always nurtured a secret desire to explore the new planet. But that role was strictly off the cards for Gens. Aside from venturing a day or two from the main settlement, exploring wasn't allowed. The new settlers couldn't afford to risk their lives on adventures, and that stricture had been cemented after the First Night Attack. Even with all the supplies they had brought, the colony wouldn't last longer than five or six years if they couldn't make it self-sustaining, and that would require the utmost effort from everyone.

"That's a beauty," remarked another farmer, Misha, as he passed Ethan on his way to the shower room, gesturing toward Ethan's face. Ethan followed the man to check his reflection in a mirror and found a black and purple bloom surrounding his eye.

"What's happening about the explosion at the stadium?" Misha asked Ethan as he went into a shower. "Did you read anything about it?"

"The Guardians cordoned off the area once everyone was out. They're going through the wreckage, looking for evidence. I haven't heard any more than that."

Ethan stripped, stepped into another cubicle, and began to wash, carefully avoiding exposing the gel on his face to water. His skin crawled at the thought that whoever had planted the bomb was living among them, pretending to be the same as everyone else—working toward the colony's success while secretly plotting its downfall. The saboteur could even be Misha. Ethan shook the thought from his head. Suspecting everyone he knew of belonging to the Natural Movement would be playing right into the terrorists' hands.

The only bright side to the situation was the fact that the bomber hadn't been able to create a bomb large enough to take out the entire stadium. If they truly wanted to destroy the colony, that would have been the obvious move. For the moment, it seemed that they didn't have access to materials to make larger or more deadly explosives.

Ethan turned off the shower and turned on the blower, which quickly dried him. After dressing, he ate breakfast before joining the rest of the farmers in the meeting room. The organizer waiting for them wasted little time in getting down to business.

"I'm sure what's at the front of all your minds is the explosion at the stadium yesterday. I don't have any news on that front, but what I will say is this, whatever the murderer who planted that bomb might think, we're not going to let him or her stop us from building a thriving community here. We're going to carry on as normal and not let the bastards stop us. Right?"

"Damned right," said a voice, and the other farmers joined in with loud agreements.

"Let's get on with it then," said the organizer. "I have the land allotments here." He swiped across a pad and a holo of the settlement and the land surrounding it appeared above the desk. Lines cut through the 3D map, marking the boundaries of the sectioned land. At the center of each block, a name floated.

The farmers got up out of their seats and went closer to see their allocations. Some asked to swap with others. Ethan had remained in his seat for a while as the rest crowded around the holo, but he decided he might as well find out where he was going to spend the rest of his life.

He went over and saw that he'd been allocated a squarish block that bordered a lake about seven klicks from town. *Well,* he thought, *Cariad said it was pretty.*

CHAPTER THREE

Cariad woke. She opened her eyes and gasped. Where was she? Then she remembered. She was aboard the *Nova Fortuna*. She'd made it. She'd survived cryo.

The lights above her were bright, blindingly bright, and she closed her eyes against the pain. She tried to move, but her limbs were leaden. She recalled her last memory: she'd thanked the medical team and said goodbye before they put her to sleep. It had been a weird, sad parting after they had cared for her so well while preparing her to be frozen. By the time she woke up—if she woke up—they would all be long dead and buried.

The team, too, had been emotional, though for some that had probably been because they believed they were euthanizing her. Yet despite the risks, despite the unproven process of cryonically preserving people for centuries, the chance had been too good for Cariad to miss. Public opposition to the launching of the *Nova Fortuna* had grown to fever pitch in the years and months leading up to her departure. If she hadn't taken the opportunity offered to her, another wasn't likely within her lifetime. As a world-class geneticist involved in the *Nova Fortuna* Project, her application had been almost a formality.

Cariad had familiarized herself with the cryonic preservation process and knew it should work, yet she almost couldn't believe she'd survived. After she'd been made unconscious, her blood was replaced with a non-aqueous, oxygenated solution that would not expand when frozen. External to her body, the solution was circulated and gradually cooled until she grew so cold that her breathing ceased and her heart stopped beating. She was lowered into a frozen slush that suspended her, avoiding pressure sores from the pooling circulatory fluid. Her body was cooled still further until she was entirely frozen.

To all intents and purposes, Cariad had died. Along with one hundred and ninety-nine other scientists—some old friends, some strangers—she was sealed within an individual chamber aboard *Nova Fortuna* weeks before the ship left. She hadn't witnessed the ship's departure from Earth's orbit, never seen the protesting mobs, never met the First Generation men and women who embarked aboard her, knowing that they would end their lives in deep space—people who would create and raise children who, before they were even conceived, were sentenced to share the same fate.

Now, the long journey was over. Cariad had survived.

She opened her eyes again and felt the smooth sheet beneath her. She moved her fingers and toes, and tried again to lift an arm. She winced as a bolt of pain came from the limb. Something seemed to have gone wrong with it. She tried to raise her head, and she winced again. She had the mother of all headaches.

To one side, out of her field of vision, a door opened, and she heard footsteps.

"Glad to see you're finally coming around," a voice said. "How are you feeling? You took quite a knock.

How's your arm?"

Cariad squinted and managed to bring into focus a man in red scrubs who looked familiar. She remembered he was one of the infirmary medics. She thought his name was Alasdair.

She became very confused. How did she know the medic's name? He was six or seven generations in the future from her perspective. And what did he mean about a knock?

Alasdair was fiddling with the infuser that was attached to her inside elbow.

"How are the others doing?" Cariad asked him, hoping that the rest of the scientists in cryo had also been successfully revived.

Alasdair replied, "There were fourteen deaths and thirty-two injuries, I'm sorry to say. You've been out around fifty hours, in case you were wondering."

"What?"

"Dr. Montfort put you into a coma to give your brain a chance to heal from the concussion. We withdrew the sedative a couple of hours ago."

"What?"

Now completely confused, Cariad tried to sit up to get a better look at her surroundings. Maybe she would see something that would help her make sense of what the medic was saying.

Alasdair laid a hand on her shoulder. "Just relax for now. You'll be feeling the effects of the sedative a little longer. I've told the doctor you're awake. He'll be along in a moment. After he's checked you over, maybe you can sit up and have something to drink."

Now that he mentioned it, Cariad realized her mouth and throat were dry and sore, as if she'd been sleeping with her mouth open. She gave up trying to move and instead tried to make sense of what was happening.

A memory of an explosion flashed into her mind. She recalled flying through the air, then nothing. She worked back from the explosion. She'd been in a stadium and resigning herself to listen to a boring speech, then... Everything came flooding back. She'd woken from cryo two years previously. *Nova Fortuna* had reached her destination. They'd held the Arrival Day celebration, and then after that there had been the First Night Attack.

She gasped again.

"Is something wrong?" Alasdair asked. "Are you in pain?"

"Ethan," Cariad said. "Is he okay?"

Alasdair smiled. "He's fine. He pulled you from the wreckage, in fact."

As Cariad closed her eyes, Dr. Montfort arrived.

After examining her, the doctor said Cariad could sit up. He wanted her to stay in the infirmary another night just in case of any after effects of her concussion. Her broken arm would be mended in about a week, the doctor said, and then she could return to work.

The doctor paused. "A Guardian, Strongquist, has been asking about you. He wants to speak to you about the explosion. I can put him off another few hours if you don't feel up to talking to him, but... "

"No, it's fine. I'll speak to him."

Cariad had a burning desire to find out who or what was responsible for the disaster. Though she had her reservations about Strongquist, she was willing to put them aside for the sake of a successful investigation.

The Guardian came into her room. "I'm glad to see you looking so well, Cariad."

"Thanks. I'm lucky I didn't suffer worse injuries, but you're even luckier than me. You weren't hurt?"

"I have to confess I'm not one for long speeches. When the explosion occurred, I'd already left the box."

"Good timing."

"Yes, indeed. I'm sorry for being so impatient to see you, but I want to catch the person or people who did this, and quickly, before they do something else."

Cariad sat up higher in bed. "Then it was a bomb?"

"I'm afraid so."

"The Natural Movement again?"

"We can't think of any other explanation."

Cariad digested the information dejectedly. After the Guardians had apprehended and executed the person who was responsible for the First Night, Attack she'd thought the threat to the colony was over. She hadn't imagined there might be more than one Natural Movement fanatic among them.

"Whoever is masterminding these attacks, it could be a Woken or a Gen," Strongquist said.

"It's more likely to be a Gen, don't you think?" asked Cariad. "Though I hate the idea. The saboteur who you executed was a Gen."

"We aren't ruling out the possibility that it's a Woken. The First Night Attack saboteur could have been persuaded to turn off the electric fence by someone else. She said she'd acted alone but she must have been lying of course. Conversely, she could have been a member of covert Gen cult that's existed since the *Nova Fortuna* departed Earth."

"You mean like a secret tradition, passed down the generations?" Cariad asked.

"Exactly."

"If that's the case, we could be talking about more than one or two people. We could be talking about tens or hundreds."

"I doubt that it's hundreds. If there were so many, it would be difficult to keep their beliefs secret, and they wouldn't be confined to single, small acts. They could do something much bigger and more damaging. A few hundred can overwhelm a couple of thousand with a little planning."

"But if the Natural Movement followers are Gens, there could still be quite a few of them."

"We already know there's more than one," said Strongquist.

Cariad sighed. The colonization was going to be hard enough without contending with a secret, subversive faction. "We seem to have lost track somewhere. How can I help with the investigation?"

"Ah, yes. I'm enlisting the help of the Woken because you may remember things from the development of the project that aren't recorded. We've analyzed the bomb residues at the site, but the chemicals used aren't particularly difficult to acquire. Anyone could have stolen small amounts while we were bringing down the supplies. So we turned our search to historical records, hoping to discover Natural Movement affiliations among the Woken or the original Gens. But we haven't uncovered anything useful so far.

"Then it occurred to me that the project scientists are living, talking historical documents. People like you, Cariad, are a source of knowledge and memories... I've been asking all the Woken to watch the news recordings from the protests and read the reports and other documents. Perhaps you'll see a face or read a name that you recognize and you may make a connection. Would you mind going over a few things and telling me of anything that strikes you as possibly relevant, however insignificant or tangential it might seem?"

"Yes, I can do that."

"Thank you."

"And when I'm up and around again, in a day or so according Montfort, I'll help with the investigation too."

Strongquist looked less happy about this proposal. "Thank you for offering, but I don't think there's any need—"

"We can't continue to rely on you Guardians all the time. We aren't babies, and now that my work with the actual babies of the colony is coming to an end, I'll be able to devote some time to ensuring justice for those who were murdered." She gave Strongquist a fixed smile.

The Guardian didn't buckle under her gaze, but he seemed to concede the fight was one he wasn't going to win. "As you wish. I've sent links to the relevant files to your account." He rose to leave.

"I want to thank you for everything you and your colleagues have done for the colony, Strongquist," Cariad said. "It isn't that I don't appreciate it. I just think the sooner we learn to stand on our own two feet the better."

"I understand perfectly." He nodded to her and left.

Cariad reached toward a nearby interface with her broken arm, winced, and swapped to her other arm. She pulled the screen in front of her and swiped it open. Strongquist's list was at the top of a string of messages from friends wishing her well. She opened the first of the Guardian's links, a vidnews report.

She checked the date. It was the day that the *Nova Fortuna* had begun its maneuvers to break free of Earth orbit: the official departure date. By that time, she had already been frozen in slush for several weeks, and she'd missed the response of Earth's population to the ship's departure.

It was quite the reaction. The recording showed massive crowds in the world's capitals and major cities. Protesting millions surged through the streets of Beijing, Washington, Moscow, London, Cape Town, Nairobi, New York, Sydney, Mumbai, and Buenos Aires. Cariad's hand rose to her mouth as she watched the rioting, fires, water cannons, and the effects of exploding nerve gas canisters.

Leading up to the final preparations, she'd been aware of the growing popularity of the Natural Movement, but she'd been working around the clock and hadn't followed current affairs closely. She also hadn't been very interested in them. As a scientist, the objections of the movement toward deep space colonization had been hard for her to understand. She'd rarely bothered to think about them. She would have better understood an angry reaction to the fact that so few were able to come along.

She wondered what she was supposed to be looking for. Did Strongquist expect she might see something significant in the mobs? After witnessing a particularly violent confrontation, she gave a shudder and silent thanks that the *Nova Fortuna* had been built in space and out of the reach of the Natural Movement followers. Otherwise, they would probably have tried to blow up the ship.

The next link led to an interview with some Natural Movement leaders at the scene of a protest. Cariad leaned closer to the screen. Here was something that might yield useful information. She scanned the faces in the background. Prominent figures in the movement wouldn't have been so foolish as to try to infiltrate the colonization project, but individuals who were behind the scenes had a greater degree of anonymity. Yet no one looked even remotely familiar.

The scene shifted to a studio interview, and Cariad's heart skipped a beat. What had moved her wasn't any of the debaters, who were Natural Movement leaders and politicians with global influence, but the large image that hung behind them. It was a portrait of a scientist. Though she looked younger in the photograph than she'd been when Cariad knew her, she recognized the woman right away. It was Dr. Crowley: the first victim of the First Night Attack.

Poor Meredith, Cariad thought. Always so warm-hearted, so ready to see the good in others, so trusting. Too trusting, as it turned out.

Cariad had warned her friend that the *Nova Fortuna* Project's ambition of creating a society free of violence was too lofty; that human aggression was innate and not a product of social conditioning. Cariad would have given anything to have been wrong if it meant having her friend back again.

Sickened by the brutality of the riot scenes and the anger from the Natural Movement leaders, Cariad closed the recording and opened another of Strongquist's links. It was a list of members of the subversive society. The Guardian had attached a note explaining that in Cariad's time, the document hadn't been in the possession of the authorities. It was a secret list uncovered by historians centuries later. He wanted to know if any of the names meant anything to her.

Cariad scanned the list. The names numbered in the thousands. For several minutes, she saw nothing familiar. She yawned. After the surge of adrenaline when she woke up, her injuries were catching up with her.

She drank some water to help her stay awake, but her mind drifted. One hundred and eighty-four years had passed while she'd been in cryonic suspension, and she had only lived through two since being revived. Yet her time on Earth seemed a lifetime away.

Memories that she'd successfully suppressed up until then began to surface. Memories of saying goodbye to her parents and two sisters, knowing that she would never see them again; recollections of the sharp sting of guilt at seeing the stoicism on her family's faces. Their parting was something she would never forget. Effectively, in her terms and theirs, they had all died at that moment.

Cariad wiped away a tear with the heel of her hand. Her family, friends, and acquaintances had all passed away while she'd been in suspension, and by the time she was revived they were turned to dust and long forgotten by anyone but her. She swallowed, trying to force down the emotions that threatened to overwhelm her, but it was no use. For the first time since she'd been brought back to life two years previously, she gave in to the grief and sorrow she had been denying for so long.

It was some time before the edge of her feelings softened and she returned to browsing the lists of Natural Movement members. Almost immediately, a name caught her eye: Frederick Aparicio. She frowned. She wasn't sure why the name was familiar. She couldn't place him in her memories of everyone she'd known on Earth. Yet she knew the name, unless her mind was playing tricks on her.

Cariad opened her personal files of vids, mails, and images from her previous life. She rarely dared to look at them, but perhaps because she'd vented her feelings, viewing the files it didn't upset her as much as she'd feared. In fact, it gave her pleasure to remember all the people she'd left behind and read their messages.

She searched all the files for the name Frederick Aparicio but turned up a blank. As she was puzzling at the problem, deep in concentration, a new mail arrived. It was from Ethan.

Heard you're awake and feeling better. Glad to hear it! I'm going to see my farm tomorrow. Do you want to come along?

CHAPTER FOUR

Ethan waited for Cariad in the lot outside the shuttle station. A regular shuttle schedule of three arrivals and departures per day had begun to run, and Cariad had mailed to say she would be on the noon arrival. Ethan had watched the shuttle fly in, appearing from out of the sky as if by magic. To him, *Nova Fortuna* was now no more than a stationary point of light at night, and in the daytime the starship was entirely invisible.

As a Gen, he now required special permission to return to his old home. The new rule rankled, especially because Woken like Cariad could come and go as they pleased. The reason given was that their roles were mostly scientific and performed aboard the starship, while Ethan's and the other Gens' jobs were confined to the settlement or nearby. Yet the delineation was clear: the Woken had freedom to travel to and from the ship and the Gens did not.

The planetside dwellers had quietly pushed back by taking control of the flitters. *Nova Fortuna* had brought thirty of the fusion-powered land vehicles to the new world. They would run for around three years before their energy ran out, but the technology to refuel or replace them was unlikely to have been developed by that time. Consequently, the Manual stated that they must only be used when absolutely necessary, such as for emergencies and transportation of materials or equipment that was too heavy to be moved by any other method.

The Gens had taken it upon themselves to bend the parameters of what constituted absolutely necessary by routinely using the flitters on trips outside the settlement. Massive road making machines were already crawling slowly across the landscape, and solar-powered electric vehicles to run on them were being assembled from kits, but neither were ready yet. The Gens were nervous about venturing into the wild with no means of escape from predatory organisms other than their own two feet. Also, they had quickly picked up on how convenient it was to ride a flitter. After growing up aboard a starship that had transit cars, they weren't used to walking long distances.

Ethan was looking forward to taking Cariad for a ride. He'd packed some food so they wouldn't have to return to the settlement to eat when they got hungry. Shuttle passengers began to emerge from the station exit, and Ethan smiled as he saw Cariad's familiar figure among them.

She spotted him seated in the flitter and waved. "Hi," she said as she approached. "How did you get permission to take one of these? I thought we were hiking out there. I wore my walking boots."

"All the farmers can use them."

Cariad's eyebrows lifted. "All the farmers? But aren't you supposed to be—?"

"Saving them for emergencies? Strictly speaking yes, but the roads out to the farms aren't ready yet, so that doesn't make a lot of sense, does it? Besides, though the creatures from the First Night Attack are nocturnal, there's always a chance something else might take an interest."

"Have any other life forms been spotted?" Cariad asked.

"No, not yet. Xenozoologists have combed the farming districts but they didn't find anything. We still put up electric fences around the farms just in case."

Cariad opened the flitter door and climbed in. There were seats for six, but the rear four were folded down to make room for a load. The flitter briefly dipped under the extra weight then returned to its former elevation.

"What happened to your face?" Cariad asked when she saw Ethan close up.

He'd forgotten they hadn't seen each other since the bombing at the stadium. She probably didn't remember being rescued.

"Just an injury from the explosion," he said. "The scar's fading now. How's your arm?"

"It's getting better. The doctor said just another few days and it'll be good as new."

"Good. And your head?"

"It's fine. I heard you pulled me out of the wreckage. I wanted to thank you."

"You don't have to thank me. Anyone would have done it."

"I know, but... " She drifted to silence, apparently unsure how to frame what she wanted to say. "It's good to be planetside again. I always feel a little claustrophobic aboard ship, even though it's as big as a small town. There's something weird about living in an entirely artificial environment. I've never quite gotten used to it."

"I never minded it. Living aboard *Nova Fortuna* was all I knew before we came here. In fact, the first time I came planetside, I was nervous. The idea that I could walk for years and never walk in the same place twice freaked me out a little, though I wouldn't admit it to Lauren."

Cariad's expression turned sympathetic, but the atmosphere between them became awkward. Ethan wondered if it was the first time he had mentioned Lauren to her. He couldn't remember. Thinking about Lauren since she passed was almost unbearably painful. Maybe he hadn't talked about her up until then.

"It's about time we left," he said, starting up the flitter. He reversed the machine from the curb and pulled out of the lot. Once they were through the gate in the electric fence, he set the flitter to automatic.

Cariad gave a surprised *Oh*, as it left the road and set off through the fern-like trees that surrounded the settlement.

Ethan chuckled. "We're heading directly to my land. The flitter doesn't pay much attention to roads. When you're floating thirty centimeters high, there's no need for them."

"I would have thought there might be *some* need for them," Cariad replied.

"Nope. Flitters go around anything that's in the way, moving or not, or they rise up and pass over. They're very safe. You never went in a flitter back on Earth?"

"I didn't. They were new technology. Anti-gravity propulsion was newly invented and the engineers had barely run all the safety tests on the flitters before they were loaded onto the *Nova Fortuna*. I hadn't even seen one in real life, only in vids. The FTL starship engine scientists had hopes that a-grav would lead them to a breakthrough, but that hadn't come by the time we left."

"This is really your first time in a flitter?" A wave of delight washed over Ethan. He'd always seen Cariad as smarter and more experienced than he was. He'd never thought he would be more accomplished at something than her.

"What are you thinking?" Cariad asked.

"Nothing much. Why?"

"You have a goofy grin on your face."

"I do?"

"You do. Is it because I said it was my first time in a flitter?"

"No... well, yeah, actually. I didn't think I'd ever have more experience in something than a Woken. You always seem to know everything and have done everything. Being around you makes most of us Gens feel stupid, if I'm honest."

Cariad's expression fell, and she turned to look out at the passing landscape.

"Is something wrong?" Ethan asked. "I didn't mean anything by what I said. I was only talking about what it's like being a Gen. I wasn't criticizing you."

When Cariad turned back to Ethan, her face remained sad. "Is that how you see me? Is that what I am to you? A Woken?"

"No. I didn't mean it like that. I was only talking generally. I don't think of you as just another Woken. You're a friend, Cariad. A good friend."

She appeared to feel a little happier. "You're a friend, too. I don't think of you as a Gen." She returned her gaze to outside the flitter. They had left the forested area that surrounded the settlement and were traveling across an open plain, where rubbery ground cover grew waist high. The flitter adjusted its height accordingly. On the horizon lay the thin blue line of the lake that bordered Ethan's land.

Ethan stole another look at Cariad. She seemed to have gotten over the downturn in her mood. He recalled her as he had first seen her in the First Night Attack, carrying a flaming brand in each hand. The image had remained in his mind and probably would forever, the light of the torches flickering across her face.

"I think I can see it," she said. "That's the lake, right? Is your land on this side of it?"

"Yes, it is. Of all the allotments, mine is farthest away

from town. The land on the other side of the lake doesn't belong to anyone yet."

"Yes it does. It belongs to everyone," Cariad said with a smile.

"Yeah, that's right. Until it's allocated."

"Maybe if your farm does well, they'll give you the land on the other side too. You could have a huge place."

"I guess so."

"Wouldn't you like that?"

The only person Ethan had told about his dissatisfaction with the idea of becoming a farmer was Dr. Crowley, his other Woken friend who had also died that terrible first night of the settlement. The profession allocation system was intended to be flexible within the parameters set by academic achievement, strengths, and temperament., but refusing to choose any of the positions offered to you upon high school graduation was seen to be anti-social. Ethan was only going to be a farmer because he didn't really have a choice. In another life, on Earth, he thought he would have done something quite different.

"Ethan?" Cariad said.

He realized he hadn't replied to her question. "Sorry. No, I'm not very enthusiastic about farming. If I could choose, I'd rather explore this new world. I used to read a lot when I was a kid, mostly when I should have been doing my homework. I read about the great explorers of the eighteenth and nineteenth centuries on Earth. They would go places where no human had ever set foot, like the southern pole. Then fewer and fewer of those places existed. Later on, people went to the summits of the highest mountains and deep into ocean trenches. They went to all the places on Earth where it used to be too hard for people to survive. They went to the Moon. Then by the twenty-second century, there wasn't even anywhere on the colonized Solar planets that someone hadn't explored.

"But this place... we know hardly anything about it. We only have information from probes to tell us what's here, and we found out on the first night that information isn't reliable. We need to know more about this planet. *I* want to find out more. But I'm going to be stuck here digging the ground and growing crops for the rest of my life." His voice had risen. He paused and gave a wry smile. "Sorry. I guess I needed to vent."

They had passed through the gate in the fence surrounding the farming district. Cariad looked out at the approaching lake in silence for a little while, then she said, "You know, you're right. What if there's some other menace out there that could destroy us? We need to know about it. If we don't, how can we defend ourselves? We're lucky that the electric fence seems to keep everything dangerous out of the settlement. What would we do if there's a life form that isn't affected by electricity? We need people like you to find out what the dangers are."

"I'd love to do that," Ethan said, "but I don't see anyone giving the order any time soon." A new Leader had yet to be elected after the bombing, and a date for a new Naming Ceremony hadn't been set. "We're nearly there. We might already be on my land, in fact. It isn't easy to tell without boundary markers, but I think this is it."

The lake stretched all the way to the horizon. If he had to be a farmer, Ethan counted himself lucky to have such a useful resource on his doorstep, though water channels to other farms would cut cross his land. Maybe the lake contained something like fish too, something that humans could eat.

He stopped the flitter a short distance from the shore, and they got out. The ground was spongy, and their footsteps left imprints as they walked across it, wading through the vegetation. Together, they went toward the wide stretch of water.

"I wanted to ask you," Ethan said, "is this place very different from Earth?"

Cariad thought a while before replying. "On the surface it isn't. The sky's blue, the vegetation is green, there are mountains and oceans, rocks and soil, and the gravity is nearly the same. That was the main reason this planet was chosen. Once the colony arrived, it would be on its own. No request for help would even reach Earth until it was way too late. So we couldn't commit to a colonization except on a world where conditions were as near perfect as possible.

"But now that I'm here, it's different in so many ways. The plants look weird. The air smells funny. The sunlight isn't quite right, and of course the night sky is totally different. And the sounds... Can you hear anything?"

"Only the noise of the wind."

"On Earth, if we were out in the countryside we would hear birds and insects, maybe frogs and other animals depending on the time of day. This planet is almost entirely silent. If I don't think about it, I don't notice, but I guess I feel it on another level. Nothing is quite right about this place. I don't dislike it, but I seem to always be a little bit aware that I'm someplace different."

A warm, humid breeze came toward them from across the lake. The sun was still high. Its rays blazed across the water surface, creating a silver sheen on the smooth expanse.

They reached the lake's edge where the vegetation gave way to black sand. Lazy ripples lapped at the shore. They were alone in the alien landscape.

"What do you think?" Ethan asked.

"It's beautiful."

CHAPTER FIVE

Cariad squatted down next to a gestation bag. Five trainee midwives stood in a half circle behind her. So far, none of them had volunteered to assist with a decanting.

"There really isn't anything to be frightened of, you know," she said. "Isn't anyone willing to try? I know it seems scary, but the chances of losing a baby are vanishingly small. I don't think a single one has been lost at the decanting stage aboard *Nova Fortuna*. It's much safer than natural childbirth. We can see if the baby's stuck or the umbilicus is wrapped around its neck or it's passed meconium. We don't have to rely on instruments to tell us what's happening. Things are going to be a lot harder planetside when you're assisting women giving birth."

She shut her eyes. That was exactly the last thing she should have said to reassure these young women and men. When she opened her eyes, however, a fresh-faced man had raised his hand.

"Great," Cariad said. "Step over here."

"Oh, I er," the man mumbled. "I just wanted to ask a question."

Deflated, Cariad said, "Shoot."

"I was wondering why you don't just open up the bags and take the babies out. Wouldn't that be a lot easier and safer?"

"Good question! So, it might seem easier to do it that way, but when the babies are squeezed out through the decanting channel the action forces mucus out of their lungs and respiratory tract, and that helps them breathe. There might be other benefits too. We try to mimic nature as much as possible because sometimes we can only guess why humans evolved to reproduce the way we do.

"That's why we play the audio of a pregnant woman's heartbeat to the babies from the embryo stage onward. Perhaps without it or other sounds their hearing won't develop normally. We can't be sure because it wouldn't be ethical to conduct an experiment to find out, so we take the precaution of exposing them to noise. On the other hand, we've removed the known risks of natural childbirth like a too-narrow birth canal."

"Is natural childbirth really risky?" asked a frightened-eyed young woman.

Cariad couldn't tell if the trainee was asking in a professional or personal capacity. "It's riski-*er*. I can't deny it. Unfortunately, the reproductive technology that's served us on *Nova Fortuna* won't last forever. It's already wearing out. We need to move reproduction planetside and increase the birth rate, which means that after this final decanting it's down to you Gens to do things the old-fashioned way. But the settlement hospital will be equipped with birthing facilities of the best quality, and those facilities are going to be staffed with the best midwives, right?"

It was an unfortunate consequence of the impersonal replenishing of the Gen population that none of them had any experience of natural pregnancies or births. Up until then, reproductive technicians had been responsible for creating and gestating the project's new babies. Working alongside the settlement doctors, the people she was training would be dealing with soon-to-be-new mothers who would probably be frightened if not terrified. What was more, the women might also have a higher risk of complications due to six generations without selective forces reducing the number of mothers who couldn't give birth naturally from passing on their genes. Still, Cariad tried to give the students her most encouraging smile.

It seemed to do the trick. The man who had first asked a question stepped forward and said, "I'll try."

"Fantastic," Cariad replied and waved him forward. "Come over here. You saw what I did, right? Make sure you have everything ready before you open the channel. I'm going to watch but I won't intervene unless I see you need some help, okay?"

When she had studied human reproductive biology, Cariad only assisted with a decanting a few times in preparation for taking her finals. The students were supposed to experience the nitty gritty of practical applications of their subject. Later on, as a reproductive geneticist, she hadn't been expected to actually decant babies. That was a job for technicians. Since being revived from cryonic suspension, however, she'd enjoyed bringing the little squirming, mewling infants into the world. She hoped she could pass on that enjoyment to these women and men.

Cariad moved out of the trainee's way as he prepared the receiving dish and checked the emergency equipment. The baby he was about to decant was one of the less active ones. The female infant hung upside down in her gestation bag, her eyes closed, a serene expression on her tiny face. She was entirely unaware that her life was about to begin.

The man paused and half-turned toward Cariad for reassurance.

"Good," she said. "You're ready to go."

He stood and activated the decant function on the panel at the top of the bag. Pulsations began to ripple the surface and fluid dripped from the channel as, slowly, it opened. The student squatted as Cariad had and held his hands beneath the channel. It was a precaution in case a malfunction or a particularly wriggly infant caused the opening to suddenly burst wide.

Now that he'd found the courage to try, the man was doing well. Time wore on, and the gestation bag pushed the baby girl into the narrow, flexible channel at its base. The trainee was beginning to look uncomfortable, probably due to squatting for so long.

"You can kneel if you want," Cariad told him. "It won't be long now."

The receiving dish gurgled as the fluid dripping from the bag was drained away.

The trainee midwives leaned closer. The moment of decanting was approaching. The baby was packed into a ball, her small, chubby arms wrapped up high around her chest. She gave a wriggle and the channel opened wider, spilling a gush of fluid into the dish below.

"Nearly there," Cariad said to the kneeling student. "Get ready."

He held his gloved hands beneath the baby's crowning head. Pink liquid soaked his hands and wrists. The top of the baby's head appeared. Centimeter by centimeter the head emerged from the channel. A small face came next, its eyes still closed. Then a tiny fist showed up, followed by one round shoulder, then another.

As the baby slid out of the collapsed bag, the man carefully took the weight of her head and body. He gently lay her down in the receiving dish. She took her first breath and a pink color suffused her skin.

"Great job," Cariad said. "Do you remember the

procedure for the placenta?"

The trainee nodded without turning around, apparently unable to take his eyes from the baby, who gently waved her arms and legs, testing out her new-found freedom. When the placenta was ejected from the gestation bag, he cut the umbilicus and picked up the baby to swaddle her. He turned around, his face wreathed in a beaming smile. "I did it!"

"You certainly did," Cariad said. "Do you want to take her to the nursery?"

The baby was breathing well and didn't seem to have any problems, but the duty doctor would check her over thoroughly.

"Sure," the trainee replied. "Do you think they'll let me name her?"

Cariad chuckled. "Maybe. It won't hurt to ask."

Like a proud new father, the man carried the newborn out of the Gestation Room. Cariad turned to the waiting students. "Who's next?"

***

By the end of the session each trainee had taken a turn at decanting a newborn, and Cariad finished the training a little less worried than she'd been when it started. Though the Gens still had a long way to go to restart natural human reproduction on a scale that would increase the population, it seemed they could at least lose some of their fear of it. Dr. Montfort would take over the students' preparation for the real thing with natural childbirth vids and whatever else he had in mind.

When the last of the trainees had left, she took a final look at the Gestation Room with its empty gestation bags, some still dripping. For nearly two centuries, the reproductive facilities had served the *Nova Fortuna* Project well, steadily maintaining a heterogeneous gene pool of two thousand individuals. But its days were finally over.

Cleaning up the room and putting everything into storage could wait until tomorrow, Cariad decided. It had been a long day. She turned off the heartbeat soundtrack and the lights and went out.

As she left, she bumped into a colleague who was on her way in. It was Anahi—an agricultural geneticist and a Woken. When she had been revived from cryo, the process had left her blind. As *Nova Fortuna* wasn't equipped with the technology to grow new eyes and optic nerves, she relied on a vision aid. A black strip of light-sensitive material wrapped around her head and connected with her brain through a contact at the back.

The crueler Gens, who weren't used to seeing anyone who deviated from standard human physiology, would make jokes about Anahi within her hearing. They said she had eyes in the back of her head and made other crass comments. In fact, she did have better than normal peripheral vision and could probably see a wider color range. However, Cariad imagined she would probably rather have had real eyes. She'd gotten to know Anahi over the years they'd both been working on the project preparations and though the older woman was likable enough, Cariad had found her to be rather brittle and not the type to take the Gens' teasing in good humor. She must have barely met the psychological standard to be allowed to join the cryo preserved contingent of the colonists.

"Did the decanting go well?" Anahi asked.

"Yes, thanks. Fifty new babies added to the gene pool. All healthy and normal."

"Good. So that's it, then. The last Gens conceived and gestated artificially."

"I hope so," Cariad said. "They're on their own for the time being, anyway. In the case of a disaster, we can always open up the shop again."

"Yes, you still have plenty of frozen eggs and sperm, haven't you?" said Anahi, "And how's the equipment?

Has it held up well? I remember you were concerned about that."

"It's still functioning adequately. I haven't encountered any failures. Have you in your section?"

"No, but everything's looking all tired and old. Rather like me." Anahi smiled.

Cariad said, "I'm sure you have quite a few more decades in you."

"Thanks, but I wasn't fishing for compliments. I wanted to speak to you about something."

"What's that?"

"Well, first of all, I want to say the Generational Colonists have done well in getting this far. Do you remember when we were placed in cryo? We thought we might never be revived, or that only one or two ancient descendants of the First Generation would be alive at the journey's end. Yet we woke up, and it was like everything had worked like clockwork. Two thousand healthy colonists with a good genetic mix. They'd followed the Manual almost to the letter in that regard." She paused. "But... "

Cariad raised her eyebrows.

"There's something... I'm not sure how to put it," Anahi went on. "The Generational Colonists... they're kind of child-like. They don't have much initiative, much get-up-and-go, if you know what I mean. They just mindlessly do things without really thinking."

"I'm not sure I understand you."

"Okay. For example, the First Night Attack. I wasn't there—thank goodness—but I heard almost everyone ran around like panicked sheep. I heard that if it wasn't for you, they would have all been killed."

"You heard wrong, then. I helped, yes, but it was Ethan—a Gen—who came up trumps. And it was terrifying. I was pretty close to running around like a panicked sheep myself. I don't think you'd be so quick to criticize if you'd been there." Cariad wondered where

Anahi was heading. Something was clearly bugging her.

"Still... "

Cariad said nothing, waiting for the other woman to speak her mind.

Anahi said, "Cariad, I think we need to resume the revival process. We need more project scientists to oversee the colonization. If we don't, we risk the entire project failing and all of us dying."

"But, Anahi... "

"What?"

"Do I have to spell it out? You're one of the last people I would expect to make that suggestion. You lost your sight, others lost the use of limbs, and some are permanently brain damaged. Some didn't even make it. Everyone we revive is at risk of serious complications or death. And anyway, I don't agree with you about the Gens. They're entirely capable of making a go of this. They might seem naive and inexperienced to us, but they were raised in an unnatural environment. They can adapt and meet the challenges. I'm sure of it. They're human, the same as us. Adapting is what we do best."

Anahi seemed pensive. "I thought you might say that."

"Huh? You thought I might say what?"

"Never mind. Look. I get it that you like the Generational Colonists. I like them too. I just don't think they're equipped for this job we've set them. And it isn't their fault. It's our fault for imagining they ever could be. Hell, it would be hard enough to colonize an alien planet even for us—people experienced at living in a planetary environment and not coddled all our lives aboard a starship.

"I think it's time to admit that we were wrong. It would have been better to freeze two thousand individuals and maintain a much smaller population of living crew, just enough to maintain the ship and begin the reviving process. That can't be helped now, but we do need more project scientists. We need their skills and their experience of living in a natural environment."

"Seriously?" Cariad asked. "Do you really think we need more people from Earth so badly we should risk their lives?"

"If we don't wake them up, they're as good as dead. Don't you think we should give them a chance of life?"

"We need more time to understand what went wrong —"

"How long do you think we should wait? The last I heard, we'd made hardly any progress in understanding why some of us were revived with no problems and others died. For all we know, it could be something to do with the way we were frozen, and there isn't anything we can do about that now. At least this way the question is decided, one way or another."

Cariad hesitated to answer. She felt that Anahi was wrong, but she couldn't put her finger on why. Her arguments seemed rational. If only the cryo organizers had thought to provide for this eventuality. All the Woken had written wills about life-saving measures if something went wrong during revival, but no one had been asked to state *whether* they should be revived. That was a given.

"Think about it," Anahi said. "I'm going to speak to some of the others and see if we can come to a consensus. I'm not going to do anything if most of us think it's too risky. But personally speaking, I'd rather be blind and living and breathing than lying frozen in sludge, possibly forever. And the Generational Colonists need more of us if the colonization is to stand a chance of succeeding."

"But even if the other Woken agree," Cariad said, "you have to get the permission of the Leader to restart the revival process."

"There is no Leader, and even if there were, why do we need his or her permission? We were the ones who organized the *Nova Fortuna* project. We were there at the beginning and we know what's needed for it to succeed. The others only exist because of us."

Cariad was becoming increasingly annoyed at Anahi's reasoning and opinions and it clearly showed on her face. The woman touched her arm in a conciliatory manner. "I just want to help the Gens, as you call them, for their benefit and our own. And to do that, we need strength in numbers. We need more of *us*."

Cariad was about to reply when Strongquist appeared. She didn't want to continue the discussion in front of the Guardian. It felt like washing the Wokens' dirty laundry in public, and she didn't quite trust the man.

"I thought I'd find you here," Strongquist said to Cariad. "I wanted to ask you something if you have a moment."

Anahi gave Cariad's arm a squeeze and said, "Think about it," again before leaving.

"What is it you want to ask me?" Cariad said, still irritated by her conversation with Anahi.

"I was wondering if you'd gotten any further with checking the resources I gave you? Did you find anything that might lead us to the stadium bomber?"

"Uh, no. I checked everything through but I didn't see anything that'll help."

Strongquist peered at her. "You seem hesitant. Do you mean you didn't see anything, or you saw something but you aren't sure how it might be useful?"

Cariad frowned. "The latter. There was a name that seemed meaningful, but I looked through all my records and couldn't see anything that would link me to the person. I think it's just my imagination running wild."

"Hmm... Maybe this person didn't have anything to do with you, but the name is familiar due to an event or encounter that you can't remember just yet. Don't forget that you were in cryonic suspension for nearly two centuries. It wouldn't be surprising if you experienced some memory loss. What was the name?"

It wasn't difficult for Cariad to recall. The name had been on her mind so much while she tried to figure out its significance, it was burned in. "Frederick Aparicio."

"Thanks. I'll check it out and see what I find."

"Are you any closer to catching the bomber?" Asking the Guardian the question was weird. It was as if they were the colony's police force, yet no one had appointed them.

"No, I'm sorry. We aren't much further on. But maybe this name will help. I'll let you know if I find anything."

"Thanks. I appreciate it," Cariad replied, wishing she knew what she could do herself to catch the bomber.

CHAPTER SIX

It was Ethan's turn with the plow. Five of the machines had been assembled from the kits brought aboard the *Nova Fortuna*. There were plenty more waiting to be put together, but the first crop was a priority. The farmers were sharing the use of the plows that were already available.

The machine was mechanical only. It had no computer controlling it or refining its operation according to variations in soil, plants, or the weather as agricultural technology on Earth had. The farmers would have to learn all the nuances of their job and not rely on support from tech, passing their knowledge and skills down to the next generation. Computers required complex parts, and those complex parts required rare, refined resources. Until the colony progressed to a level capable of providing those resources, it would rely on human ingenuity.

Ethan stared at the instruction manual, then at the plow, then at the manual again. The farmer who had brought the plow over had explained its operation. It had seemed straightforward while he was listening, but Ethan was having problems matching his memory of the farmer's words with the machine in front of him. His difficulties probably had something to do with the fact that he had no interest whatsoever in operating it.

Heaving a sigh, Ethan approached the machine. Maybe he could learn how to work it by trial and error. There wasn't anything around for him to collide with, so he wasn't likely to do any harm. He didn't even have a house yet to run into. He rolled the plaspaper document and pushed it into his back pocket before grabbing the bars on either side of the cab door and pulling himself up and in. He sat in the driver's seat and stared at the controls. They seemed simple enough. Some steered the machine and others operated the plow.

"Hey," called a voice.

Ethan jumped nearly out of his skin. A short woman was standing right next to the cab, squinting up at him from under a cap, her hands on her hips.

"Sorry," she said. "I didn't mean to startle you. I guess you didn't hear me arrive."

A flitter rested on the ground behind her.

"I'm your neighbor," the woman went on. "Name's Cherry." She held up her hand.

Ethan leaned down and shook it. "Ethan. But I thought my neighbor was—"

"He got reassigned. I took over his land. Always wanted to be a farmer, and here I am! Can I join you up there? I think I'm next in line for this plow. Thought I'd get a handle on it."

"Sure."

With some difficulty due to her shortness, Cherry climbed up into the passenger side of the cab. "Have you figured it out yet?"

"Honestly? No. I was just about to start it up and take it from there."

"Sounds like a good idea to me," said Cherry. "Do you have the instructions? Can I take a look?"

Ethan pulled the thin book out of his pocket and gave

it to her. Then he pressed a button. The engine started.

"Doing good so far," said Cherry, not looking up from the manual.

Ethan wasn't sure if she was being sarcastic. He had finally recognized her. Cherry had been two grades above him at school. Then he remembered something else that made him pause.

"Aren't you going to start driving it?" Cherry asked. "You should go to a corner of your land and begin there."

"Wait a minute," Ethan said, "I'm trying to figure out what you're doing here. Why are you a farmer? You were top of your grade in math and science."

Cherry rolled her eyes. "Just because I was good at something doesn't mean I have to like it. I didn't want to do any of the jobs my grade average qualified me for. I wanted to be farmer. I can't think of anything else I'd rather do."

"So they let you change jobs? Just like that?"

"Not exactly *just like that*, but it wasn't too hard. Things are in disarray at the moment with no Leader. I think they just got tired of arguing with me in the end and gave me permission to take over the land after it became vacant. They only wanted me to go away and stop bothering them."

"Really?"

"Yep. So... Are you going to drive this thing or not?"

"Er... Do you want to try?"

"I'd love to."

Ethan jumped out of the cab and walked around the plow to the other side. He climbed into the seat Cherry had vacated as she moved across to the driving seat. She turned her cap around so the bill faced backward and, giving Ethan a grin, she pressed the accelerator. The plow lurched violently forward. He grabbed the side of the cab to prevent himself from being thrown out.

"Sorry," said Cherry.

He slid his door closed and Cherry did the same, then she set off. As they drove along the rough ground bounced them up and down and threw them from side to side. Cherry began to laugh and so did Ethan.

"Where do I go?" Cherry asked.

Ethan turned and pointed to the side of the lake where his land bordered the shore. It was as good a place to start as any.

Cherry swung the plow around so hard Ethan thought it was in danger of toppling over. He held on tight.

"Whoops," Cherry said.

"Take it easy. What's your hurry? We have all day."

"I know," Cherry replied as she stopped the plow at the edge of the lake where the vegetation gave way to the shore. Her expression turned more serious. "But it would be great if I could plow and sow my own land soon. The sooner this colony is self-sustaining the better."

"I don't think anyone would disagree with you on that," said Ethan, "but, let's face it, none of us knows what we're doing. This is an expensive item of equipment that we can't replace. It might be good to take things slowly, step by step."

Cherry's look darkened further. "You mean none of us *Gens* knows what we're doing."

"I guess I do mean that. We grew up aboard the ship, while the Woken and the Guardians—"

"Don't say it."

"Don't say what?" Ethan asked.

"You were about to say they're more experienced than us, better than us, just because they grew up on Earth."

"Yes, something like that. The Woken went to college. They worked hard to become the world's top scientists. They didn't have everything provided for them like us. And they know how to handle living planetside."

"And I suppose you think that makes them better than us?"

"It depends what you—"

Cherry said, "I can't believe I'd hear an opinion like that from you, Ethan. Everyone likes you so much because you helped save people in the First Night Attack. But if the others heard what you just said..."

"What? What did I say?" He thought he'd only stated the obvious. "I didn't say anything bad about Gens. I don't think there's anything wrong with us. But we're different from the Woken and the Guardians. There's no denying it."

"And there I was thinking of asking you... " Cherry shook her head.

"Asking me what?" When she refused to answer, Ethan said, "Wait a minute. You aren't really here because you wanted to help me with the plowing, are you?"

"Yes, I am."

"No, I don't think so. It doesn't make any sense that someone as smart as you would want to be a farmer. Why are you really here?"

Cherry wasn't meeting his gaze. "I do want to be a farmer, but don't worry about it. It doesn't matter. I think I better go. I'll walk back to my flitter. Bring the plow over when you're finished with it, okay?"

Before Ethan had a chance to reply, she jumped down out of the cab and set off along the shoreline.

His brow knitted in confusion, Ethan slid over to the driver's seat and took the manual out of his back pocket to study it again. The engine was humming, and he only just heard another sound over it—something like a gasp and thud. He checked over his shoulder to locate the source.

A mass of thin, writhing threads from the lake had Cherry by her ankles. She was on her stomach being dragged into the water. She was terrified and her mouth gaped in a soundless scream.

Ethan leapt from the plow and was at her side in moments. He grabbed her arms and pulled as hard as he could. Cherry finally managed to scream, and the shriek she gave cut through Ethan's mind. He was immediately back to the First Night Attack hearing the almost inhuman howls of settlers being digested alive.

No matter how hard he pulled, he couldn't break the threads' hold on Cherry. They were winning the dreadful tug of war. Cherry was slowly inching backward to the water's edge. The prehensile threads were also squirming up her body toward Ethan, seeming to seek out the source of the resistance.

Desperately, he cast about for something to cut the threads, but all around him was nothing but vegetation, sand, and water. All he had with him were the clothes he was wearing. The moment he let go of Cherry, the threads would drag her into the water. Then there would be nothing he could do to save her.

"Please," Cherry gasped. "Please help me. Please."

"I'm trying. I can't pull any harder." As he spoke, Ethan's hands slipped on her arms, and Cherry jerked closer to the lake. She gave another shriek. Ethan quickly grabbed her again and tugged with every ounce of strength he had, but he could only maintain a stalemate against the threads.

There was no one for kilometers around and even if he managed to comm someone, the struggle would be long over before help arrived.

"I'm going to have to let you go, just for a moment," Ethan said through a clenched jaw.

"Noooo," Cherry howled. "Don't let go."

"I have to. I have to run back to the plow. Try to hold on to the sand as hard as you can. Fight with everything you've got. Don't let them drag you into the water." When she didn't answer, he said, "Cherry. Do you understand? Don't let them drag you into the water."

Her face was drained of color but she managed a brave nod.

"Good. Three. Two. One." He released his grip and flew back to the plow. As he swung the machine around, he push down a lever that looked like it might lower the blades. His heart surged as the long, sharp slices of metal moved downward. But then his heart fell as the turning machine brought him in sight of Cherry.

She was scrabbling and clutching the ground like a wild thing, but she seemed to be having no impact on the inexorable tugging of the threads. She was nearly at the water's edge.

Ethan pushed the accelerator forward and the plow surged ahead. He would need to drive it into the lake to avoid cutting Cherry with the blades.

The plow entered the lapping waves. Ethan hoped the water wouldn't drown the engine. He drove toward Cherry. He had to turn even deeper into the water or he would hit her. Her feet were submerged and only the threads that were wrapped around her legs remained visible.

The threads jerked and pulled her deeper. The plow blades churned the water close enough to Cherry to freeze his heart. He passed just beyond where he guessed her feet were, and the water filled with clouds of black sand and hundreds of pieces of thread, still wriggling as they bobbed to the surface.

He was past Cherry. He looked back. She was in the same spot. He turned the plow, watching her all the while. She pulled up a leg so that she was on one knee. Then she was up and running.

He steered the plow toward her. After running for half a minute into the vegetation, she seemed to calm down. She stopped, looked around and found him, then sped over.

She climbed quickly into the cab, covered in wet

sand, grazed, and still looking terrified. She grabbed Ethan and sobbed into his chest. He comforted her until her weeping finally slowed.

Wiping sand from her face and body, she said, "What the hell were those things? They were going to drown me. If you hadn't saved me, I'd be dead."

"I don't know. When I think of the times I've walked along that shore by myself... " Ethan shuddered. "We should head back to town and tell someone what's happened."

"Yeah. Let's go. We can use the flitter."

Ethan pushed the accelerator and turned the plow toward the place where Cherry had left the vehicle. "Only... " he added.

"What's wrong?" Cherry asked.

Ethan peered back at the lake, then around at the low vegetation.

"Only what?" asked Cherry.

"Those threads, or tentacles, or whatever they were, there were so many of them, and they were capable of moving an adult human."

"You don't need to tell *me* that."

"It was the first time the creature or creatures attacked one of us. But they didn't evolve to eat people, if that's what it had in mind."

Cherry said, "I think I know where you're going. You mean whatever it usually eats is human-sized or bigger. I think I'm going to be sick."

She wasn't speaking figuratively. She leaned out of the cab and vomited. When the spasm was over she leaned back, looking exhausted, in her seat.

Ethan said, "Sorry. I shouldn't have mentioned it."

"It's okay. I was going to do that anyway. Have you ever seen any large creatures out here? I haven't."

"No, but the plants are knee height. It wouldn't be hard for a large animal to conceal itself. All it would have to do is stay still and it would be impossible for us to detect. We could have walked right by something and never known it."

"I think I'm going to be sick again."

"The electric fences we set up aren't enough. We need the xenozoologists to go over the area again with a fine-toothed comb. I don't trust their report that the place is safe for farming. Not after today. When we get back, I'll comm the ship."

"You mean you have to ask the Woken for help?" Cherry asked. "Why? Why can't we handle this ourselves? Why do we always have to go running to them at the first sign of trouble?"

"It isn't like that."

"It's *exactly* like that."

They drove the rest of the way back in silence.

CHAPTER SEVEN

An announcement was to be made in the stadium. Cariad's gaze roved the gathering crowd as she waited. A gaping hole in the seating remained from the bomb explosion. All loose material had been stripped away by the Guardians for investigation, and the structure temporarily braced for safety. To Cariad, it was a stark reminder of the terrible event, and the sight of it made her newly fixed arm ache in psychosomatic sympathy.

The mood was in somber contrast to that at the Naming Ceremony. Most of the noise came from people maneuvering between the seats. No one was saying much, and what was said was conveyed in low voices, as if in fear of being overheard. Guardians had scanned the stadium thoroughly for any explosive devices and found nothing, but the tension and unease in the atmosphere was almost palpable.

Cariad noticed another marked contrast: at the Naming Ceremony, Gens and Woken, and even Guardians, had intermingled and seated themselves randomly, but now the groups were mostly sitting apart. She could identify the Gens and Woken even at a distance due to their clothing styles. Both groups clothed themselves from the ship's printing facilities, but the Woken sported the fashions of Earth at the time they'd left—Cariad wore the same exaggerated swirls and folds in muted shades herself—the Gens, however, favored tighter, more body-defining shapes and bolder colors.

A patch of dark gray in a corner of the stadium represented the Guardians. They made up the smallest group, only ten or twelve of them. Cariad knew Strongquist and a few others by name. The faces of the rest seemed to constantly change, as if they were serving shifts planetside or aboard *Nova Fortuna*, which, she reflected, was probably the case.

She'd sat among Gens, but no one was speaking to her. Looking around, she noticed that people were avoiding her gaze. The Gens' attitude toward her seemed to have changed within the last few days. Even those who hadn't been planetside during the First Night Attack knew who she was, and previously everyone had been friendly. Now she was beginning to feel like a pariah.

Something was happening within the colony. Groups were defining themselves into factions. Cariad was strongly reminded of her conversation with Ethan about the Gens' feelings about the Woken, and Anahi's attitude that the settlers were divided into the Gens and *us*. The divisions didn't bode well for the future but Cariad didn't know what to do about them.

"Hey."

It was Ethan. He sat next to her, and Cariad's spirits rose immediately. She had one friend at least. He must have sought her out among the crowd.

"Hi," she replied. "How are things down at the farm?"

"You didn't hear what happened?"

"No, I haven't heard much news. I've been busy."

He related a story about a farmer being attacked by

an organism living in the lake.

"That must have been terrifying. Was she okay?"

"She didn't suffer any permanent damage that I know of. Do you know what this announcement is about?"

"I've no idea. I just received the message, the same as everyone else."

The stadium sound system gave out low rumbles, indicating someone was about to speak. The background noise dropped to silence, and all gazes turned to the newly constructed speaker's box. A prominent Gen called Garwin was standing there facing the crowd. Strongquist was in the box with him and another Guardian. A woman, she sat at the back and Strongquist was standing behind Garwin. Anahi also appeared in the box.

"Gens, Woken, Guardians," Garwin began, "thank you all for coming here today. This meeting is long overdue. We've never gone so long without a Leader."

The general mood seemed to soften a little. Garwin was well-known and well-respected among the Gens. An older man, he had stood for election to be the Leader several times but had never won, probably due to his reputation for philandering. While not particularly frowned upon in Gen culture, Cariad had guessed it gave the impression that he was unreliable.

He was a good speaker, however, and the Gens were prepared to listen to him.

"I'm pleased to tell you the election process will begin soon," Garwin continued. "I'm not going to be standing again. Don't worry, I don't need it spelled out to me. You don't want me, and that's fine." He spoke wryly and without rancor. Some Gens began chanting *Garwin for Leader*, but the chant quickly faded when no one joined in.

He raised a hand. "My chance has come and gone, my friends. As I said, the election process begins soon. We have important things to talk about before that happens." He paused, as if to gather his thoughts. "It's been thirty days since we arrived at our new home, and what a tumultuous time it's been. Counting the Gens and Woken who died in the First Night Attack and the stadium bombing, fifty-five people have been lost to us, and more have suffered serious injuries. The other day, we also nearly lost two more in a wildlife attack out by the lake."

He looked down and shook his head before raising it to speak again. "Friends, we aren't well prepared for the dangers of our new lives. Whoever we elect as Leader has a tough job ahead of him or her, the toughest leadership job ever in the history of *Nova Fortuna*. But electing a new Leader isn't enough. If we're to succeed and make this colony viable, we need to improve our game.

"All our lives, we Gens have followed the guidelines laid down for us in the Manual, but we weren't ready for what we found here. How could we be?" He spread his hands wide. "We only knew how to live aboard a starship. We'd never known danger, so how could we protect ourselves against it?

"Sure, we learned basic ideas about survival, but learning is one thing, practice is another. We've been doing our best, but it isn't enough. We need more guidance. We need people with experience of a real world to lead us."

Cariad had assumed that Garwin was going to try to dispel the unrest and calm people's fears, but the man's last few sentences brought her to a sharp focus. His words had begun to sound worryingly familiar. They were very similar to a certain person's opinions she'd heard only a short time ago. She was surprised to hear them coming from the mouth of a Gen.

She glanced around. The people nearest her were frowning.

"It's time for a change," Garwin said. "There's an old

Earth saying I've heard: desperate times call for desperate measures. It's time that we rethink what we've been doing and invent a new way forward, a way that will save lives and bring us the success we need and deserve. I'd like you to listen to someone who has thought up a plan for that new way. It's a plan that promises to solve these problems we've been having and ensure a thriving, healthy colony for all."

The previous warmth that Garwin's appearance had generated entirely drained away. Puzzled or concerned looks were turning angry.

Anahi stood.

Cariad suddenly became very conscious of the fact that she was a Woken sitting among hundreds of Gens.

"Thank you, Garwin," Anahi began. "Thank you for your wonderful introduction to my proposal." She turned to the crowd. "My name is Anahi, and I am what you call a Woken. I was revived two years ago along with roughly half of the rest of the cryonically preserved. I wanted to speak to you today to give you my perspective on what's been happening. To say things have not gone according to plan would be a gross understatement. People have died. People have been injured. As some of you are no doubt aware, we are already behind schedule according to the Manual.

"I'm sure a few may be pointing the finger of blame at the Natural Movement, whose terrorists and saboteurs we've unfortunately brought along with us. And you would be entitled to do that. It was they who precipitated the First Night Attack, and it was a Natural Movement terrorist who planted the bomb in this very stadium. But the Natural Movement are not the only ones at fault here.

"We, the Woken, must also take some of the responsibility for the problems that have occurred. It was we who unknowingly allowed Natural Movement members to infiltrate our ranks. It was we who were foolishly lax in putting security in place that might have prevented their terrorist acts. It was we who failed to anticipate the problems our new colony would encounter with native species.

"My friends, I'm here today because I want to tell you we wish to make amends. Though Earth's best scientists did their utmost to create a viable plan for humanity's first deep space colony, we could not conceive of how that plan would play out in reality. Here, in our new home, we are finding that the information brought to us by probes was inaccurate. This planet harbors far more dangers than we realized.

"But all is not lost. The Guardians are helping us root out the Natural Movement members, and we Woken can fix other problems. We can start anew, armed with fresh knowledge, gleaned from on-the-ground experience. We want to help, not only for our own sakes, but for yours. *Nova Fortuna* was built for you. This planet is yours." Anahi held up a finger. "But.

"You need a new plan. A new Manual, written to see you through these fledgling days, based on everything we now know, and everything that our current experiments discover. We Woken need to be more proactive. Simply put, we need more control of the colony. I would like to propose that, while this emergency situation continues, Generational Colonists take a step back. When we have assessed what needs to be done, we will tell you. We will guide you as we did during your time aboard *Nova Fortuna*, as we guided your ancestors for generations.

"In order to do this, the next Leader should be a Woken."

That did it. Angry murmurings had been growing around Cariad as Anahi spoke. At her last sentence, the murmuring broke out into yells and shouts. Expletives were hurled at Anahi. "Friends, friends," she called. "Listen to me. Listen to what I have to say. This would be a temporary measure only, until... "

The noise from the crowd was so loud it drowned her words. Anahi gave up and returned to her seat. Strongquist stepped forward. Simultaneously, Guardians appeared from the tunnels that led to the stadium field. Armed Guardians.

Cariad clutched her seat. No Guardians had carried weapons since the First Night Attack, when they had fired at the predators that had invaded the camp. Their firearms were slim, sleek weapons, clearly far in advance of the weapons brought aboard *Nova Fortuna*. She could hardly believe they were being used to control the Gens.

For it was the stands filled with Gens that the Guardians went toward. They let the Woken stand alone. A shocked hush settled on the crowd.

Strongquist began to speak. "Please, do not be alarmed. The armed guards are for your own safety. I understand that you are upset at Anahi's proposal. I anticipated that it might not be well received, and I'm sorry to say that I was correct.

"I want to make it clear that we do not want anyone here today to be hurt. We want to protect you. That, after all, was our role during the First Night Attack, and that has been our aim since then. You have called us your Guardians, and we will not shirk that task. So, please, do not be alarmed. When emotions run high, crowds can get out of control and then people get hurt. Remain calmly in your seats, and no one will be in any danger.

"We will give more information about the election for the new Leader at a later date. Meanwhile, I would like to answer the many inquiries we have received about the state of things on Earth. Gens and Woken alike are naturally very curious about their old home. I wanted to take this opportunity to satisfy that curiosity. In order to do that, I have brought Faina here to speak to you. She is our captain. She can outline the pertinent facts for you."

The Guardian woman stood. Her dark gray, short hair matched her uniform, and when she spoke, her voice was crisp and loud. "Gens, Woken, thank you for this opportunity. I acknowledge that the time for answers is long overdue, and I apologize for that. We felt that you were all psychologically vulnerable after the First Night Attack."

Cariad and Ethan shared a puzzled look. Whatever the Guardian was about to say, it didn't sound like anything good was coming up.

"I will first answer the question that's on many lips," Faina said. "I'm sorry, but *there is no going back*. It's true that our ship travels faster than light. It's also true that we could take *some* of you back to Earth tomorrow, but it is an Earth that none of you would want to live on. Earth is full and its resources depleted. Mars is full. Ganymede and Ceres are full. There is nowhere for you to go.

"Gens and Woken, your new home is a difficult place to live. There's no denying it. But it's your home. It must be, so you must make the best of it. The Guardians wholeheartedly endorse Anahi's proposal that the next Leader should be a Woken. We are prepared to enforce this. This colony must succeed, and the Woken have the expertise to ensure it. We are lending them our support to safeguard everyone's survival."

Faina sat down and no one rose to take her place. The announcement was over. The armed Guardians moved away from the stands, walking backward toward the center of the field. It was the signal that the audience was free to leave, or perhaps that they had to leave.

The Gens filed silently out of their seats.

"I can't believe it," Cariad said quietly to Ethan as they stood to take their place going down the stairs.

"Me neither," he replied. "There's going to be trouble. The Gens already held a grudge against the Woken before this."

"And Anahi doesn't respect the Gens," said Cariad. They reached the bottom of the stairs. "I want to talk to her. I'll see you later."

"Okay. Take care."

Cariad sped around the edge of the field until she spied the person she wanted and walked quickly over. She caught up to Anahi as she was about to enter an exit tunnel. Strongquist, Faina, and Garwin were ahead of her.

The Woken stopped and turned when Cariad touched her arm. She pulled the older woman to the side of the tunnel, out of the way of the crowd.

"What the hell are you doing?" Cariad whispered fiercely. "Do you have any idea what you've started? They already dislike us."

"So what? All children hate their parents. And that's what they're like. Children. They need our guidance and now they're going to get it, whether they like it or not."

"You're an idiot," Cariad hissed. "You've handed over military control to the Guardians. This isn't supposed to be a military state. What's wrong with you? We're supposed to be building a new kind of society here. A better society. Not another Earth, with people murdering each other."

"Ha," Anahi exclaimed. "Weren't you one of the ones who insisted on bringing weapons along? Look, the situation's only temporary, okay? Until we get things back on track. I'm not prepared to sit around while some stupid Gens cock everything up. When the colony is working, and when the Gens gain some more experience of living in the *real* world, then we'll hand back control. But not until then."

Maybe Anahi believed her own words. Cariad wasn't sure. Maybe she really was that deluded. Whatever she thought, if history was anything to go by, the Woken had just started the events that were going to repeat it. A battle for independence and control was coming.

"I thought you were going to propose that we revive more Woken," Cariad said. "Like you said at the final decanting."

"Oh no," Anahi replied. "Why would I propose that to the Gens? We don't need their permission to restart the revival process. At least, now we don't."

CHAPTER EIGHT

Ethan stood at Dr. Crowley's grave, hardly able to believe that it had only been just over a month since they had buried her. The remains of the other victims of the First Night Attack were also buried in the small graveyard, along with those who had died in the stadium bombing. The soil on the bombing victims' graves was still fresh, while on Dr. Crowley's, the moss-like, native ground cover had already overgrown it and was creeping up the gravestone.

Ethan cleared the tendrils away, detaching them with some difficulty as their roots gripped tightly to the artificial stone. When he had cleaned off the surface, he sat on the ground and stared at the inscription:

Meredith Crowley
Star voyager, your journey is over
May you rest in peace

Far beyond the graveyard, a roadmaker trundled along, its square, bulky form inching across the horizon, dark against the lighter sky. Even with the intervening distance, its deep bass hum penetrated as it turned the native soil and rocks to firm, cambered dirt roads.

Some days, Ethan almost forgot that Dr. Crowley had died. Then the memory of that awful sight of her trapped beneath the alien predator would resurface like a wound torn open, and his grief would rise up fresher than ever.

He wished that she were still alive. Everything seemed to be going wrong and he didn't know what to do about it.

He wondered what Dr. Crowley would have said about what happened at the stadium meeting. He suspected she wouldn't have approved of the Woken's proposal to take over the leadership of the colony. She would have definitely protested the Guardians' use of guns to control the Gens. He was certain of that because she and Cariad had argued about having weapons aboard *Nova Fortuna*. Dr. Crowley had been against the idea. She'd believed the colony should be founded upon non-violent principles.

He recalled one of their talks they'd had not long after they'd become friends. They'd met in *Nova Fortuna's* Main Park as they usually did, beneath the Clock. Ethan had spent the morning studying the fertilizer requirements of root crops, and he was numb with boredom. He perked up when he saw the older woman waiting for him, reading an interface she held in one hand.

"Doctor," he said. "Sorry I'm late."

"Are you? I hadn't noticed." Dr. Crowley looked up at The Clock. "Only a few minutes." She closed her interface and slipped it into a pocket. "Where would you like to go today?"

The time they spent together usually followed the same pattern: Ethan would suggest a section or facility aboard *Nova Fortuna* for them to visit. Dr. Crowley would explain the history behind the place as far as she knew it—the space colonization project had involved tens of thousands of people and she wasn't familiar with all its aspects.

Ethan found it fascinating to hear about the building of *Nova Fortuna* from the perspective of someone who had actually been there when it all took place. Dr. Crowley would name long-dead space architects and engineers who she had known personally, but to him they were historical figures.

That day, however, Ethan hadn't been in the mood for a trip into the past. "How about we go to the Observatory?"

"You want to go there again? I think I've told you all I can remember about it."

"Yeah," Ethan replied. "That's why I want to go. I'm kinda tired and I don't think I'll take much in today. It would be good to relax for a while."

"Sure, if that's what you want."

The Observatory was quiet as usual. They sat down and reclined the seats until they were nearly lying flat.

"Is something bothering you, Ethan?" Dr. Crowley asked after some moments of silence.

"What makes you say that?"

"You're quiet. You usually have lots of questions for me. It isn't just that you're tired, is it?"

"I'm okay. I'm just bored of my course."

"Agriculture? I remember you telling me once that you would rather be an explorer than a farmer. I think if that's what you want to do, you should do it."

"It isn't as easy as that. Exploring was removed as an option when they revised the Manual."

Dr. Crowley's *pfft* of disgust came through the darkness. "You know what I think of the New Manual. I'm sorry, Ethan, but no one gave Gens the mandate to rewrite the Manual. Scientists and engineers with decades of experience in the outer planets put those guidelines together. I appreciate that it's Gens who will be impacted by the rules, but that doesn't give them the right to change them. No explorers? Nonsense. And forcing people into occupations they have no interest in or aptitude for is even more unwise. I have to tell you, I have grave reservations about the success of the colony if we follow the revisions that were made to the Manual. *Grave.*"

Subdued somewhat by the older woman's ire, Ethan didn't respond.

After a short while, she continued, "I would hate to see our new home go the way of Earth. I don't know what you understand from the vids and learning resources, but politicking is one of the greatest flaws in human nature. The lust for power and desire to control others is a highly addictive, corrupting drug. I've read the revised Manual, and that motivation to change things for the sake of leaving a mark, to know that the new guidelines would affect others for generations, is written clearly between the lines. It worried me to see it. Perhaps I'm only a foolish old woman, but I had hoped we would leave such evils behind. I'd hoped that such things were taught, not instinctive, and that if we could shape the Gens' education to promote egalitarianism and empathy, you wouldn't develop such traits. It seems, alas, that I was wrong.

"Ethan, I've been meaning to tell you this for some time, and I suppose this is as good a time as any: you have some wonderful qualities, and I believe you should put them to better use. I hope you don't mind my frankness when I say that you seem to think less of yourself because you weren't top of the class at school. But after getting to know you, I have to conclude that the education system we devised did you a disservice. Either that or the guidelines in the Manual for teaching were also revised. You strike me as a very intelligent, capable young man. What's more, you're very personable. You would be very popular if you put yourself out there more."

Dr. Crowley's words made Ethan uncomfortable. He

wasn't sure how he'd given the doctor such a positive impression. Was she trying to make him feel better about not wanting to be a farmer?

"What I'm trying to say is," Dr. Crowley continued, "it wouldn't hurt you to have a little more faith in yourself. You have a lot to offer. Don't be afraid to speak out if you think something isn't right. Believe me, it seems there will be plenty of people vying for power in the not-too-distant future, and they won't be the ones who should be leading the colony. It's people like you—people who don't want to lead—they're the Gens who will serve the colony best."

Watching the stars move slowly past, Ethan weighed his friend's words. "That's good of you to say that, Dr. Crowley, but I don't think I'll be leading anyone anywhere. I just can't see myself doing that."

"Can you see yourself being a farmer?"

"Nope."

"We have a long way to go yet. Think about what I said. The colony will need a very special Leader after Arrival."

A stiff breeze had started to blow through the graveyard, and the chill brought Ethan out of his reverie. While he'd been musing over the past, shelf clouds had risen, towering tsunami-like overhead. The roadmaker had edged farther along the horizon.

For the first time since he'd had that conversation with Dr. Crowley in the Observatory, Ethan began to wonder if there was some truth to what she'd said. After the First Night Attack, as the Guardians prepared to execute the Natural Movement saboteur, Strongquist had called him a hero. It was true that he'd been one of the few to keep his head during the attack. Maybe Dr. Crowley had been right when she'd said he had more to offer the colony than he'd thought. Maybe he could do something to stop what was happening with the Woken and the Guardians.

"Hi, Ethan," came a voice from behind him.

He started and turned. It was Cherry. "Hi."

"Sorry I made you jump."

"It's okay, but you do seem to have a habit of appearing from nowhere."

"But it's always good to see me, right?" She smiled impishly, and Ethan was forced to smile in return.

"I guess so."

"So much enthusiasm," Cherry exclaimed sardonically. "That's what I like."

"Well—"

"I'm just messing with you. I was looking for you because I wanted to ask you to come along to a meeting."

"What kind of meeting?"

"A meeting about what happened at the stadium."

"Right. Who's going?"

"Some Gens. You'll see when we get there. They wanted me to invite you."

"No Woken?"

"No. Definitely no Woken."

Ethan thought about it. "Okay. I'll come."

"Good. I was hoping you'd agree. And, Ethan, I'm sorry for saying that you were taking the Woken's side that day out of the lake. I thought about it, and I don't think you're like that."

"No problem," Ethan said, thinking her reversal a little odd.

"Shall we go?"

Ethan stood, stretching his stiff muscles, and walked with Cherry back to the settlement.

She led him to a newly built shop. In time, it would sell groceries. Cash vouchers were to be introduced to start a fledgling economy until a commercial network and credit system was set up. For the moment, the place functioned as a storehouse for supplies. The colonists collected them according to their allowance every day. By the time Ethan and Cherry arrived, that day's rations had been given out and the building was quiet.

Cherry took Ethan around the back and they went through a door that led to the stockroom. Food supplies in sacks and large tubs filled it to the ceiling, and the musty odor of dried grains and beans tinged the air.

They walked inside and Cherry opened the door to another back room. This was packed with chairs and people. Only one corner was empty of chairs and a man stood there, obviously addressing the meeting. The man was the last person Ethan had expected to see. It was Garwin.

"Ethan," he said. "Good of you to join us. Come in, come in."

The attendees shuffled chairs aside so that Ethan and Cherry could move from the door to spare seats.

"I had just begun explaining the situation to the newcomers," Garwin said. "I know it must be confusing, hearing me say one thing in the stadium and another thing here. The fact of the matter is, I and a few others have seen the way things were going for a while now. Since before Arrival Day, even. We didn't think the Woken would continue to leave control of the colony to us Gens for much longer. We knew what would happen, and we knew we would need someone on the inside when it did. So I've been friendly with the Woken and gone along with what they've said. I've made them believe there are Gens who are sympathetic to their position and support them. Believe it or not, they really think there are some of us who like to be treated like we're inferior."

This elicited both chuckles and grumbles among the listeners.

"The Woken trust me," Garwin went on, "idiots that they are. I believe they'll tell me what they have planned, and we can use that information and turn it against them. We can take back control. We have the numbers and pretty soon we'll have the weapons too."

It was a resistance meeting that Cherry had invited Ethan to. Suddenly her professed change of opinion about him made sense. They were hoping to bring him over to their side, and after the events at the stadium, he wouldn't take much persuasion. He didn't think any Gen would.

"Yes. Weapons," Garwin continued. "That's one reason you see a lot of farmers here. We've singled you out because after the creature in the lake attacked Cherry you've been allocated guns for protection while you're out in your fields. We're lucky the decision was made before the stadium announcement. I believe they're regretting their decision already. It's my prediction that the Wokens' next move is going to be to tell the Guardians to relieve you of your weapons at the earliest opportunity. So what I'm saying is, if you already have a gun, don't give it up. Make an excuse. Tell the Guardians you'll bring it in, then don't. Tell them you were never given one, or you lost it. They think we're stupid, so it's more than likely they'll believe you. Hell, just refuse if you want to, but don't give up your guns. We'll store them, ready for the day we fight back. Right?"

Ethan found himself nodding along with the rest. He'd received a weapon three days previously.

"Ethan," Garwin said. He held up an arm outstretched. "Come up here."

With the gaze of everyone in the room upon him, Ethan felt he had no choice but to comply. However, going up in front of the other Gens didn't make him as uncomfortable as he thought it would. Things had gone too far. They were being wronged. They couldn't trust the Woken or the Guardians anymore, and he agreed with Garwin that they had to do something about it. *He* would do something about it.

As he stepped through the chairs, someone began to clap. Garwin motioned downward with his hands to quieten the clapper.

"We mustn't make too much noise," he said. "We don't know who might hear."

He put an arm over Ethan's shoulder and spoke to the audience. "Here he is: the man who saved hundreds of lives in the First Night Attack. He's quick-thinking, brave, and he doesn't give up. With Ethan on our side, we can't go wrong."

"That's right," called a voice.

To his surprise, Ethan found himself speaking. "I'm just another Gen like all of you. What's happening to us isn't right, and I'll do my best to fight alongside you to change it. But I want to say one thing: don't think all Woken are the same. They don't all agree with what's going on. We have friends among them who'll help us."

From some expressions, he could tell that not all of them believed him, but they were keeping their opinions to themselves for the time being.

"Wise words," Garwin said. "And I'll also say, the Woken have friends among us. Though I'm not one of them." He grinned broadly, eliciting some laughs. "So be careful who you speak to. Is there anything else you'd like to say, Ethan?"

"No, I'm done for now."

"Right." He addressed the room. ""Going forward, I think we should hold each meeting at a different place, day, and time. Between now and the next meeting, we need to watch and learn everything we can about what the Guardians and the Woken are doing. Everyone: watch, listen, and remember. Don't make a record of anything except in your own heads. Don't write anything down. The next meeting is... " He gave the details. "Finally, farmers, don't give up your weapons. Thanks, everyone. Until next time."

The meeting began to break up. Those nearest the

door slipped out. The rest waited, chatting before leaving in small numbers at irregular intervals so that their movements weren't too noticeable. Garwin spoke to Ethan about the inner circle of Gen insurgents. As Ethan listened, he was surprised to discover that certain Gens had banded together months previously, even before Arrival, and begun preparations to fight the Woken, guessing they would try to assume control.

"The only thing we didn't factor into the equation," Garwin said, "was the Guardians. It was quite a surprise when they turned up."

"A pleasant surprise at the time," Ethan said, recalling how it was only through a Guardian's intervention that he was saved from a grisly death.

"Maybe. They've shown their hand since then."

"I can't disagree," Ethan replied. "But I think something else is missing from your equation: the Natural Movement. What about them? Where do they fit into all of this?"

"I confess that we don't have that figured out yet. Who they are, how many they are, whether they're Woken or Gens—we're as much in the dark as anyone else."

Ethan wasn't sure if it was due to the man's convincing speeches on both the Woken and the Gen sides, or due to something more subtle about his manner, but he didn't think that Garwin was being entirely open.

Someone tapped Ethan on his shoulder, signaling that it was his turn to leave. He said goodbye to Garwin and went out. It was dusk and the shelf clouds had risen higher, looming swollen and black over the small town.

When Ethan arrived at the farmers' hostel, a Guardian was awaiting him. She told him he had to surrender his gun.

CHAPTER NINE

As far as Cariad knew, she was the first of the colonists who had been invited aboard the *Mistral*. At least, she'd never heard of anyone going to the Guardians' ship before, and that news would have spread through the colony like wildfire.

The *Mistral's* shuttle had arrived for her not long after she received the comm from Strongquist. He'd said that he wanted to talk to her the stadium bombing and that it would be more convenient if she were to go to the *Mistral*. With *Nova Fortuna's* reproductive facilities mothballed and human reproduction planetside only just starting up, she was at a loose end and eager to help with the investigation. She was also eager to learn more about the mysterious Guardians and their intentions.

The colonists' relationship with the Guardians had never been formalized. No agreements made or guarantees given. The late arrivals had stuck to their story that they were there to help protect the colony from the Natural Movement plot to sabotage it, and according to the Guardian captain's recent words at the stadium, they were also generally intent on safeguarding the colony's success. On the surface, it all added up, but the Guardians' apparently ready acquiescence to Anahi's request for armed support of her move to increase Woken control made Cariad deeply uneasy. What else might the Guardians do if asked? Where would they draw the line?

Guardian technology was far superior to that of the *Nova Fortuna.* That much was clear from their weapons, the medical assistance they offered, and their shuttles. Cariad imagined that the same would be true of their ship. What she'd seen of the small, sleek vessel seemed to indicate it, most importantly the fact that it had caught up to the *Nova Fortuna* at the end of her long journey by the means of its faster-than-light engine.

If the Guardians used that technology to help the colony, that would be to the good, but if they changed their attitude neither the Gens nor the Woken would be able to do much to resist them. In truth, these visitors from an Earth Cariad had never known held the fate of the colony in their hands. She also worried that the colony might end up depending on them, and then they would have the ultimate control. Despite the fact that the Guardians had arrived in the nick of time during the First Night Attack and saved many lives, Cariad wondered if things might have turned out better overall without their presence.

She sat alone in the small passenger cabin of the *Mistral's* shuttle as she was carried over, wondering what it all meant. The Guardians' shuttle was smaller than *Nova Fortuna's* transport craft but its superior quality and capability was clear. Cariad's seat conformed perfectly to her body, and the shuttle had wide windows in the passenger cabin, unlike *Nova Fortuna* shuttlecraft. The vessel's movement was smooth and unaccompanied by engine noise, and it seemed to Cariad that it was moving incredibly quickly.

Below, the planet surface skimmed past and the

Mistral soon loomed up. Cariad had seen it before through *Nova Fortuna's* scanners, but up close it looked even more impressive. Its proportions perfect, the ship's designers clearly hadn't focused only on its FTL capabilities. The ship was also an aesthetic masterpiece and in marked contrast to *Nova Fortuna's* massive, chunky wheel. She wondered if the Earth engineers had built any more and if people had set out to leave the crowded Solar System and start new deep space colonies.

The next moment, the shuttle was docking. As soon as the portal opened, air infiltrated the cabin. It smelled different from that aboard *Nova Fortuna*. Circulation and filtration units worked hard on the colony ship to eliminate odors, but after a trip planetside the slightly sweaty, moldy smell of the interior was distinct. The air aboard the *Mistral* smelled clean and mildly fragrant.

Strongquist was there to meet Cariad. His dark eyes were deep and unreadable, as always. "Thank you for coming."

"It's my pleasure. I admit I'm curious about your ship. Am I the first you've invited aboard?"

"You know, I think you are."

"Ha, you say that like it wasn't intentional," Cariad joked. "You must know how curious we all are about you." She was skating close to the line of politeness. She didn't want to overstep it and cut short her welcome, but on the other hand, she wanted to take advantage of the favor Strongquist was showing her.

Strongquist's expression became grave. Had she pushed things too far?

"Curiosity is to be expected, I guess." He left his response at that, shutting the conversation down. "Come this way, please."

As they went through the ship's corridors, one of the first things Cariad noticed the total absence of grime. *Nova Fortuna* had her sanobots—simple, fist-sized, self-repairing machines that constantly crawled the surfaces of the ship, brushing and wiping as they went. They would automatically discharge into the trash chutes and return to recharging stations when they ran low on power. But sanobots weren't perfect. There were areas they couldn't reach and others that, for some reason, their programming missed, resulting in certain ever-present patches of dirt.

Whatever was maintaining the cleanliness aboard the Guardians' ship was doing an excellent job. Not only were there no perma-grime spots, every surface gleamed like new.

Cariad asked what was cleaning the ship.

Strongquist replied with a word that sounded like gibberish.

"I never heard that word before. Is it a trade name?"

"No, it's just what we call the nano that cleans the ship."

"Weird. It sounds like a word from another language."

"No. It's English."

Cariad's brows knitted. She was no linguist, but it didn't sound like any English she knew.

"You have to understand," Strongquist said, "English has evolved since *Nova Fortuna* departed. You would probably find modern English difficult to follow."

"I thought I was speaking modern English."

"No, you speak mid-third millennium English, as do the Gens because their learning and leisure materials are all in mid-third English."

"Wait a minute," Cariad said. "How can I understand you if English evolved so much after we left?"

Strongquist gave a rare smile. "You can understand me because I'm speaking mid-third English. Here we are."

They stepped into a small room that had consoles on every wall.

"I've been doing some more investigating into the name you gave me," said Strongquist. "I've been searching the data bank of recordings we have from twenty years before and after *Nova Fortuna* departed."

"Twenty years after we left?" Cariad asked. "Why so long?"

"While the *Nova Fortuna* was within a reasonable distance from Earth, transmissions could have been sent and received pertaining to the Natural Movement's attempt to sabotage the mission."

"But not after twenty years?"

"Perhaps, but it was less likely. There was also a limit to how much data we could bring. We have millions of zettabytes."

Cariad was about to ask another question, but Strongquist said, "I have something I want to show you."

He looked toward the empty space in the center of the room. A holo started up, though Cariad hadn't seen the Guardian do anything to start it. She wondered if he was using a mind interface. Researchers had been working on prototypes in her time, but no one had been able to tolerate the web insert in their brain.

She was looking from an above-head view down into a lobby, as if the camera had been stationed on the ceiling. Glass walls allowed a view of a street and on the opposite wall a line of elevators stood. The lobby was empty. From the dim light shining in from outside, Cariad guessed it was either around dawn or dusk. If it was dusk, the place seemed quiet.

"What am I looking at exactly?" she asked Strongquist.

"I don't want to suggest anything to you," he replied. "Please, just watch and tell me what you notice."

A figure appeared, coming down the street. A man wearing clothes from Cariad's time. As the man approached the glass doors, they opened. He came into the lobby and went to the elevator. While he waited, another figure entered. A woman. Both were dressed for office work. Their clothes were light and cool, suggesting that it was summer.

It was a very ordinary scene, but a strong sense of displacement struck Cariad. These people she saw arriving for work were long dead, though from her perspective they'd been alive only two years previously. She was now living in a future people of her time had only dreamed of, yet to the Guardians she was a living relic, speaking an archaic language.

The man and woman had entered an elevator and disappeared, but more people were arriving.

"It would help if you would tell me what I'm looking for," she said, her feeling of dislocation giving away to frustration. She wanted to catch the Natural Movement terrorists, not play Strongquist's games.

"I can't," Strongquist said. "If I did that, I couldn't rely on what you tell me. The human mind is very suggestible. Eye witnesses are notoriously unreliable."

Witnesses? Was something about to happen? Was a bomb about to go off? Cariad scanned the scene.

"It would be helpful if you would watch the people," Strongquist said.

The lobby now held eight workers. Another appeared and joined a group that had congregated around an approaching elevator. The new figure was a man. Something about his features attracted Cariad's attention. She leaned forward to look more closely. It was hard to see his face clearly due to the camera angle. But there was something about him...

She touched Strongquist's arm. Immediately, the scene froze. He'd stopped it somehow.

"What do you see, Cariad?"

"That man." She pointed, her finger poking through his face in the holo. She hesitated. The feeling was tenuous. She didn't trust it, especially as the holo had frozen when the man's face was slightly turned away. "Can you let it play on?"

The holo started up, and, as if on cue, the man turned and looked upward, almost directly at the camera. It was like he was aware and concerned that he was being recorded, though from the direction of his gaze, it was clear he couldn't see the camera. The elevator doors opened. He stepped inside and was gone. The holo played on.

Cariad turned to Strongquist. "I think I recognized that man."

"Good. Where do you know him from? Do you remember?"

Cariad mentally replayed the moving image of the man's face. "Not right now. I can't place him, but I'll think about it."

"I have other scenes I can show you to help jog your memory."

"You do? I'd like to see them."

The holo was replaced by another. It was a laboratory at night.

Cariad asked, "So you were showing me that man among other people hoping that I would pick him out?"

"Exactly. If I'd shown you only his image, you might have been convinced you knew him simply because it would be obvious he must be important in some way. I needed you to pick him out from a crowd of strangers."

"Wait a minute," Cariad said. The holo stopped. "Who is the man I saw?"

"Oh. I was hoping you would know."

"Huh? If *you* don't know who he is, what makes you think *I* would know him?"

Strongquist only looked at her.

The penny dropped. "It's Frederick Aparicio, isn't it?"

"We believe so."

"So I did know him, or I wouldn't have recognized him. But where from?" Cariad thought back to the time of the *Nova Fortuna* project. She was sure that Frederick Aparicio wasn't a distant relative. She was also sure he hadn't been a work colleague either. The work on the project had been intense and relationships extremely familiar. Everyone had spent most of their waking hours on the job. Some had even slept on site.

Perhaps Aparicio had been one of the more peripheral workers. They'd numbered in their thousands. But if that were the case, why did his name and face stick out?

"Should I play the next holo?" Strongquist asked.

"Yes," she said. "But I wanted to ask, how are you controlling it?"

Strongquist smiled. "The lesson in modern tech will have to wait for another day, I'm afraid. Now, if you don't mind...?" His eyebrows gestured to the scene in the lab that was frozen in midair in front of them.

"Okay. Go ahead."

***

Cariad watched four more holos of Frederick Aparicio before Strongquist said that was all they had on him.

Cariad couldn't tell him any more at that time but said she would let the Guardian know as soon as she remembered anything. "Can I take the recordings with me to watch them again?"

"Yes, of course," Strongquist said. "I had them converted to play on *Nova Fortuna's* drives." He took a vidring out of his pocket and handed it over. Cariad took it, wondering why, if she could have watched the holos on *Nova Fortuna*, the Guardian had brought her there.

"Would you like a tour of the ship before you go?" Strongquist asked.

"I'd love it."

He took her to the bridge first. It was surprisingly similar to *Nova Fortuna's*. Much less instrumentation adorned the consoles, however. The Guardians present didn't offer any greeting but one stood up as Cariad walked in. She recognized Faina, who had addressed the crowd at the stadium.

"Cariad. Welcome to the bridge. Strongquist said he was bringing you aboard. What do you think of the ship?"

Did Cariad detect tension behind the woman's words? Or was it a subtle anger directed at Strongquist? The man's expression was as enigmatic as ever.

"I haven't seen a lot of it yet, but it's very interesting," she replied. "Amazing, even. Everything's so much more advanced than on the *Nova Fortuna*. It's to be expected, I guess. But coming here, I feel like I've stepped into the future. Our ship was the pinnacle of human technology when we left but I'm going to struggle to see it like that now."

"Don't forget that our ships serve separate purposes," Faina said. "*Nova Fortuna* was built for stamina, not speed, and it was intended to be home to two thousand. Our ship was built for speed and... not for comfort."

The slight hesitation was almost unnoticeable. Almost. What had Faina been about to say before she changed her mind?

"But I could talk forever about my ship," the Guardian continued. "Don't let me keep you. I'm sure Strongquist has plenty more he'd like to show you."

Cariad would have loved to stay longer to discuss the Guardians' ship's specs, but Strongquist was already ushering her away. As they went down the corridor, Cariad asked him, "So Faina speaks mid-third English for our benefit too?"

"Yes, that's right."

"You all learned the language before leaving Earth?"

"No. We learned it on the way."

"You all speak it so well. I can't hear a trace of your original accent. How long did it take you to learn?"

"Not long. Would you like to see the FTL engine?"

"You can actually see it?"

"Oh yes."

By the time her visit was over, Cariad had seen the living, eating, and recreational quarters, supply hold, and the engineering section. Several times she attempted to extract more information from Strongquist but he politely and adeptly deflected her inquiries. She was left with few answers and a growing sense of unease.

CHAPTER TEN

It had been agreed that they would stash the weapons in a certain shed for farm equipment. Conscious of the fact that he was openly carrying the gun after he'd informed a Guardian that he hadn't been issued one, Ethan headed quickly in the direction of the tool shed. Evening had fallen, and the settlement seemed unusually quiet. Perhaps the emptiness of the streets would work in his favor.

As he passed the corner of a building at the end of the lot, a hand grabbed his elbow and pulled him around and out of sight of the road. It was Cherry, standing in the shadows.

"Something's going to happen at the tool shed," she said. "I just went there to hide my weapon with the others. The place is crawling with Guardians."

"Really? What are they doing?"

"Just hanging around in the street. Loitering."

Ethan gave a snort of derision. "When did a Guardian ever loiter?"

"That's my point. I think that somehow they've figured out what we plan to do. They're waiting for us to bring over our weapons and then relieve us of them.

Quite a few farmers went there already. I think they're caught in the shed, not wanting to leave with Guardians in the area."

"I won't take mine over, then. I'll find another place to hide it."

"Exactly what I was thinking."

"Wait," said Ethan. "That's no good. We can't leave the others to get caught. How many Guardians did you see?"

"Five. But I can't swear there aren't more. It wasn't like I stuck around and surveyed the place."

"And how many Gens in the shed, do you think?"

"Twenty of us have guns. I guess most of them are there by now."

"Twenty against five is pretty good odds," Ethan said.

"Twenty untrained Gens against five highly trained Guardians with superior weapons, don't forget."

"I'm not forgetting."

Their gazes met as they each made their decision.

"If we were fast... " Ethan said.

"And if we approached from the east... " said Cherry.

Simultaneously, they nodded.

Fifteen minutes later, after making a wide circle around the tool shed through several streets, the two Gens prepared to close the final distance. The Guardians wouldn't be expecting anyone to approach the shed from the direction of the shuttle field. No Gens took the regular shuttles to the *Nova Fortuna* anymore.

If they rushed down the street, they could join the other farmers before the Guardians knew what was happening. Alone, a Gen didn't stand a chance against a Guardian, but together they might be able to resist the attempt to take their weapons. At the very least, it would be a show of strength and an open demonstration that the Gens were not going to take their suppression lying down.

Ethan and Cherry were at the end of the street.

Cherry had been correct. Five Guardians were spread about, doing bad impersonations of people hanging around with nothing to do. In their formal uniforms, the effect would have been almost comical if it weren't for the fact they were armed.

The rest of the colonists had clearly gotten the message that something confrontational and dangerous was about to go down, because this part of the settlement was entirely deserted.

"Okay," Ethan whispered. "Let's go."

Their weapons at the ready, they set off running down the street, stooping low and trying to make as little noise as possible.

Their efforts paid off. They made it nearly a third of the way before a Guardian noticed them. She called out for them to stop. Neither Ethan nor Cherry even broke pace. Ethan gripped his gun tighter and sped up. There was no sense in trying to avoid detection now.

"Hey," the Guardian called more harshly. "Stop right there. Now!"

The farmers in the shed must have realized what was happening because the door opened a crack. Light from inside spilled out.

"Stop or I'll shoot," shouted the Guardian, but Ethan was almost at the door. It was widening in front of him. A hiss and a burst of warmth came from behind him, then he was through the door and inside the shed.

He spun around. Where was Cherry? She was flying into the shed right behind him. With a slam, the door closed.

Ethan grabbed Cherry's upper arms. "Are you okay? I thought you were hit."

She shook her head, panting. "A round hit the sidewalk between us."

"That was lucky," a man said. It was Misha.

"I don't think so," Cherry replied, still gasping. "They were so close, they could have hit either of us if they'd wanted. I think they were only trying to scare us."

"That's something," said Misha. "They aren't prepared to kill us just yet."

"Let's hope it doesn't get to that," said a woman called Phy.

The door rattled in its frame. Someone was trying to open it, but it had been locked after Ethan and Cherry went in. A succession of loud, hard knocks sounded out. "Open up," a Guardian said. "We're taking your weapons into safekeeping. If you just hand them over, no one will get hurt and there won't be any repercussions. We know exactly who you all are. If you don't comply, you'll be breaking colony laws and you'll be subject to punishment."

"What's that, I wonder?" said Misha "The punishment, I mean."

"They'll have to decide what law we're breaking first," Cherry said. "I don't think there is one referring to weapons. They aren't mentioned in either the old or the revised Manual."

The door resounded with another loud knocking. "Come out. You have one minute until we force you."

Ethan went over to the door. "You're the ones acting illegally here. Guardians have no jurisdiction in this colony, even if we were breaking any laws, which we aren't. You fired on me and Cherry with no provocation. If you don't back off and leave us to go about our legal business, you will be the ones in contravention of colony laws. We give you one minute to vacate this area."

"Ha," said Misha. "That told them."

But as he turned from the door to face the farmers, Ethan's expression was grave. "What I want to know is, how did they know what we were doing here?"

The implication of his words lay heavy. Gazes were shared around the room. Someone had informed the Guardians about the plan to stash the weapons in the tool shed. There was no other explanation for them being there. One of the reasons they'd chosen the tool shed as the hiding place was because it wouldn't be unusual to see farmers come and go from the place. It was very unlikely that a Guardian had noticed their movements and guessed what they were doing.

Seconds dragged past in silence.

"I can't believe anyone would do that," Cherry said quietly. "Who would do that?" Her eyes searched the faces of those around her.

"Someone on the lookout for themselves," said a woman.

The farmers shifted uneasily, waiting for the Guardians to make a move. They stood and sat in the cramped space, surrounded by shelves filled with powered farming tools. It occurred to Ethan that the tools could double as weapons in a pinch, then he winced at the thought of the kind of damage they would inflict on the human body.

More than a minute had passed. The Guardians seemed to have backed down on their threat.

"Should I look outside?" Misha asked.

"No," Ethan replied. "Wait a little longer. They might be expecting us to open the door out of curiosity. It would make forcing us out a lot easier."

Another minute passed, then another. By the time half an hour had passed, the farmers were growing fidgety. Ethan felt the same way. The waiting was unbearable. He almost yearned for the Guardians to burst in.

Abrupt knocks made the entire room of farmers jump. "We demand that you open up on the authority of the Leader of the *Nova Fortuna* colony."

"Well, that was quick," Cherry said to Ethan. "You told them they didn't have any authority, so they went and got the authority."

"We do not recognize the legality of your demand that we leave," Ethan retorted. "*Nova Fortuna* has no

Leader."

"The newly elected Leader is Anahi. On her authority, we demand that you leave."

"Shit," Ethan said. "They've elected that Woken."

"Who's elected her?" Cherry asked. "We didn't vote."

"I bet they've changed the rules so that we can't vote," said Misha. "They're just doing whatever they want to get their way. I don't know. Maybe we should give up and leave quietly? They said there won't be any repercussions."

"I don't believe that for a minute," Ethan said. "They know exactly who we are. We've declared our hand. There's no turning back now. I'm for fighting them." He held up his weapon. "Who's with me?"

Cherry followed suit and raised her gun. One by one, the rest did the same. All except Misha. Finally, he raised his weapon too.

Ethan said, "We won't open the door except as a last resort. We can fire through the shutters. My guess is that one or two Guardians are directly behind the door. The rest are probably either next to them or across the street, ready to grab us if we run. Set your guns to stun."

"Stun?" Cherry asked. "Isn't that a bit stupid? I'm pretty sure they aren't planning to stun us."

"You said you thought they deliberately missed us when we ran in here."

"That was before they had the authority of the self-appointed Leader. Now they can do what they like."

"We don't know that," Ethan replied. "And I'd rather avoid more loss of life. Too many people have died already."

Her brow wrinkling in disapproval, Cherry turned the dial on her weapon.

"Right," Ethan said. "You two on these shutters. You two on those." He motioned the farmers he'd pointed at to their positions. "Cherry, you and me are aiming for long range targets."

He took up a position facing the crack between one set of shutters. The pair of farmers he'd nominated stood on each side, ready to fire through at an angle.

Cherry went to the other side of the room, and stood with her rifle at her shoulder, left foot forward.

Ethan gave a nod, and the shutters opened. The gaps were just wide enough to shoot through. Pulse slugs hissed from every weapon, and in the enclosed space the air was tinged with their faint, acrid after burn.

From outside came the *Uhhh* of a pulse reaching its target followed by the sound of a body hitting the ground. A flicker of movement passed on the opposite side of the street and Ethan's finger jolted on his trigger. The figure was gone. He didn't know if he'd scored a hit.

A massive blow hit the door. At the same time, a pulse round hit one of the shutters. Half of the round made it through and grazed Misha's face. He gasped and dropped his gun, his hand gripping the spot.

"Close the shutters," Ethan shouted. As they swung to, another massive blow hit the door, but it held. Then it began to smoke. Having failed to batter it in, the Guardians were firing their weapons at the door. The smoke quickly thickened.

"Move back," Ethan said. "The minute you see any of them come through, start shooting." Some of the farmers spread themselves along the wall on each side of the door. Others found positions around the room where they were able to take aim.

Ethan held his rifle grimly at his shoulder. He could hardly believe that only a few weeks previously, at the execution of the Natural Movement saboteur, Strongquist had patted his shoulder and called him a hero. Now he was in armed conflict with the people who had turned up to rescue them—the people the Gens had named Guardians because they believed they would help protect them from the dangers of the new world. Now, it looked like they needed defending from their Guardians. How had it come to this?

The smoke from the door was filling the room. The melting material gave off a choking and unpleasant reek.

Any minute, the Guardians would be through and the firing would begin. Ethan wished he'd had a chance to talk to Cariad. She was a Woken. If he didn't make it, he hoped she would sort out the colony's strife.

CHAPTER ELEVEN

Cariad headed toward Anahi's quarters, determined to make the woman think twice about her actions. Visiting the Guardians' ship had been an interesting distraction, but Anahi's not-so-subtle move to wrest power from the Gens had grated on Cariad more and more in the intervening hours. She was damned if she was going to stand by and allow someone take the colony in a direction that made a mockery of everything it was supposed to stand for.

Anahi lived in the agricultural area of *Nova Fortuna,* which spanned three kilometers of the Outer Rim. She was responsible for developing crops that would grow in the conditions of the new planet. Some of the fields that had helped sustain two thousand Gens during their long space voyage had been converted. They now held the new planet's soil in experimental beds where Anahi could test the newly modified crops.

In the years before Arrival Day, Cariad had enjoyed going to the fields. The massive lights mimicked nearly temperate climate levels of daylight, and the growing plants gave the air a "green" smell, so she felt almost as though she were back on Earth. During those two years since they had both been revived, Anahi had seemed a cordial enough colleague when they'd met during Cariad's visits. The emotional delicacy Cariad had noted before departure had been the same but Anahi had never been unpleasant. Cariad wondered how long she'd been planning to move the colony to Woken control.

On her way to the residential section of the agricultural area, Cariad spotted Anahi working in a field. The older woman stood up from a crouch, shears in hand, holding a handful of plant stalks. Cariad changed direction and made her way down a muddy path toward her.

Anahi's vision aids really did seem to give her eyes in the back of her head, Cariad mused, as the woman turned around when she approached, even though she'd been facing away. Anahi's arms fell limp. "I thought you would be along sooner or later."

"I wish it had been sooner," Cariad said, standing at the edge of the rice paddy. "Can we talk?"

"If you like, but you aren't going to change my mind." Anahi put the cut stalks in a trug and squatted down once more.

"Firstly," Cariad said, "it's clear that you have the backing of most of the Woken because no one spoke out against you, but you have absolutely no mandate for what you're doing."

Anahi shrugged. "The Generational Colonists had no mandate to revise the Manual. That didn't stop them. I'm not doing anything different than they did, except that I know what I'm doing."

"Do you? When the Gens changed some parts of the Manual, they were only trying to exercise some control of their situation. They didn't choose this life. We consigned them to it. It shouldn't come as a surprise they want a say in their destiny."

Anahi was examining the base of a plant. "I don't

disagree. And, in fact, I don't blame them for what they did. As you say, it's a natural human reaction. However, they had no automatic *right* to do it, so when you come here and tell me that we have no *right* take control away from them, I can only point out the hypocrisy of your position."

"But we're the ones who wrote the Manual," said Cariad. "If anyone should abide by its rules, it's us. Do you want to demonstrate that it's acceptable to seize power and do whatever you like? That's a dangerous precedent to set."

"I didn't hear your protests when you found out about the revisions they'd made after you were revived." Anahi deposited another handful of stalks in her trug and leaned in to cut a third.

"You're not getting it," Cariad exclaimed. "We can't change everything just because we think we know better."

"No. *You're* not getting it." Anahi stood and pointed her shears at Cariad. "We can and should change things because we *do* know better. If you had a dog, would you let it run through traffic because it saw a rabbit? If you had a child, would you allow it to wear summer clothes when it was freezing outside?" She walked over to Cariad, her basket hooked over her arm.

"Look at these rice plants. They're growing pretty well, don't you think? If none of us had survived cryo, do you think a Gen could have modified them to grow in this soil? Of course not. Even the ones who specialized in genetics have next to no practical experience. It would have been years before they grasped the techniques required to do the work I do. If I wasn't around, they would have been forced to grow seed suited to Earth soil, which would give half the yield. Back home, it wouldn't matter. There's enough surplus food that no one starves from a few crop failures, or there used to be anyway. Here, low yields could mean the difference between survival and death."

"You're being ridiculous," retorted Cariad. "You did survive cryo, and here you are, doing your work. No Gen would have stopped you. The entire colony recognizes the importance of what you do. You didn't have to seize control in order to modify crop genes."

"Didn't I?" Anahi seemed to glare behind her visor. "There are two thousand Gens and only a hundred of us with another hundred still in cryo. All it would take would be one madman, Cariad, one cultist or schizophrenic—"

"That would never happen. All the First Generation's and all the stored gametes' genes were screened for mental illness."

"Or one power-hungry idiot," Anahi continued, regardless, "to persuade the rest of them to follow him, and who knows what could happen? They could decide to murder us all in our beds. There's no protection for us out here. Or at least there wasn't until I asked the Guardians for their support. Up until now, the Generational Colonists could have done whatever they liked."

"Now I'm thinking *you're* the one who's insane."

"I'm not mad," Anahi said crisply, pushing past Cariad on the narrow path, "I'm pragmatic." She set off toward the glasshouses that bordered the fields.

Cariad followed on her heels. "You're reacting to a situation that you think might happen. You're punishing the Gens before they've done anything wrong."

"Helping someone isn't a punishment, and they need our help."

"No, they don't, and it is a punishment if it's unneeded and unasked for. Wait up a minute." She grabbed Anahi's shoulder, forcing her to stop and turn around.

Though her eyes were covered by her vision aid, the woman's anger was evident from her thin, set lips.

Cariad asked, "Are you sure that "helping" the Gens is what this is all about?"

"Yes, I am. Helping them, and helping us. It's the only sensible thing to do in the circumstances. Are you aware they have already begun using the flitters whenever they want? And some are leaving their designated professions? Choosing to do whatever they fancy instead? We don't have that kind of wiggle room. Maybe in two or three generations we might, but not now. We can do this, but only if people stick to the plan."

"Bullshit," spat Cariad. "No one was going so far off the guidelines to make a difference. I know what this is about. It's all about you, Anahi, isn't it? You want to be the one in control, don't you? You didn't like the idea of Gens being in charge. It scares you. Or did the decades in cryo give you some kind of god complex?"

"You're talking nonsense." Anahi marched toward the glasshouses.

Cariad watched her go, her guess about Anahi's motivations gnawing at her. Was she right? If she was, the scientist posed an even greater danger than Cariad had thought.

As she decided to leave and consider her next move, she saw Anahi stop. She was answering a comm. The message seemed to agitate the scientist. She began to run, and as she went, her carefully gathered plant stalks spilled out of her basket. Anahi didn't pay any attention. She reached a hut and went inside.

Curious, Cariad jogged after her. When she peered in at the door, Anahi was at an interface speaking to a Guardian. The background showed that he was at the settlement. Cariad ducked outside again. Anahi was facing away, but that didn't mean she couldn't see her. Cariad leaned against the wall and listened to the conversation.

"The Gen farmers are refusing to give over their

weapons," the Guardian was saying. "We have them confined in one place—an equipment storage building. Apparently, they were going to stash all the weapons there. They noticed our presence, unfortunately, and locked themselves inside. They're refusing to come out or surrender their arms."

"You have to get those guns off them," Anahi said. "We can't allow them to have any firepower. The Guardians must be able to control any potential unrest."

"We know, but as one of them pointed out, we actually don't have any jurisdiction in the colony. By trying to force them to surrender their arms without the proper authority, we're breaking colony laws. Under colony law, only the Leader has the authority to order the use of force. Currently, there is no Leader."

This seemed to stump Anahi for a moment because Cariad heard no immediate reply, then the Woken said, "Well, that's simple then, isn't it? I declare myself Leader. I authorize the Guardians to use all necessary force to seize the weapon of any Gen."

The Guardian hesitated.

"What?" Anahi challenged. "What's wrong? Do as I say."

"I'm not sure..."

"Look, we revised the Manual to allow a Woken to become Leader, right? But we didn't define how the Woken Leader would be chosen. Nowhere does it say that the Woken Leader has to be elected. Until that part is decided and ratified, anyone can declare themselves Leader. That's exactly what I'm doing."

When the Guardian still gave no reply, Anahi said, "I'm *ordering* you to force entry to the place where the Gens are confined and seize their weapons. Do you understand?"

After another moment's silence, the Guardian's reply came. "Yes, Leader."

Cariad was frozen in shock.

The Guardian asked, "I'm assuming we set our weapons to stun?"

After a moment's pause, Anahi replied, "As I said, use whatever force is necessary to seize the Gens' weapons."

Cariad couldn't let this insanity continue any longer. She ran into the room. Anahi turned to face her. Behind the scientist, the interface screen was blank. The Guardian she'd been speaking to had left to carry out Anahi's orders.

"Call him back," Cariad yelled. "Someone's going to get hurt."

"Nonsense. The Generational Colonists will give themselves up. They're just testing their boundaries."

"You're insane. You really are. You ordered the Guardians to take the Gens' weapons? But they need them. They're facing deadly life forms down there. They have to be able to defend themselves."

"We cannot allow them to have weapons that could be used against us."

Cariad stepped so close to Anahi, their noses were almost touching. She glared into the black light-sensitive screen of the woman's vision aid. "Call the Guardian back."

"No."

"I warn you, this won't stop here. I won't rest until you're made to answer for your actions. If anyone's hurt down there, you'll pay for it."

Anahi laughed. "I think you over-estimate the support you'll have. The Woken are on my side in this. They're just as tired of the Gens' stupidity as I am. Do what you like. You'll be fighting a lonely battle."

Cariad had no time to argue with the unbalanced woman. She had to do something to stop the carnage threatening to occur at the settlement. She ran out of the hut and sprinted to the nearest transit car station. She would go planetside. It seemed the only option.

As she was sitting in the transit car to the shuttle bay, wishing that the vehicle would go faster, her comm chirped. It was Strongquist. Guessing that he wanted to talk to her about Frederick Aparicio, she pressed the 'busy' button. Immediately, the comm chirped again. She answered. "I can't speak to you now." No point in appealing to *him* about the situation at the settlement. The Guardians were clearly on Anahi's side.

"Are you going to board a shuttle?" Strongquist asked.

Wondering how he knew, she replied, "Yes, I am. Why?"

"I believe you may be aware of the developing standoff between Guardians and Gen farmers at the settlement?"

"Yes," Cariad said angrily. "Your people are about to cause a disaster."

"I was hoping you had received news. It is regrettable. Unfortunately, our protocols state that we obey colony law or, failing that, the orders of the colony Leader."

"*Unfortunately* you're a bunch of fools. You're following the orders of a madwoman. I think the cryo's turned her crazy. She's megalomaniacal."

"So you're going down to the planet to intervene?"

"Yes, I am."

"That's good."

"What?! If you think it's a good idea to intervene, why don't you do it yourself? Why don't you call off your buddies?"

"I'm afraid I can't. We have to follow protocol."

"Even if someone might get killed?"

Strongquist seemed to struggle for an answer. "We respect the Leader's judgment. Any threat to human life is acceptable if it's for the greater good of the colony."

The transit car was pulling into the shuttle bay station. "So what you're telling me is, I'm on my own in this?"

"As I said, we will follow the Leader's orders."

"Thanks a lot." Cariad closed the connection and ran for the shuttle. It was just about to leave. When she went into the passenger cabin, it was empty. The shuttle was the last of the day. It would pick up Woken who had been working planetside and bring them back to the ship.

On her way down, Cariad tried to figure out a way of removing Anahi from the Leader's position. Persuading the other Woken was going to be a struggle. They were sympathetic to Anahi's cause. Ever since being revived, most of them had been distant from the Gens. Cariad realized that she'd been remiss in doing nothing about the growing divide.

She silently cursed Strongquist and the rest of the Guardians. She could hardly credit that they would allow themselves to be turned into the colony's bully boys. Anahi had availed herself of extremely dangerous, powerful allies, and Cariad didn't know what she could do about it.

We must follow the Leader's orders. If Anahi ordered them all to walk out of an airlock, would they do it? Her thoughts turned to the Gen farmers who were refusing to give up their rifles. Was Ethan among them? Her stomach clenched at the thought.

By the time the shuttle touched down, Cariad was no closer to figuring out how she was going to defuse the crisis. She sped past the waiting line of scientists and out of the shuttle bay. She'd recognized the farmers' equipment shed behind the Guardian while he was talking to Anahi. It was on the edge of the settlement.

The streets were quiet. Darkness had fallen and the solar-powered lamps had come on. A dull thump echoed in the distance. It came from the direction where she was heading, and sounded like something heavy striking a hollow place—like a battering ram striking a door. She sped up. She was only a couple of streets away.

Another thud.

How could she make the Guardians stop? *We must follow the Leader's orders.*

She couldn't comm Anahi and demand that she call them off. The self-appointed Leader would never agree.

As she rounded a corner, Cariad almost stopped in her tracks. *The self-appointed Leader.* Anahi had declared herself Leader, saying that there were no laws in place governing a Woken Leader's appointment. So unless Anahi had put laws in place in the intervening time...

She was in the street that held the equipment shed. Guardians were grouped around the door. A haze was rising from the pulse fire they were aiming at it, attempting to burn the thing down.

"Hey," she yelled from the end of the street. A few of the Guardians heard her.

"Stop what you're doing. I demand you leave those people alone." Cariad ran up to the group.

The Guardians paused their pulse fire. One said, "We're following the Leader's orders."

"I know. But the leadership has changed. I'm now Leader of this colony, and I command you to withdraw."

CHAPTER TWELVE

Voices were coming from outside the door. New voices. Ethan thought he recognized one of them. "I command you to stop," a woman was saying. "Lower your weapons immediately."

There was further discussion that Ethan couldn't quite hear—an argument that went on for some time. He heard the words "Leader" and "Manual" mentioned. Then, after a long, quiet pause there was murmuring followed by the woman's speaking again, this time through the door.

"Whoever's inside, this is Cariad. I've ordered the Guardians to stand down. You are not in any danger. You're free to leave and no harm will come to you, I swear."

Cariad.

"Open the shutters," Ethan said. The room began to clear of haze. After taking off his shirt and wrapping it around his hand, he opened the hot door. Cariad was directly outside, flanked by Guardians.

His first impulse was to grab her into his arms, but something made him stop. Guilt? A sense of disloyalty to Lauren? No, it was something else.

"Ethan," Cariad said with relief. "I thought you might be here. I'm so glad you're okay. Has anyone been injured?"

"Yes, but nothing major."

He stepped aside to allow the rest of the farmers to come out. The Guardians also moved back to make room for the men and women. The farmers watched them suspiciously as they filed by, their weapons clutched close to their bodies, dark and angry expressions clouding their features. The rift between Gens and Guardians and Woken yawned wider.

Cariad glanced at the Guardians before saying to Ethan, "Can we talk in private?"

He nodded and they went in the opposite direction to the departing farmers, also leaving the Guardians behind.

"See you later," Cherry called. She didn't look too happy about him leaving with Cariad.

As soon as they were out of earshot of both groups, Cariad laid a hand on Ethan's upper arm and said, "I'm so sorry. I've been trying to talk some sense into Anahi, but she's gone crazy. I can't reason with her and I don't know what to do about it. She also seems to have most of the Woken on her side."

"What did you do?" Ethan asked. "How did you get the Guardians to back down?"

"That's another crazy thing," Cariad replied, and went on to explain that she had temporarily declared herself Leader.

"You mean the Guardians just did as you asked? Just because you said you were the new Leader?"

"Yes. That's exactly what happened."

Ethan glanced back at the Guardians in the distance. "So what would happen if I declared myself Leader and told them to go and arrest Anahi?"

"I don't think that would work. Since Anahi changed the Manual, it has to be a Woken."

"Then maybe you should tell them to arrest her."

"I thought about it, but I don't want to do that, and I'm not going to contest it when she takes back the Leader's position, as she inevitably will. Too many of the Woken think like her. It wouldn't be long before I found myself arrested. Up until now, Anahi's been tolerating me. She was trying to bring me to see her point of view. I don't think even after this incident she would do anything rash against me. Most of us Woken go back a long way. But I definitely don't want to push it. I can only work to change the situation if I have my freedom."

"So what *are* you going to do?"

Cariad's expression told Ethan that his question stung. Perhaps he had been too harsh, but on the other hand, he didn't see how any of the problems were the fault of the Gens. They'd all mostly been doing as they were supposed to. None of them had deviated much from the Manual, despite—in his own case—a strong desire to. It was the Woken who were changing the rules. It was the Woken who had slipped up and allowed a Natural Movement saboteur aboard the ship. Cariad was a Woken too.

"Maybe I should speak to the others privately and try to make them see sense," she said. "If I can change enough minds we might be able to transition back to a more equitable situation peacefully. I know most of the Woken well, Ethan. They aren't bad people. They're just worried about the long term survival of the colony. They will be shocked to find out what happened here today. I hope it won't take much effort to persuade them that Anahi is unstable and needs to be stopped."

Ethan didn't have much faith in Cariad's plan. He thought that her personal closeness to the Woken was blinding her to their faults. Yet he didn't have a better solution, or at least not one that didn't involve potential violence.

"Okay," he said. "But I'll tell you this, Cariad: we may

not be as well-educated, experienced, or sophisticated as you Woken, but that doesn't mean we'll tolerate being controlled by you for very long. We were brought up with the Manual. We know exactly what it says, and nowhere does it say that the Woken are to take charge of the colony. You're supposed to be here to join and support the colonization effort. You aren't our shepherds and we aren't your sheep."

The adrenaline of the fight at the shed was fading and his delayed emotional reaction was flooding in. His tone had risen. With some effort, he controlled his anger. "We outnumber the Woken forty to one, and we're armed. Don't imagine we'll ever surrender. All our lives it's been drilled into us that this world is ours —that we're going to make it a home for our children and grandchildren. If it comes to consigning our descendants to what's basically slavery... What I mean is, you Woken might be able to turn the Guardians on us, but we won't go down without a fight, even to the death."

He found himself leaning menacingly over Cariad. She had turned pale with shock. He stepped back. An apology rose to his lips but didn't make it out of his mouth. Though it pained him to have spoken so bluntly and threateningly, he'd meant every word of what he'd said. It wouldn't hurt to impress the seriousness of the situation upon her so she would convey it to her friends.

Cariad hung her head, uncharacteristically deflated. His conscience twinged. Perhaps he had been too frank. She was, after all, his closest friend despite being a Woken, she'd saved many Gens from a horrible death in the First Night Attack, and she'd defused the situation over the weapons.

But then Cariad's head rose, and she had a sharp look in her eye. "Has it ever occurred to you to ask yourself why this has happened? What is it that's made Anahi take these steps to remove control from the

Gens?"

"She wants the power, of course," Ethan replied, "like most of the Woken. When it came down to it, in spite of what it says in the Manual, some of you can't stand to see us in control. Some of you can't bear it that your pet project you worked so hard on has been handed over to someone else."

"You're wrong," Cariad replied. "That isn't it at all, or at least not for most of us. You're forgetting that I was there when the Manual was written. Hell, I even wrote some parts of it myself. We knew that what we were demanding of you wasn't fair. The people who embarked on the voyage were in full knowledge that they were never going to set foot on a planet again, but their children didn't agree to that, and neither did their children. We knew we were demanding the sacrifice of thousands of people to see the project through to the end and make the dream come true.

"We decided that the minimum we could do in recognition of the nameless individuals who lived and died aboard a starship would be to gift the planet to you, the Final Generation. We'd put you in the position you were in. You hadn't asked to be there. We wanted you to be in control. We wanted it to be *your* world, and we would only be there to help."

"So what changed?"

"Can't you even guess, Ethan? When we were revived, we found out that somewhere along the journey, the Manual had been rewritten. People who had never seen Earth, never breathed a natural atmosphere, and who never would, thought they were in a position to dictate what should happen. We didn't like it, but we didn't say anything. We left you in control.

"Now think back to the First Night Attack. How did all the Gens behave, with you the only exception? It was near total panic. They couldn't deal with the emergency. And what's been happening since? You're doing as you like. Changing roles, using equipment in ways it isn't supposed to be used, putting yourselves in danger.

"I don't agree with the way Anahi's gone about it, but I can't deny that she has a point. If we allow you to continue as you have been, acting stupidly with no thought of the future, this colony might fail. If we sit by and let you do what you want, we could all end up dead. All that work, all that sacrifice by tens of thousands of people will be for nothing."

"That's exactly what I'm talking about," Ethan said. "Why can't you trust us? You made us after all. You, Cariad, are personally responsible for our genetic inheritance. What you're saying is, you got it wrong. That's what you can't stand. You think you messed up. That's what's bothering you. That's why you want to take back control. The real problem is that we don't mindlessly obey. Do you want a second chance? Do you want to create people who will do as they're told? Your children have grown up and you don't like it."

Cariad's hands were clenched into fists at her sides, but she didn't offer a return argument. "I'm going back to the ship. I'll speak to the others and see what I can do."

Ethan couldn't stand the hurt look on her face. He also couldn't take back what he'd said. When he didn't reply, Cariad walked away. He watched her go. She glanced back and their gazes met, but still he said nothing.

***

After waiting for Cariad to turn the corner, Ethan went to see Garwin. The older man's job as a "Priority 1" worker had qualified him for one of the first private homes that had been constructed. He was a mechanic and chief supervisor overseeing the construction of the plows, roadmakers, and other machinery involved in creating the infrastructure of the settlement. Most of the rest of the Gens were housed as Ethan was, in large, temporary dorms and barns while they waited for more permanent homes to be built.

As soon as Garwin opened his door and saw who had come to pay him a visit, he glanced from side to side along the street, which was empty. He pulled Ethan quickly inside, his usually open, friendly features creased into an expression that mixed irritation with concern.

"Not a good idea coming to my house, Ethan," he said quietly the moment the door was closed and they were alone in the dim, quiet hall of his small home.

"Sorry," Ethan replied. "I didn't think about it. Did you hear what—"

Garwin's wife, Twyla, had stepped into the hall from the living room. She was a tall, raw-boned woman. Her welcoming smile seemed fake. "Hello. You're Ethan, right? I didn't know you were one of Garwin's friends. There's no need to stand and talk out here. Why don't you come in and have something to drink?"

Twyla gestured for them to follow her and turned away. Garwin shrugged. Ethan guessed that his wife might not be privy to his subversive activities. He went through with him to the living room of the prefabricated house.

The room's pale gray walls were brightened up with cut-out prints of brightly colored flowers, which made the place seem less utilitarian. Ethan was reminded of conversations he'd had with Lauren about how they would decorate their farmhouse.

"Tea or coffee?" Twyla asked.

"Tea would be fine," Ethan replied.

Garwin said, "Sweetener?"

Ethan was about to say no, but an almost imperceptible nod from Garwin made him alter his response. "Er, yes please."

"Oh, we don't have any sweetener," Twyla said. "We don't use it."

"The store's still open," Garwin said. "Maybe you could go and get some. It'll be handy for guests."

"I guess so. Sit down, Ethan. You're our first visitor, you know." She went out into the hall.

As he took a seat in the armchair of their matching living room set, Ethan began to speak, but Garwin held his finger to his lips. He said, "I know why you've come, Ethan, but I'm sorry, I'm no further along with that plow than I was yesterday. Like I said, the kit was incomplete, and I'm waiting for the missing part. It has to be printed and sent down. Until I receive it, there's nothing I can do. It isn't like I can just open another container and take it from there. Those things contain thousands of parts."

The sound of the front door closing came through from the hall, and Garwin went out to check that Twyla really had left.

When he returned, Ethan said, "I didn't realize your wife doesn't know what else you do. Maybe I should go."

"No, it's okay. You're here now. We might as well make the best use of the time till Twyla returns."

"You heard about—"

"The assault on the shed? Of course. That news is probably halfway back to Earth by now."

"We need to talk about that," said Ethan, "but it'll have to wait for another day. We don't have time at the moment. But I just wanted to tell you, we learned something important today. The Guardians will do whatever the Woken tell them, and they're prepared to use lethal force. We nearly didn't make it out of that shed. We can't let them catch us out again. What I want to know is, what are we going to do to protect ourselves?"

"I totally agree," Garwin replied. "That's a question that needs answering immediately. We've been playing it too safe with plenty of talk and precious little action.

It's time to take control of the situation. We need to go on the offensive. The biggest problem we have is that nearly all of us are down here. The Woken are up there... " He pointed at the ceiling. "And as well as the force of the Guardians at their disposal, they have most of the technology and control."

"So what can we do about it?" Ethan asked.

"I'm not sure, but I had an idea. If the situation doesn't improve, as long as we stay here, we're at their mercy. They know exactly where we are and what most of us are doing most of the time. But we do have some things on our side. We've been trained in everything we need to build a civilization on this planet. It's been our one collective purpose in life since we were born. The Woken are a bunch of scientists. Sure, they know more than us, but do they have the numbers or the raw power to make a colony on their own? They might not realize it, but they need us more than we need them."

Ethan had an idea what Garwin meant, but it was almost too radical for him to comprehend. "What are you saying?"

"Look, we already have enough supplies down here to last us another year, plus tons of equipment. Most important of all, we have skills. Skills that are perfectly suited to the job ahead. But if we remain where we are, the Woken have us exactly where they want us. They're going to exploit us for their own ends."

"You're suggesting that we leave and build another settlement someplace else, aren't you?"

"Exactly."

CHAPTER THIRTEEN

As Cariad went to the meeting that Strongquist had called, her wish for easy solutions to the problems that dogged the colony was peppered with pessimism. Anahi's behavior was unhinged, yet Cariad doubted that she could convince the woman of that, nor any of the Woken who supported her. She'd tried speaking to them as individuals but she hadn't made much headway. Rather, she seemed to have turned some of them against herself. And after the confrontation over the weapons, the Gens were also unlikely to be in a conciliatory mood.

When she reached the room aboard the *Nova Fortuna* they were using for the meeting, Anahi had already arrived. She was the only person there, but she didn't acknowledge Cariad when she went in, preferring an icy disregard, no doubt due to Cariad's interference in the standoff over the Gens' weapons. Cariad sat down and the strained silence continued until Strongquist stepped in closely followed by Faina. With an air of statesmanship, Anahi stood and welcomed the newcomers.

She had re-assumed the role of Leader as soon as

she'd learned of Cariad's trick. Then she'd immediately altered the legislation to prevent any further usurping of the position. The move had been inevitable, but Cariad was a long way from backing down over the issue.

The two Guardians sat together opposite Anahi, looking oddly twin-like side by side in their uniforms. Cariad had taken a seat at the end of the table. Strongquist had said he was also inviting some Gens. She had high hopes over who one of them might be. It would make sense for the Guardian to invite prominent members of the Gen community, especially those who had been involved in the incident at the equipment shed.

Garwin entered first. Cariad approved of Strongquist's choice. The man was sympathetic to the Woken concerns and well-liked among the Gens. They would listen to him. As the older, broad-shouldered man took a seat next to her, the person she'd been hoping to see also entered the room. Ethan. They exchanged small smiles. Cariad was relieved their friendship seemed to remain intact despite their recent falling out.

Strongquist leaned his elbows on the table and clasped his hands together. "Thank you for coming, everyone. I hope you'll agree it's long past time that some of us tried to take these problems the colony has been experiencing in hand. I'm hoping we can thrash out some steps toward solving them today."

"Wait a minute," Anahi said. "Are these all the people you invited? I wasn't expecting so few. I suggested several names to you, but none of those people are here. Shouldn't we have a little more expertise on board before we make any major decisions on the future of this settlement? And I'm not sure what she's doing here." The black strip of her visor turned to Cariad. Her face was stony.

"Leader," Strongquist began. Cariad balked at his

use of the designation for the mad woman. "I didn't intend that any decisions about the future of the *Nova Fortuna* colony be made at this time. Instead I believe we should address the widening schism between the Gens and the Woken. We need to make an effort at conciliation and a meeting of minds. I propose that we address that concern first. We need to find a way to avoid further violence and to move toward returning to the previous atmosphere of mutual goodwill."

"I'll suggest a way to avoid further violence," Ethan said bitterly. "You Guardians can stop your military tactics and the Woken can stop using you to control us. Let us Gens go about our business freely. We haven't done anything that calls for our control by armed forces, and even if we had, so what? This colony is ours, as the Manual says and the Woken used to say, until they changed their minds."

Cariad raised her eyebrows. He was right, but she was surprised to hear him speak so forcefully in front of Anahi and the Guardians. Ethan was growing in confidence day by day.

Strongquist's expression was pained. He leaned back in his seat. "What happened at the equipment storage unit was a situation that got way out of control. We should have found a better solution than an aggressive confrontation like that."

Ethan asked, "So we can have your guarantee that the Guardians will never threaten the Gens again?"

Strongquist looked at Faina for a moment.

Faina answered Ethan's question. "It's important that you understand our mandate is to support this colony at all costs. We must avoid the loss of life as far as we possibly can—the Guardians who were trying to retrieve the weapons from the tool store were firing on stun setting—but if, in the direst circumstances, we must use deadly force to ensure the success of the colony, our mandate allows us to do that." As she finished speaking, her pale brown eyes seemed to lose all warmth.

"What the hell are you saying?" Cariad exclaimed. "You're telling us that Guardians have the right to kill "for the good of all?" Who gave you that authority? No one here did. Not one person aboard the *Nova Fortuna* or planetside has that right." She looked pointedly at Anahi. "And who are the Guardians to judge what's best for the colony and what isn't? You can't see the future. You can only guess, like the rest of us."

"*Damned* right," Ethan exclaimed, hitting the table with his fist. "The first Gen you kill will be the last. It'll be war."

Into the tense silence that followed the outbursts, Strongquist said, almost apologetically, "I don't recall anyone objecting to the execution we carried out following the First Night Attack."

Cariad and Ethan's gazes met. The Guardian's point was a good one. Not one person had challenged their actions when the Guardians killed the person who had turned off the electric fence, resulting in many horrible deaths. But at that moment, everyone had agreed who the enemy was. It was now that they might suddenly become the enemy that they objected to the Guardians' license to kill.

"This is all nonsense," said Garwin in a conciliatory tone. "How can it be for the good of the colony to use lethal force? The First Night Attack was a special case, and if we ever catch the bomber who blew up the stadium, we'll make another exception. But for the general settlers—Gens and Woken alike—we need every one of them. There are only just over two thousand of us. I'm not a geneticist, but isn't that the bare minimum needed for the genetic diversity to colonize a planet? Aside from the moral objections to murdering people, we can't afford any more bloodshed. We need every single person."

Anahi spoke. "Actually, no. We don't." She paused for effect, a wry smile on her lips. Garwin and Ethan looked confused, but Cariad knew what she meant.

Anahi went on, "We have enough eggs and sperm stored to replace every Gen ten times over. It wouldn't be easy of course. We'd have to reopen the reproductive labs, gestate the infants, and then care for excessive numbers of them at a time, but it's feasible. I think we could do it."

"You're insane," Cariad said. "Whether we could do it or not is immaterial. You're talking about threatening the lives of thousands of people just because they won't do what you want. And what if this next generation you raise from babies also disobeys you? Do you plan on murdering them too? On and on, until our supplies run out and at last the colony fails?"

"Stop downplaying the Gens' actions, Cariad," Anahi replied. "You need to stop making excuses for them. You know as well as I do the expertise and care that went into crafting the Manual. If they pick and choose what they follow and what they ignore, it puts the colony and all our lives in jeopardy. If they won't do as they're told, they have to be stopped. And if I have to command the Guardians to take whatever steps necessary to make them comply, I will do that."

"Aside from the insane logic of your thinking," Cariad said, "you're forgetting that Manual was written on another planet centuries ago. We were both there, remember? We both helped to write it, and at the time, we acknowledged that we couldn't anticipate every eventuality; that the Manual was a guide only."

"And yet it's the best guide we have," Anahi retorted between her teeth. "If anyone's going to make a decision to deviate from it, it should be us."

Cariad shook her head. "*You*, you mean. There's something wrong with you, Anahi. Seriously. You aren't the person I worked with on the *Nova Fortuna* project."

She turned to Strongquist and Faina. "I believe Anahi may have suffered brain damage while in cryonic suspension or during revival. She should be medically examined and treated if necessary. It's only manifested over the last few weeks, but she's becoming more and more irrational with each day that passes."

"How dare you," Anahi shouted, rising to her feet. She took a breath as if to launch into a verbal attack, then she smiled and sat down. "Why should I care what you think, Cariad? If I'm suffering from brain damage, how is it that most of the Woken agree with me? You must be just about the only dissenter, which makes me wonder why Strongquist even invited you to this meeting."

"Cariad performed a great service to this colony," Strongquist said, "and I believe that many Gens and some Woken respect her opinion. Despite your assertions, she is as influential as anyone sitting around this table."

Anahi simmered but she didn't reply.

"So what's the way forward?" Garwin asked. "We need to find a way to make things work between all parties. I'm sure none of us want the Guardians put in a position where they feel the need to exercise their mandate."

"The way forward is to return to how things were," said Ethan. "We elect a Gen Leader and we get on with making our new home habitable—without interference."

"No," said Anahi. "The proposal of a Gen Leader is off the table. I won't countenance it and neither will the rest of the Woken. If you ever prove capable of following the rules we set out, maybe we'll think about it, but I doubt that's going to happen in the near future."

Ethan's expression darkened. He was about to respond but Garwin laid a hand on his arm. An unspoken message passed between them that Cariad couldn't interpret. "I have a solution that I believe both sides might agree on. How about this? If, whenever a Gen sees the necessity of deviating from the Manual, they send up a request along with their reasons for it. Then Anahi, as Leader, can grant it or not."

Ethan shot Garwin an indignant look. The older man gripped the younger's arm tighter. Ethan looked down and remained silent. Something ulterior was clearly going on between the two men but Cariad couldn't guess what it was.

After a few moments' consideration, Anahi replied, "I think I could live with that." A collective breath exhaled. The mood in the room lightened a notch, though not on Ethan's part. He remained gazing downward, a frown creasing his brow.

The attendees began to shift in their seats. The meeting seemed to be drawing to a close, but Cariad still had questions. "Strongquist, do you have any updates on your investigation into the stadium bomber?"

"Only in the negative sense, I'm afraid. I inquired of all the Woken about the name you recognized from the list of Natural Movement followers, but no one else remembers him. We've also gone through all the backgrounds of every Woken, revived or not, and we haven't turned up a single lead."

"Are you saying the bomber was a Gen?" Ethan asked.

"No, I'm not saying that," Strongquist replied. "But now that we've thoroughly explored that avenue of inquiry, we are turning to the Gens. Of the two groups, it's the least likely to harbor Natural Movement members. That's why we looked into the Woken first. But if the Natural Movement infiltrator died with the First Generation, it's possible that the cult has been passed down somehow from one generation to the next."

Cariad said, "Okay, there's one more thing I want to talk about. You told us today that the Guardians have a mandate to save the colony at all costs. That's the first I or anyone else heard about it as far as I know. Let's be frank: we're almost entirely in the dark about you. You've told us hardly anything about who you are or what's happened on Earth since we left. Are you from the Global Government? I guess you're military, seeing as you're armed. But whose military are you? And how come you're so intent on making a success of the colony?"

Strongquist looked uncomfortable but nodded. He couldn't twist his way out of answering Cariad's questions put directly and in front of others. "All good points. Yes, we are from the Global Government. We were sent to save you when the Natural Movement's plan to sabotage the colony was discovered in the historical records, as you know. But we are also here to protect the colony because you represent humanity's hope. As Faina said in the stadium, Earth, Mars, and the Outer Moons are overpopulated. They're also polluted and low on resources.

"When we set off, longer than eighteen years ago, the situation was dire. Now, it's probably at crisis point. The Solar System is not a place you would wish to return to. The one reason that the resources required to build our ship and send us here were allowed was in order to save you. You are humankind's hope. If the *Nova Fortuna* colonists succeed, there is a chance for the rest of humanity."

"Do you mean that if we make the colony viable, we can expect refugees from Earth?" Cariad asked.

"As far as we're aware," Faina replied, "no refugee ships have departed Earth to come here. The Global Government is struggling to keep everyone fed, let alone anything else. It would find it hard to justify spending the billions needed to build a ship that would only save a few thousand people. Besides, overwhelming a fledgling colony with thousands more mouths to feed wouldn't be in anyone's best interests.

"Which isn't to say that, at some point in the future, you might not receive some arrivals hoping for a fresh start. But I don't think you need to worry too much about that right now. However, if the colony flourishes, it will prove that deep space colonization could be the long-term answer to the problems in the Solar System." She placed her hands palm downward on the tabletop and leaned forward. "We want you to succeed. Humanity needs you to succeed. We'll do whatever it takes to ensure that."

"Success at any cost?" Cariad asked bitterly. "If it means killing innocent people who just happen to have a different opinion? Is that a price worth paying? I didn't think that was what we were trying to build here."

"If their opinions are invalid and their actions harmful," Anahi said, "we have every right to deny them, with force if necessary. If someone gets hurt as a result, is that our fault? But anyway, we have the Guardians' word that they won't harm anyone unless it's absolutely necessary for the sake of the colony.

"Now, it's time to move on from this circular argument. I have an announcement to make: starting tomorrow, the process of reviving the remaining individuals in cryonic suspension will resume. We've looked at the problems that led to failures in the past, and we believe we've ironed them out. With more Woken around, we'll have the benefit of additional expertise. Everything should go more smoothly. I'd appreciate it if you could lend a hand with the process, Cariad. I understand that you oversaw many of the more successful revivals after you'd recovered from your own."

Cariad hesitated, surprised. The invitation was the

last thing she'd expected from Anahi. She was sure the woman must hate her following her recent interfering. Then she remembered the saying: *Keep your friends close and your enemies closer.* Was this Anahi's way of keeping an eye on her?

It didn't matter. The saying worked both ways, and several of her friends were still lying frozen in slush. If an attempt was going to be made to revive them, she wanted to be there. "Sure. I'd be happy to help."

"Good," said Anahi. "I thought you would agree. I put someone rather important to the top of the list. The colony needs a clear sense of purpose and direction, and so tomorrow you can be in attendance at the reviving of Aubriot."

Cariad's heart sank.

CHAPTER FOURTEEN

Ethan watched the curve of the planet's surface straighten out as the shuttle sank lower into the atmosphere. Below, the regular lines of the settlement were clear to see, carved on the natural landscape. After the heat of the meeting his emotions were finally calming, and the sight of the settlement and the planet they had yet to name provoked an unfamiliar feeling in him.

The only sensation he could liken it to was how he used to feel when returning to the kindergartners' dorm at the end of the day when he was a little boy. His spirits would rise when he saw the room and his caregivers. Even the smell of the place had made him feel warm and content.

His feeling at that moment in the shuttle was similar, only stronger. He was looking forward to returning to the farmers' temporary housing, and maybe tomorrow he would go out to his farm, though he would stay well away from the lake. He'd planted seed with Cherry's help. Perhaps the shoots would be showing.

Though *Nova Fortuna* had arrived only two months prior, Ethan already felt a kind of bonding with the new planet that was greater than anything he'd felt in all his years aboard ship.

Garwin, who had been dozing in the seat beside him, stirred and woke up. He peered over Ethan and out the window. "Nearly there."

"You know, I never thought about the planet much until now," Ethan said. "I always focused on whatever we were supposed to be doing here. It was always, what do we have to do now according to the Manual? What do we have to watch out for? What do we have to do exactly right? That's what you and I were brought up to do, wasn't it?"

"As far back as I can remember," Garwin replied. "From the moment I left my milk mother until Arrival Day, everything I did, everything I learned, was aimed at one purpose. Build a colony. Survive."

"That's how I saw things too. But look at it. Did you ever see such a wonderful sight?"

Garwin smiled. "Never. Not in any vid of Earth. Not even in art."

"And you know what?" Ethan said, "It's ours. It belongs to us. Living here is what we were created for. We mustn't ever let anyone take it away from us."

Ethan was finally understanding what the feeling in his gut was—for the first time, he was seeing the planet as home. Not only that, he knew he would fight to his dying breath for his right to live there however he wanted. The conflict with Anahi and her supporters wasn't about Woken versus Gens, or minor points like whether flitters should be used for non-emergencies, it was about protecting his home, his territory, and his independence.

They didn't say much more as the shuttle made its final descent and landed, but as they were leaving the shuttle field, Garwin asked Ethan to follow him. It was soon apparent that they were going to the flitter shed.

A Gen called Verney was guarding the vehicles.

Ethan only knew him by sight. Verney's job was to check that the Gens who borrowed the flitters had the authority to do so. The man took no notice when Garwin went in and beckoned Ethan to do the same.

Inside, the space was full of the boxy, flat-bottomed vehicles, their covers down. Only one was missing from its bay now that it was nearly evening.

"Are we going somewhere?" Ethan asked.

"No," Garwin replied. "Or at least *we're* not, not today. I wanted to bring you here so that we can talk without being overheard."

Garwin moved closer and held Ethan's gaze firmly. "With most of the Woken remaining shipside, we have the planet virtually to ourselves at the moment. If we find a site for another settlement soon and transfer everything and everyone there little by little... Well, we could do it under their noses. It's us Gens who are in charge of most everything down here. We could manage it if we were careful. Then, once we've built our defenses at the new place, the final few who are managing the facade of a working settlement can transfer over. When the next Woken or Guardian visits, they'll find a ghost town. What do you think?"

"I think it's a great idea," Ethan replied. He glanced around the shed. "I'm guessing this is the reason you brought me here."

"You guessed right," Garwin said. "I can't leave my job for long periods without it being noticed, but you have the perfect excuse to be away from the settlement. Everyone will assume that you're working on your farm, and no one's likely to check on you. You're also a lot younger than me, Ethan. I have to admit I'm not up to spending hours traveling about these days. Verney here will let you take a flitter no questions asked.

"I want you to look for a place. Somewhere like this area, where the vegetation isn't too dense and the ground is flat. Somewhere that seems safe. As soon as you've found it, we'll build a fence, set up a generator, and start bringing supplies over. Before we know it, we'll have a new home."

As the impact of what Garwin was suggesting settled in, Ethan didn't answer right away. Garwin mistook his silence for a reluctance to agree. "You'd be doing it for Gen autonomy, don't forget. But if you want to think about it... I understand it's a lot to ask."

"No, no. It isn't a lot to ask at all. All my life I've wanted to be an explorer. You just gave me the perfect opportunity. I'll start out at first light tomorrow."

***

When Ethan returned to the flitter shed the following morning, he was surprised to find someone besides just Verney there. She seemed to be waiting for him.

"Hi," Cherry said. "I hope you brought plenty to eat. I couldn't sneak much off the table at breakfast."

"I have plenty of food," Ethan replied, "but Garwin didn't mention anyone else coming along."

"He didn't? He must have forgotten. I suggested that two people should go. You know, in case something bad happens. Then the other one can go and get help."

"Makes sense, I guess." Ethan scanned the identical flitters in their bays before pointing at the one nearest the door "We'll take that. Jump in. Wait. Did you bring your weapon? We don't know what we might find out there."

"Of course. What did you think I was gonna do? Leave it at home and let the sluglimpets get me?"

"The what?"

"The creatures that ate people in the First Night Attack."

"Is that what we're calling them now?" The memory of Lauren's corpse threatened from the edge of Ethan's mind. He suppressed the image.

Cherry said, "A Woken gave them some long, scientific name that no one can remember, but *we're* calling them sluglimpets. You know, like the animals in the vids at school. Half slug, half—"

"I get it. You know they're a lot bigger than slugs and limpets? Don't imagine that if one attacks you you're going to flick it off."

"Of course not. I wasn't there on the first night, thank the stars, but I heard all about it." She had climbed into the flitter. "Are we going to set off now?"

Ethan climbed in the other side. He put his bag next to Cherry's on the back seat and started the vehicle. As it rose thirty centimeters above ground and hovered, the interface screen came alive, displaying a map of the immediate surroundings. Satellites launched from the *Nova Fortuna* mapped the terrain and weather systems for several hundred kilometers around, broadcasting the data to the surface. As long as they stayed with the flitter, Ethan and Cherry would know exactly where they were.

The sun was just coming up and the streets were quiet. Ethan drove the flitter the shortest route to the gate in the electric fence. It opened automatically, and they were soon heading out across the fields. Ethan took them in the direction of the lake, as if he were heading toward his farm. As soon as they were out of sight of the settlement, however, he veered sharply to the right.

Cherry had been training her weapon on random items in the landscape, turning to keep them in the sights as they passed by. At Ethan's change of direction, she lowered her gun and peered at the interface. "Where are we going?"

Instead of replying, Ethan took one hand off the steering disc and touched the interface image with his finger and thumb, pulling it smaller and increasing the scale. The flashing red dot that signified their flitter slowed its pace rapidly on the larger map. Their direction was obvious.

"The ocean," Cherry exclaimed. "Great idea."

A grin spread across Ethan's face. "We'll be the first humans to ever see it up close."

"But what if they have those thread monsters that live in the lake there, only ten times bigger?"

"Don't worry. We won't go too near the water. Only look at it from a safe distance."

***

They'd been traveling for around two hours and the sun was well up when Cherry put the flitter cover down. The wind was invigorating. They were passing through a wide valley that meandered between high hills. Below them was what looked like an ancient, dry river bed, filled with water-rounded boulders.

"Do you think," Cherry said, "when the Woken and the Guardians see that we've all left the settlement to strike out on our own, they'll come looking for us?"

"I don't doubt it."

"And will they be able to find us?"

"They'll find us for sure. We can't go far. We don't have the equipment or the time. If we did, maybe we could hide on the other side of the planet. Then, it might be a long while before they found us. Hiding from them forever isn't the point though. What we want to do is get out from their control. If they come after us and try to force us to return, we'll have to put up enough of a fight for them to conclude that it isn't worth their while to make us come back.

"I hope it doesn't come to that. I don't think most of the Woken or the Guardians are bad people. They just don't trust us not to mess up. I don't think they'll do us much harm if we make it clear that all we want is to be left alone. They probably wouldn't go so far as to turn us into slaves or anything like that. At least, not according to Cariad. She said one of the aims of the *Nova Fortuna* project was to create a better society. Fighting each other isn't better, it's taking a step back.

I can't believe they would really want that."

"But without us, what'll they do?" Cherry asked. "There aren't enough of them to create a settlement by themselves."

"At the meeting Garwin and I went to on the ship, Anahi said they could start up the generation cycles again. Create new babies and bring them up. Maybe they'll do that. Or return to Earth, though it sounds like conditions are bad there. But if it's only the Woken who go, maybe the Guardians could fit them in their ship. I don't know. They can do what they like. It isn't our problem."

He sniffed. "Does the air smell strange?"

Cherry breathed in deeply through her nose. "Yeah, it smells kind of... Hmm... hard to describe."

Ethan checked the interface. The dot that represented their flitter was at the blue edge of the ocean, but the scale of the map was large. He widened the image with his fingers and took another look. They were nearly at the ocean, but hills on their right were obscuring their view. Ahead of them, the valley petered out and ended in a narrow gap.

"We're almost there," said Ethan, excitement rising in his chest. "It's through that opening." He pushed the accelerator and pointed the flitter's nose at the patch of sky between the final hills of the valley. He peered ahead. Was it only sky that he could see? Or was that different blue at the bottom something else?

The flitter cleared the last tens of meters. Ethan's eyes soaked up the ocean view that spread out before them. Less than a second later, the flitter's nose dipped and suddenly they were zooming vertically down.

Cherry screamed as she fell forward. She hadn't fastened her safety belt. Ethan grabbed her with one hand while desperately pulling at the steering disc with the other to return the flitter to horizontal. He was hanging forward. Only his safety belt was preventing his certain death.

Cherry's fumbling fingers quickly found and fastened her belt. Ethan could concentrate on controlling the flitter.

"What's wrong?" Cherry yelled. "Pull it up." The rocks below were zooming up toward them.

"I can't. I'm trying. It won't move. It's sticking to the cliff. Oh, wait. I've got it." Ethan pressed the screen. The flitter responded instantly. A handful of meters from the base of the cliff, its nose lifted until it was horizontal once more.

"That was close," Cherry exclaimed.

"Yeah. No traveling without safety belts from now on."

The flitter's default setting was to remain thirty centimeters above the ground and Ethan hadn't changed it. The vehicle had done what its program told it, maintaining a short distance between its base and the nearest surface. Only the nearest surface had been the cliff face. Ethan checked the screen. They were five meters above sea level. Blue waves were below and all around them.

"This," said Cherry, "is amazing."

Ever since he'd been a young child, Ethan had wondered what it would be like to see an ocean. He'd also wondered how it would feel to set foot on the solid ground of a planet, but the concept of an ocean was something else. It was fairly easy to imagine standing in a landscape. The *Nova Fortuna* had Main Park, and he anticipated that a landscape would be similar, only bigger. To an extent, he'd been right.

But it had been almost impossible for him to grasp the concept of a vast sea of quadrillions of liters of water. Not like the expanse of space, empty and barren, but somewhere where entire ecosystems lived and died under the waves. Vids of oceans on Earth had seemed unreal, like cartoons. The most water he'd ever seen in one place was the contents of the vats that fed the showers. Water was a precious commodity aboard *Nova Fortuna*. The idea of enough of it to fill an ocean boggled his mind.

Ethan nodded slowly. The expanse surrounding them had robbed him of words. He drove the flitter higher, well out of the reach of ocean thread monsters, and brought it around to see the place where they'd exited the hills. The gap they'd come through was clear. Judging from the worn boulders that lay on the beach below the gap, their death-defying plunge had been along the route of what had once been a waterfall leading to the ocean.

The dried-up waterfall wasn't the only geographical feature to capture Ethan's attention. All along the cliffs on either side of it were dark holes. Caves.

CHAPTER FIFTEEN

For a place where Cariad had spent one hundred and eighty-four years of her life, the cryo chamber didn't look much like home. In fact, it reminded her of a morgue, and she was glad that she hadn't asked to see it before she'd been frozen in suspension all that time ago on Earth. The coffin-sized receptacles that held the bodies were slotted into the wall behind steel doors, and their -101 Celsius temperature chilled the room, frosting Cariad's exhalations.

Beside each door was a panel that displayed the temperature, the occupant's name and number, and his or her physical condition—sensors constantly scanned for evidence of decay. In the event that the temperature rose or the sensors detected a deterioration in the subject's condition, the individual was supposed to be revived immediately. The cryo units had functioned perfectly up until then, though that hadn't prevented problems from occurring during the revival process.

Anahi had come along to the cryo chamber, as well as Dr. Montfort, the Woken physician who had treated Cariad after the stadium bombing, and Alasdair, the medic who had also attended her. Montfort was a cryonic revival specialist who had joined the *Nova Fortuna* Project just before departure. None of the physicians who had put the subjects in suspension had applied to be one of those preserved, which had only served to highlight the riskiness of the procedure. Dr. Montfort had been one of the first to be revived by the Gens and the only person in that initial batch to survive the process unscathed.

Alasdair was preparing the equipment on the cart that would transport the next person they would attempt to slowly return to life, Aubriot, to a revival room. As Cariad watched the medic, she wondered which of the open doors and empty holes of vacated cryo units had been hers. It would have been easy to read the panels and find out, but she didn't want to know from which of those hollow graves she had arisen.

"Everything seems perfect," Montfort said, straightening up from his squatting position next to Aubriot's chamber. He turned to Alasdair. "The cart's ready?"

"Yes. I've double checked all the equipment. It's at the correct temperature."

"Then let's begin." Montfort's tone had the air of someone enjoying a long-anticipated treat. He seemed about to rub his hands together in glee. The doctor squatted down again and inserted a card into a slot before swiping the display screen. He pressed the keys that appeared. There was a click. The seal was broken. The door slowly, smoothly swung open.

Montfort keyed in another instruction, and the cryo unit slid out to its fullest extent.

It was a transparent box, its sides and base threaded with fine wires. Inside the box was a semi-transparent white gel, and suspended within the gel lay a human body. Aubriot. He was pale, entirely hairless, corpse-like. Cariad's stomach twisted. She had passed many decades in the same state, a hair's breadth from death.

"Excuse me," Alasdair said as he wheeled the cart over to the opened unit. Cariad stepped out of his way, and he positioned the cart parallel to the box. Two slim metal arms lowered and slid under it. The arms lifted and retracted, so that the box moved over and into the cart. The cart's monitoring equipment sprang to life, drawing data from the contacts on the base of the box.

"Looking good," said Montfort as he checked the readings. "Let's go."

Alasdair activated the cart's electric motor and guided it toward the chamber exit.

Cariad followed in its wake with the others. Feeling like she was in a funeral procession, she grasped for a distraction. She asked Montfort, "How have you altered the revival process to reduce the rate of complications?"

"I thought you might ask me that. I haven't done anything very sophisticated. I've slowed the process down and increased the monitoring. I analyzed all the data we had on the revivals we completed. I think we were too ambitious in our estimation of how long it would take organs and nerves to resume normal functioning. The problem was, the information on successful revivals that took place prior to the *Nova Fortuna* project was sparse."

"Yes," Cariad said. "Not enough data to base our predictions on."

Montfort continued, "I've set the revival equipment to automatically halt the moment the monitors pick up an abnormal reading. We'll wait a while before resuming the process. If the readings continue to register as abnormal, I may make the decision to lower the patient's temperature and resume suspension before any further damage is done."

"That sounds sensible," Cariad said.

Montfort asked, "Did you do something similar with the few you oversaw?"

Before Cariad could answer, Anahi interrupted. "So if something goes wrong, you're saying we won't revive Aubriot?"

"That's correct," Montfort replied. "Better to remain in suspension with the chance of revival later than risk permanent impairment or death, don't you think?"

"I'm not sure I agree," Anahi said. "I've adjusted to my sightlessness, and we have the materials and skills to fashion other disability aids. I'd rather be here and blind than still in suspension. However, I'll bow to your superior judgment. For now."

Anahi was clearly determined to have Aubriot up and around, at almost any cost. It wasn't hard for Cariad to guess why. Anahi wasn't a natural leader, but Aubriot was. She was clearly hoping to align him to her cause and profit from the man's dictatorial skills.

The procession proceeded to the revival room. The equipment it contained was highly specialized. From the warming unit that would gradually increase the temperature of the cryonic suspension gel by points of a degree at a time to the cell nutrient supply system, all the devices were geared to the sole purpose of returning a long-frozen human body to normal health.

Entering the room brought back strong memories of Cariad's moment of her own awakening, which she'd relived after the bombing. The place was decorated in pastel shades intended to be easy on eyes that hadn't worked for nearly two centuries. She recalled the pale yellows and blues as the first thing she'd registered as she'd slowly come to, when her new life had begun.

Alasdair and Montfort placed Aubriot's cryo unit inside a white plastisteel container for the first stage of the process.

"Attach him," Montfort said to Alasdair. "I'll be back in a moment." As he passed Cariad and Anahi, who were watching from the door, he said, "There's no need to hang around. You know that nothing interesting is going to happen for a few days." He added, to Anahi, "I'll keep you informed of progress, Leader."

He walked away down the corridor, and without a

word to Cariad, Anahi also left.

Alasdair was busily connecting wires and flipping switches.

Cariad asked, "How many revivals have you assisted with, Alasdair?"

"I was involved with most of them." He glanced at her with a smile. "In case you're wondering, yes, I helped with yours. Don't you remember?" He inserted a final jack and stood back before taking a slow walk around the revival container and double-checking the readout screen.

Cariad moved into the room, recalling her glimpse of Aubriot's prone figure in frozen slush. He'd been lying on his side in the recovery position.

"What's it like for you, watching us return to life?" she asked.

"Weird at first," Alasdair replied. "But you get used to it." He folded his arms and frowned for a moment before saying, "Your revival was straightforward. Textbook, in fact. But you were young compared to the rest. Others weren't so lucky, of course. We did what we could, but sometimes their hearts just refused to start, or just when we thought they were fine, their hearts would stop and nothing we did would get them going. Or everything would seem normal but their reflexes were dead. Then, when they regained consciousness they couldn't move their arms and legs. Or everything worked physically, but their brains were mush—sorry, I didn't mean to sound so callous."

"I know, and it's okay," Cariad said. "We all knew the risks. Thanks for bringing me back to life."

"No problem."

"So, what does Dr. Montfort's new process entail exactly?"

"Nothing much for seventy-two hours. We'll begin internal warming afterward, through the circulatory system, bladder, stomach, intestines, and lungs—"

"Lungs?"

"Sure. It's another of the doctor's innovations. We spend the first nine months of life with our lungs filled with amniotic fluid, and the patients don't begin breathing until right at the end of the process."

"Of course. How long will it be before you know the revival is successful?"

"Montfort said ten days before we replace the suspension fluid with blood. I think it's at least another five days after that before we attempt to start the heart. I'd say three weeks minimum, but you're better off talking to the doctor about that."

Three weeks. A lot could happen in three weeks.

Cariad turned to leave.

"Did you know this man, Aubriot, back on Earth?" Alasdair asked.

She'd almost forgotten he was a Gen. So very few of them remained aboard *Nova Fortuna*, she'd grown used to thinking of everyone she encountered as Woken.

"Yeah, I knew him. I'm surprised you don't too. Didn't you cover the founding of the *Nova Fortuna* project in history at school?"

"I did. I wasn't that interested, though. It's hard to care about a place so far away and events that took place so long ago. So Aubriot was a founder?"

"He was the primary financier." When Alasdair's expression still failed to register understanding, she added, "The owner of Mercantor Enterprises?"

"Ohhhh." Recognition dawned on Alasdair's face. He looked down at the frozen figure and took a step back as if he was frightened of disturbing him. "I had no idea he came along."

"Really? It was his primary condition before contributing to the funding. He liquidated all his assets and sunk every last cred into the project. Even so, he barely scraped the fifty-one percent holding required to have the final say in board decisions. Aubriot was first on the list for cryonic suspension. It looks like he was forgotten in the race to revive the key scientists."

"You mean he gave up everything? The ability to have whatever he wanted, and taking a chance of never waking up, just to be a part of the colonization?"

"That's the short version," said Cariad. "The long story is that he took his majority holding and used it to ensure he did everything in his power to make sure he survived and the colony was a success. I know Aubriot personally because the minute the preparations began, he insisted on knowing about everything that was happening, in detail. He questioned everything too, even stuff he had absolutely no understanding of. Made all the scientists and engineers dumb it all down until he thought he knew what it all meant. Then he would challenge our decisions and suggest different ways of doing things, insisting we try them out, claiming to know better. Made all our lives hell, basically, with constant interference, as if preparing for humanity's first deep space colonization project wasn't hard enough."

Cariad drew breath. The sight of Aubriot was causing long-forgotten memories to resurface—his constant, obsessive observation and criticism had driven her crazy. More than once, she had been tempted to slap his smug face when he doubted her assertions, which were based on ground-breaking world-renowned research she had personally conducted.

Alasdair said, smiling, "I'm guessing you wanted to know when he wakes up so you can be as far away as possible?"

"Hmph, something like that," Cariad replied. "No, not really, Alasdair. You know the problems we've been having? I think Anahi plans on gaining Aubriot's support to tighten her grip on the colony. Reviving Aubriot is like trying to put out a fire with gasoline."

Alasdair frowned.

Realizing he probably didn't know what gas was, Cariad said, "A very bad idea."

"Gotcha."

"So I'm going to do the opposite of what I want to do. I'm going to stick to Aubriot like glue, hoping for some damage control."

"Okay," Alasdair said. "I get it. So do you want me to tell you as soon as he's awake?"

"Can you do that? You aren't worried about getting into trouble with Anahi?"

He shrugged. "Maybe. But we could pretend you happened along at the right time. Anyway, I don't care if she guesses what I did. I hate that crazy bitch."

"I really appreciate it," Cariad said. "I want to warn you, though: the second he's awake, stay the hell out of his way. Aubriot is going to be so pissed he wasn't the first to be revived."

CHAPTER SIXTEEN

Ethan could hardly believe his luck in finding what seemed the perfect place for a new, Gen-controlled settlement on his very first scouting trip. He'd considered exploring farther before telling Garwin of his and Cherry's find, but Cherry had been as excited as him and had wanted to show Garwin the place right away.

As they sped along on the flitter, returning to the site, Garwin was with Ethan at the front of the vehicle. Cherry was watching for dangerous life forms from the back, her weapon at the ready. Shelf clouds were building darkly and threatening rain, but Ethan estimated they had two or three dry hours ahead of them.

"I have to say," Garwin remarked, "it feels good to get away for a while. I don't seem to step far from the workshop or home these days."

"How is work going?" Ethan asked. "Are there many more machines to assemble?"

"Hundreds. And I also have to deliver and sometimes install them, and instruct on their operation. Then people are always forgetting how something works, or breaking it. I'm always busy. I don't see my work letting up for years to come. I'll have to start training some youngsters soon, too. Otherwise no one will know how to fix anything when us older mechanics retire."

"Will Twyla get suspicious while you're out here now?" Ethan asked, remembering that Garwin's wife wasn't yet aware of the subversive movement he headed. They would have to tell all the Gens what they were doing soon, but after the fight at the farmers' equipment shed, Ethan didn't think they would face many objections to their plan to create a new settlement free from Woken or Guardian interference.

"No, it's fine," Garwin replied. "She's used to me disappearing for hours."

"Those are the hills I was telling you about," Ethan said as they appeared on the horizon.

After passing a few more kilometers in silence, Garwin said, "I'm going to reserve final judgment until I've seen these caves. But I want to say, I'm not entirely convinced by the idea of building the settlement there. I agree that caves would be terrific hiding places. I don't think the satellites or the *Mistral's* scanners will pick us up once we're inside. But what seems a sanctuary could easily turn into a trap. We might be able to prevent an attacking force from getting in, but they could also prevent us from getting out. All they have to do is lay siege to the place, and eventually they'll starve us into submission."

"I thought of that," Ethan said. "But these caves are full of passages. We can probably find plenty of exit routes to escape from if we're under attack. We don't have to be trapped."

Garwin nodded. "Okay. Let's see."

"Fasten your safety belts," Ethan said. "We're nearly at the old waterfall."

Ethan had disengaged the default setting on the flitter. This time when they zoomed out over the ocean, the vehicle didn't drop precipitously down the cliff.

Glancing at Garwin's profile, Ethan saw a grin growing wider over the older man's face as he surveyed the ocean spreading wide in front of them. The rising clouds had only marginally dimmed its deep blue.

"Whatever we find at these caves, Ethan," Garwin said, "I'm glad you brought me here today."

Spitting rain began to hit them. They would have to get under cover soon to avoid the approaching downpour. Ethan's gaze roved the cliff face for a few moments before locating an opening large enough for the flitter. He flew the vehicle over and settled it down on the floor, which was thick with soft dust.

Ethan stepped out. His boot sank a couple of centimeters into the dry material. Reaching into the flitter, he picked up his weapon. After his encounters during the First Night Attack and Cherry's experience by the lake, he wasn't taking any chances. The cave went back ten meters or so before the interior was lost in darkness.

"Not bad," Garwin said, looking around. "Not bad at all. And I could make out plenty more entrances in the cliff. If the place is safe, and if it has other exits, maybe this would make the ideal setting for our new settlement." He took a bag out of the flitter. Inside it were helmets with lights. "After you told me what you'd found, I made these. If we decide to move here, we can fix up a permanent lighting system, but for now, these will come in handy."

He turned on the lights before handing a helmet each to Ethan and Cherry. Ethan put on his and went deeper into the cave, his boots sinking in and leaving deeply ridged footprints at every step. The first human footprints ever in that place. The light beaming from his helmet bobbed in time with his steps, illuminating more of the back of the cave. The walls were smooth, as if water had once flowed through it. The other caves he and Cherry had examined had looked the same. He imagined the cliff face filled with pouring spouts of water.

"Let's see how far back it goes," Ethan said as Cherry and Garwin came up behind him.

"Yes, but no splitting up," Cherry replied. "And if we're in danger of getting lost, we come out immediately, okay? No one else knows we're here, and I don't want to die just yet."

The farther in they went, the narrower the cave grew. They didn't appear to be in any danger of getting lost. It was one long tunnel. Gradually, the floor rose. The roof remained the same height, however, so that they were soon stooping.

A black gap in the wall opened on Ethan's right. "I'm going to take a look in here. If it goes somewhere, I'll call out."

The gap was tall but only wide enough to squeeze through by turning sideways. Ethan eased in, the reflection from his helmet light brightly reflecting on the smoothly polished rock. He was temporarily blinded. The narrow space soon opened wide, but he stopped when he was through, waiting for the green glare that was affecting his eyes to fade.

As he blinked, his view of the space he had entered became clearer. He was in a bowl-shaped chamber. The floor sloped down to the center, and at the far side a hole opened in the ceiling. At one time, he guessed that water might have entered the chamber from above and pooled temporarily before running out and down the tunnel to the ocean. There was no other exit.

Ethan spent a few more moments assessing the chamber. It was entirely dry, and so deep within the cliffs that he guessed the cool temperature would remain steady. He couldn't see any signs of animals or their droppings. The area would make a perfect storage place.

He left to give Garwin and Cherry his assessment, turning sideways once more and edging through the gap. As he emerged into the main tunnel, the first thing he noticed was the lights from his companions' lamps moving oddly. Then he saw the reason for the odd effect: they were locked in a close embrace.

Garwin and Cherry were kissing with an intensity that indicated a passionate, intimate relationship. Ethan felt his face grow hot with embarrassment. He took a step backward into the gap and paused a moment, resting against the wall while he decided what to do.

He scraped his helmet against the rocky surface, making plenty of noise. When he returned to the main tunnel, Garwin and Cherry were standing apart, looking like they'd hardly moved the entire time he'd been gone.

"It doesn't lead anywhere," Ethan said. He explained what he'd seen. "Maybe we could use it for storing food."

"Great," Garwin said. "This site is looking better and better. Let's see if we can find another exit, and maybe we'll have time to explore a few more caves before we leave."

"Yeah," said Cherry. "Maybe some of them link up."

A few more gaps appeared in the walls and ceiling as they went on, but they weren't like the first. They were shallow dead ends. They came out and went to another cave. After exploring two more, the sun was getting low in the sky, and they decided to call it a day. Garwin and Cherry sat in the back while Ethan flew the flitter through the growing twilight. The surrounding hills grew colorless and dark as the sun disappeared. The only sound was wind. It was fresh and humid after the rain that had fallen while they explored. Ethan didn't turn around while he drove, leaving Garwin and Cherry to their privacy.

The sight of them kissing had awakened mixed

emotions in him. First had come the shock. Ethan had heard the rumors about Garwin, but it was another thing to be confronted with the evidence. Next came the ache and grief of Ethan's memories of Lauren. Finally, he felt something he realized he'd been denying to himself. As well as Lauren, the image of his friends' embrace had brought Cariad to his mind. He missed her and regretted their recent disagreement and unhappy parting.

CHAPTER SEVENTEEN

Cariad surveyed the offerings at the buffet for that evening's dinner. Balls of yeast, flavored and colored to look like meatballs, floated in tomato sauce. Rolls of steamed rice were wrapped in layers of dried seaweed. Algae strips nestled among assorted fungi. Deep-fried crickets rested on a bed of taro mash. Cariad helped herself to some meatballs and salad and carried her tray to a table.

The remaining refectory in use aboard the *Nova Fortuna* was much quieter than it had been before most of the Gens had gone planetside. Though at the time she hadn't much liked the noise and bustle they created, Cariad found that, now they were gone, she missed the crowds. Their absence had also made seating arrangements more noticeable and fraught. Now that only a hundred or so Woken were eating in a room designed to hold five times their number, who sat with whom and who sat alone was extremely obvious.

Cariad had adopted a default position. She assumed that her vocal opposition to Anahi meant that no one would want to be seen fraternizing with her. She always sat at an empty table. Occasionally an old acquaintance would take the political risk of sitting down with her, but often no one did. She didn't really mind or blame anyone, but sometimes she felt the absence of company.

She opened her personal interface and propped it up before digging her fork into the meatballs. She re-examined the links Strongquist had sent her regarding the investigation into the bombing. Frederick Aparicio stood out in her mind, but it stubbornly refused to yield any more information about the man.

The more she thought about it, the more she was convinced that he had to be significant. He'd been on the covert list of Natural Movement members, yet though she'd had nothing to do with the organization, she knew his name and she recognized him. The answer was buried somewhere deep in her mind, if only it would let the memory through. Long experience of fathoming out scientific problems had taught her the best thing to do was to try to avoid thinking about the thing that was bothering her. She should try to put Aparicio out of her mind altogether, then the link would probably pop out to her soon enough. But, naturally, the more she tried not to think about him, the more he sprang unbidden into her thoughts.

She chewed thoughtfully on a mouthful of algae and fungi salad as she gazed at the frozen image of the man's face, staring up at the camera in the lobby of the building where he'd worked. He'd been a systems engineer, Strongquist had told her. It seemed an odd profession for a member of the Natural Movement. The Guardian had said a fair proportion of the movement's members had occupied technical professions. Supposedly anti-science, they'd been possessed of that all-too-human trait of hypocrisy about their beliefs.

"Frederick," Cariad murmured, "how did I know you?"

"Are you working?" asked a voice.

Cariad looked up to see Rene, a young soil biologist

who had been her roommate when they were both recovering from cryonic suspension.

"Not on anything productive," Cariad said, closing her interface.

"I won't disturb you if you're busy."

"It's fine. Please, sit down."

Rene put down her tray next to Cariad's.

"Thanks," Cariad said as her friend joined her.

"For what?"

"Sitting with me. I'm not exactly popular at the moment."

"You mean for standing up against our new, self-appointed Leader? You're more popular than you think. More than a few of us feel the same as you. We're worried about the direction all this is heading, but we aren't sure what to do about it."

Cariad put down her fork. "You aren't sure what to do? It's easy. Stand up to her."

"I only said some of us. Anahi has plenty of followers who think she hasn't done anything wrong. And you know what we scientists are like. We hate getting involved in things that might take us away from our work. But don't think you're alone, because you aren't." Rene picked up a fried cricket with her fingers and bit it in half. She crunched up her mouthful. "Some of us want to swing things back to a more equitable situation with the Gens too, but we don't know how."

"If you really want to do something," Cariad said, "you can start by speaking out. Let Anahi know that she doesn't have a unanimous backing for whatever she wants to do. That might make her think twice before introducing yet another rule to crush Gen autonomy. Or it might not. I don't know. I think she may be mentally unstable, and nothing anyone says or does will deter her. But it's worth trying."

"You're right. We should do that."

"And when you hear anyone praising what she's

doing, challenge them. Remind them why we're all here. What our intentions were for the colony. They seem to have been forgotten, but you remember, don't you? You remember the kind of world we wanted to build?"

"I remember. We wanted to leave behind corruption and selfishness and start afresh with better ideals. If the colony were made up of people who had been brought up without of the influences of human societies, it wouldn't be unequal or cruel and uncaring. That was the idea. I guess we thought wrong."

"Did we? Maybe if we hadn't come along too, the Gens would have achieved that. Maybe it's our presence that's creating the problem. But we shouldn't give up on that ideal. Things were going okay until Anahi decided to seize power. We can put things right again if we're given the chance. I'm sure of it."

"You think all these problems are due to our being here?" said Rene. "I guess that old saying is true. Wherever you go, there you are. We've brought the contagion with us. Even the Natural Movement came along for the ride."

"As if we didn't have enough to contend with," Cariad said. "But that has something to do with what's happened. People are frightened, and when they're frightened, they see enemies everywhere, even in people who are really their friends. Maybe if we catch the Natural Movement saboteurs, the Woken and Gens would put aside their differences and reconcile."

"Maybe." Rene ate the other half of her cricket.

"I couldn't ever learn to enjoy those things," remarked Cariad. "Too many legs."

"I like them. Full of protein too." She popped another small one into her mouth.

"What I wouldn't give for a cheese sandwich," Cariad said, looking at her meal. She pushed her tray away. "On rye with mayo."

Rene chuckled. "Are we going to have one of those

"foods I miss" conversations? They only make it worse, you know. Unless you hid some cow eggs and sperm aboard the ship, I don't think you'll be eating cheese again anytime soon."

"No," Cariad replied wistfully, "no cow eggs or sperm, or pigs', dogs', cats', chickens, or ducks'. No salmon's, trout's, tuna's, or oysters'." The decision to not introduce any Earth animals to the new world had been beyond debate. Any escapees in the alien environment could be disastrous, putting the ecological systems entirely out of balance. Growing Earth crops was risky enough. As for insects bred aboard *Nova Fortuna,* they were only available to eat on the ship. None would ever be taken down to the surface. On the new world, all food would be plant-based.

The mention of animal gametes tickled a memory at the back of Cariad's mind, but the sensation was so slight that she barely noticed it.

"The thing I hate about it all," said Rene, "is going down to take soil samples. I feel so uncomfortable working among the Gens. I feel like I should wear a sign that says "I'm on your side." I try to tell them that, but I don't think they believe me." She ran her fork around her plate, scooping up the last of her taro mash as she went on, "One of my last thoughts before they put me under for suspension was that I was looking forward to meeting the people who would be there when I was revived. I thought it would be cool to meet people who had grown up on a starship." She ate her forkful of food and asked, "Did you guess that the coloring and build of the Gens would homogenize like they did?"

"To be honest I didn't even consider it," Cariad replied. "We selected for health mostly, absence of recessive gene conditions, and sociability. Intelligence and other factors were a crap shoot. We predicted that we needed a range for a successful society." She frowned. The topic of the conversation was ringing a bell in her mind.

"What's wrong?"

"I feel like there's something important I've forgotten, something to do with the gene selection process."

"Does it matter any more?" Rene asked. "That was a helluva long time ago. If you forgot something, there's no going back now."

"No. It isn't that. It's... what were you saying?"

"I was talking about how the Gens all ended up black-haired and olive-skinned. I was wondering if you or the other geneticists knew that would happen."

"And I said... " Cariad gasped. "That's it! That's how I know Frederick Aparicio."

"Excuse me?"

"Frederick Aparicio. *That's* why I recognized him. Sorry, Rene, I have to go." Cariad got up. "Thanks for the talk. Remember to tell the others what I said: stand up to Anahi. Show her she's going to be held accountable. See you soon."

She hurried out of the refectory. She needed to speak to Strongquist. As she sped down the corridor to her quarters, where she would be able to comm him in private, the memory of Frederick Aparicio sitting opposite her in her office on Earth played as clearly as if it had happened yesterday.

As soon as she reached her cabin, she opened a comm to the Guardians' ship. She had to wait to speak to Strongquist, and as she was waiting, she puzzled over something. The Guardians had all the documentation relating to the *Nova Fortuna* Project, from start to finish. So why hadn't Strongquist come across Aparicio in a simple search of the records?

CHAPTER EIGHTEEN

Cariad's face was vivid in Ethan's mind. He was glad he'd invited her to spend a day planetside with him, but he was also conflicted. The building of the new settlement in the ocean-side caves was progressing rapidly, and he knew the secret would weigh heavily on him while he was with Cariad on their planned excursion.

He wasn't comfortable about hiding what the Gens were doing from someone who had grown to be a close friend. The problem was, the secret wasn't his to tell. It was something that involved all the Gens. He couldn't betray them by telling a Woken about it, even though he personally trusted her not to act on it.

It was inevitable that Cariad would find out. There would come a time in the not too distant future that all the Woken and Guardians would discover the old settlement was nearly empty and most of the supplies gone. What would she think then? She would know he had deliberately withheld the truth from her. Would she understand? Or would she be hurt that he hadn't trusted her? He didn't know. All he could do was hope that one day he would get the chance to explain, and that eventually she would forgive him.

The only alternative was to avoid seeing her for

weeks. He couldn't bring himself to do that. She was the one person he'd felt close to since Lauren and Dr. Crowley had died.

The shuttle from the ship wouldn't arrive for another hour, but Ethan had nothing else to do, so he went to the flitter shed to borrow a vehicle. He planned on taking Cariad out to his farm to show her the green shoots sprouting in his fields and the small progress he'd made on the pre-fabricated farmhouse. In truth, Cherry had done most of the field work on his farm as she had turned out to be extremely adept and efficient at using the machinery. Perhaps that was one secret he wouldn't need to keep.

The flitter shed was nearly empty. Most of the vehicles were being used to ferry equipment and supplies to the caves, with the Gen in charge, Verney, turning a blind eye to the practice. Ethan took one of the few remaining vehicles and flew it out and through the streets to the shuttle field. An office had recently been constructed there to process shipments and passenger arrivals and departures. A step in the settlement plan that had been too prominent to avoid, the Gens had built the office, but it was to be their final construction on the settlement.

Ethan parked the flitter in the lot and leaned back in his seat, putting his hands behind his head. He settled in for the wait, enjoying the pleasant anticipation of the afternoon with his friend. He looked up in the direction of the shuttles' usual approach. The sky was unusually empty of clouds. In a while, he would see a glint of light, the first sign of the descending shuttle as the sun reflected from its metal skin. He estimated that Cariad would have already boarded. He imagined her in her seat, looking out the window or reading her interface, her expression serious and intent. He liked how she always thought deeply about things, but he also loved it when she laughed.

The interior of the flitter was warming up in the sunshine, making Ethan sleepy. Soon, he was in a light doze, and memories mixed with dreams played through his mind.

He remembered a time when he was very young, kindergarten age. He was at Main Park with his class and teacher, and all his classmates were playing or running through the grass and trees. Main Park had been one of his favorite places when he was a little boy. He loved the bright lights there, which his teacher had told him helped the trees to grow, and the smell of the air. It was cleaner and fresher than anywhere else. He was also fascinated by the Clock. Every time his class went there, he would look up at it to read the numbers. Each time they were different. The numbers at the end of the line changed as he watched, and they counted down, which was strange. All the other clocks he'd seen counted up.

His teacher had told the class that the Clock was counting down to a special event called Arrival Day. Ethan didn't understand what that meant. He thought that to arrive somewhere you had to travel there, like when he went from the children's dorm to school on the transit car. He didn't understand how they could be traveling when nothing around him moved. His teacher had said that Arrival Day would be when they reached their new home.

He was looking up at the Clock, watching the numbers change, when someone tapped him on his shoulder. He spun around just in time to see a little girl running away. She was from another class. He didn't know her name. As she was running, she looked over her shoulder and giggled. Then she stopped and grinned. "You can't catch me."

"Yes, I can," Ethan exclaimed, and took off after her.

The girl gave a squeal and sped away, darting behind some shrubs. Ethan followed, but the girl had disappeared. He paused. Where had she gone? She had to be on the other side of the bushes. He ran quickly around, just in time to see the flick of her ponytail and flash of her heels before she vanished.

Ethan ran after her as fast as he could, but the girl was too quick. They ran around and around a large shrub, panting and giggling. Ethan was getting dizzy. He wanted to catch the girl, but how? He had an idea. He quickly about-faced and ran back the other way. A moment later, he collided with the girl and they bounced off each other before falling down onto the grass. Immediately, the girl stuck her knuckles in her eyes and began to sob loudly.

Ethan got up, concerned. He rubbed his forehead where he'd hit it. He hadn't meant to hurt the girl. He'd only been playing.

Her crying attracted the attention of Ethan's teacher. She came over and frowned at him, standing and apparently unharmed, and then at the girl, who was sitting on the ground and sobbing. She looked accusingly at Ethan.

"What's wrong? Are you hurt?" she asked the girl. "What happened, Ethan? Did you hurt her?"

Ethan didn't reply. He *had* hurt the girl, but only by accident. He hadn't meant to.

The girl took her hands from her face and said, "Oh no, he didn't hurt me. We only bumped." She stood up and straightened her playsuit. Wiping away her tears, she gave Ethan a smile.

"Okay," said the teacher. "Well, be a little more careful, both of you. If you want to run around, look where you're going."

The teacher went away, and the girl invited Ethan to play a game she'd made up using little sticks. It was a neat game. Ethan had a lot of fun and was sad when the teacher said it was time to go back to school.

He waved goodbye as the girl's class left the park in

a crocodile line of pairs. His new friend turned back and waved too. He hoped he would see her again the next time his class came to the park.

As he stood and watched the girl leave, the park turned strange and fuzzy. His teacher's voice, telling him to hurry up, became distant and indistinct. The sadness he'd been feeling at his friend's departure grew stronger and more painful. He had an ache in his chest that felt like someone had stabbed him. Ethan looked down. The agony was so great, he expected to see a knife handle protruding from his heart.

He jerked awake, squinting in the sunlight that was now shining directly on his face. The flitter was unbearably hot. He opened his door, and refreshing, cool air rushed in. The pain from his dream still gripped him. *Lauren.* He'd dreamt of the first time they had met. His face was wet and he was breathing heavily.

He slumped back in his seat. *Lauren.* Her death still hurt so much. Some days he would almost forget she was gone, but on others the memory would hit him like it was yesterday. He didn't think he would ever get over losing her, or the appalling sense of helplessness when he remembered the moment he'd failed to save her life.

He wiped his face on his shirt sleeve and checked the time. Almost an hour had passed. The shuttle would be arriving soon. He would have to try to brighten up a little for Cariad's sake, though after his dream he felt almost guilty for arranging to meet with her. It didn't feel right that he should go on living, meeting new people and doing new things, while poor Lauren's life had been cut abruptly short.

Ethan squinted up at the sky in the place where the approaching shuttle should soon appear. There it was. He'd seen the tell-tale flash as the sun hit it. Within moments he saw it properly, the silver wedge swooping down. In five minutes it would land and Cariad would be out soon after when she'd passed through the new arrival procedure.

His sad mood began to lift a little. He would enjoy Cariad's company for a quiet afternoon out at his farm. As the shuttle approached, he raised his hand to shade his eyes.

A flash burst from the speeding ship, so bright it blinded him. An ear-splitting boom followed. Ethan blinked, desperately trying to bring back his vision, while his ears rang from the noise. When he could finally see, the sky was filled with smoking, flaming, spiraling parts, plummeting to the ground. Dimly, Ethan heard screams and shouts of disbelief.

He was frozen, unable to process what he was seeing. His hand was still shading his eyes, his mouth agape.

Debris from the shuttle began to rain down. Twisted pieces of metal pierced the shuttle station office and the lot. Outside, moaning, screaming, and sobbing continued, but Ethan couldn't speak. He couldn't move.

Cariad had been on the shuttle.

The shuttle had exploded.

Cariad was gone.

CHAPTER NINETEEN

Cariad had only been speaking to Strongquist for a moment when an emergency announcement broke into the line. A shuttle had exploded. Her news about Frederick Aparicio died on her lips. The interface screen in her cabin switched from Strongquist's image to a vid of the vessel exploding. It was a view from the planet surface. Her legs were suddenly weak. She sat on her bunk.

"Are you seeing this?" Cariad asked Strongquist.

"Yes," he replied. "I'm sorry to say."

In horror, Cariad watched the recording of the shuttle debris falling like rain on fire. Numbly, she tried to process the news. No one could have survived the explosion. How many had died? Each shuttle carried two pilots and four cabin crew. How many passengers had been aboard?

She gasped.

"Cariad?" Strongquist asked.

She'd arranged to go planetside to see Ethan. She'd planned to travel on that shuttle, but her realization about Aparicio had wiped the arrangement from her mind. She should have been one of the passengers.

Her stomach clenched. Ethan would have been waiting for her. He would have been at the shuttle field. He would think she was dead.

And he might have been hurt by the falling debris. Had there been planetside casualties too?

"I have to contact someone urgently," she told Strongquist. "I'll speak to you soon."

"Of course," the Guardian replied, "but you said you had something to tell me about Aparicio. If you have any more information on him, I must know immediately. I don't think this explosion is an accident."

"You don't?"

"It's extremely unlikely that any vessel belonging to the *Nova Fortuna* Project would spontaneously explode. The shuttles were built well for their era and are very safe. We'll investigate, of course, but my guess is that this is another Natural Movement sabotage."

"No," Cariad exclaimed. "When is this going to stop?" She paused to collect herself. "What I have to tell you about Aparicio isn't much, but it might help. I'll comm you again in a couple of minutes."

"I'll be waiting."

Cariad closed the comm to the Guardians' ship and tried to open one to the planet surface. If she couldn't contact Ethan directly she could at least leave a message at the farmers' dorms. But the comm line wouldn't open.

Everyone aboard *Nova Fortuna* had to be attempting to comm the planet, she realized. Most shuttle passengers were Woken, traveling to the surface to take samples or make observations. Their friends aboard ship would be trying to find out if, by some miracle, they had survived.

Nevertheless, Cariad tried to open a line again. She had to let Ethan know she was okay. Another ship-wide announcement broke in: "Ship-to-surface comms have been temporarily suspended. Preliminary reports on the shuttle explosion state that twenty-seven passengers and six crew were aboard. Guardians are at the scene surveying the wreckage. No survivors are expected."

Thirty-three deaths. The shuttle had been unusually full. Most of the time they only carried ten or fifteen passengers. Thirty-three more people had died, most of them Woken. Cariad wondered who they were. She dreaded finding out.

Why had the Natural Movement targeted a shuttle? If the bomber had wanted to kill a lot of people, they only had to blow up one of the dorms, where hundreds of Gens slept. But they'd picked a shuttle, and an exceptionally full one at that. The intention was clear: kill as many Woken as possible.

On her interface screen was a frozen image of the explosion. The passenger manifest and the names of the pilots and crew began to scroll across it. Cariad's eyes were filling with tears. Many of the names were familiar. They were women and men she'd worked alongside for years preparing for the departure of the *Nova Fortuna*.

Despite all the previous setbacks to the colonization, for the first time since her revival, Cariad felt hope slipping away. After the First Night Attack, and even after the stadium bombing, she'd clung to the belief that the colony would win through. She'd seen the saboteurs as serious but solvable problems. All the colonists had to do was catch the perpetrators and move on.

But then Anahi had started up her mad, divisive schemes, including reviving the powder keg that was Aubriot. And now the Natural Movement had struck again, giving them all a brutal reminder of their lethal threat and the fact that even the Guardians with their advanced technology had failed to identify them.

For several long moments, despair crushed down on Cariad. She questioned why she'd joined the project, why she'd left Earth and everyone she loved. She remembered her parents' and her sisters' last embraces. In those final moments, they had all clung together tightly. Guilt at her decision wrung every fiber of her being. How could she have put her family through that dreadful parting?

There she was, light years away and nearly two centuries later, and everything she'd dreamed of was collapsing around her. She was about to be a participant in humankind's first failed attempt at deep space colonization. She'd subjected the people she loved to deep pain and grief and deprived herself of their love and companionship for nothing.

Then, as Cariad recalled the final look her mother had given her before they parted forever, something shifted deep inside her. Anguish and surrender were replaced by anger and determination. She wiped her eyes. She would not let the Natural Movement or Anahi win. She would fight for the colony with every gram of strength she had. She owed it to her family and she owed it to herself. She refused to accept that they had all suffered for nothing. She would make the colony a success or die trying.

Hope remained. She had her friendship with Ethan, for one thing. Woken and Gens could work together. They could get through this.

Again, she tried comm the settlement but nothing was working. When would they lift the suspension? A security alert sounded and the ship's comm announced, "The Leader has declared a state of emergency. Shuttle flights and private comms are prohibited indefinitely. Please await further instructions."

No private comms? How could she contact Ethan? And Strongquist? Cariad got up. She had to find Anahi and try to talk some sense into her.

***

The self-appointed Leader was at the official suite designated for the position. The Leader's Residence included an office as well as living quarters. Traditionally, anyone could make an appointment to speak face to face with the Leader. By the time Cariad arrived, the office was crowded with people, appointments notwithstanding. It seemed like almost all the remaining Woken were crushed inside along with many of the Gens who worked aboard the ship.

Cariad spotted Anahi in a corner, trying to speak to the crowd, but her voice was drowned out by the hubbub. People were discussing what had happened and shouting out questions. Cariad tried to push her way through to get closer to Anahi, but the office was too tightly packed. As she was trying to figure out a way to speak to her, Anahi got up on a chair and waved her hands, asking for silence.

"Please," she said as the noise died down, "I'm doing everything I can to keep control of this situation. We mustn't panic. That's exactly what the bomber wants. They want to undermine this colony."

"It was another bomb," a voice exclaimed. "I knew it."

"That hasn't been confirmed yet," Anahi said, "but for now I'm treating the explosion as an act of terrorism."

"Do the Natural Movement really want to undermine the colony?" asked a Woken, a meteorologist. "It seems to me the saboteurs have switched tactics. Now they're targeting us Woken. They want us all dead, and they want the Gens in control."

"We don't know that," said Anahi, irritation giving her tone a sharp edge. "We don't know anything yet. It's early days. We mustn't speculate. The Guardians are already examining the wreckage to find out the cause. If the Natural Movement is responsible, the Guardians might find evidence that will lead us to the saboteur."

"When will we be able to comm planetside?" a plump young Gen maintenance worker asked. "I want to talk to my wife. She'll be worried about me. And when will I be able to go home?"

"These are all questions I'm not able to answer right now," Anahi replied, her irritated tone intensifying.

Cariad cupped her hands around her mouth. "Anahi," she called over the heads of the crowd. "I have information that might help the Guardians catch the bomber. I have to comm Strongquist."

Anahi's black visual aid turned in her direction. She gave a huff of frustration. "Very well, Cariad. Come with me into the back office." She climbed down from her chair and the crowd eased apart a little to allow Cariad through. When she reached Anahi, the older woman unlocked a door at the back of the room and motioned her inside. When the two were through, Anahi closed and locked the door with a sigh. "My interface, over there." She pointed. "It's the only one that comms outside the ship."

Cariad wanted to speak to Anahi about her decision to ban private comms, but speaking to Strongquist was more urgent. She opened the interface.

The Guardian answered immediately. "Cariad. It's good to hear from you. I've been trying to comm Anahi to tell her I needed to speak to you urgently, but she didn't reply."

Cariad looked at Anahi, who said, "Things have been a little busy around here, in case you hadn't noticed."

Cariad returned her attention to Strongquist. "I remembered where I met Frederick Aparicio. I know who he was."

"Excellent," Strongquist said.

"Okay." Cariad took a breath. "He was one of the First Generation applicants." Now that she'd finally recalled the man, small details of her encounter with him kept popping into her head. "His application was rejected. Subnormal sperm count."

"What's this about?" Anahi interrupted. "Who was

this man?"

Cariad briefly explained how she'd been helping Strongquist with his investigations.

"I see," Anahi said. "Are you certain you remember who this man was? There were tens of thousands of applicants."

"I remember him because he appealed," Cariad explained. "He took it all the way to the Supreme Court. Don't you remember?" she asked Anahi. "There were about twenty rejected applicants who argued for their right to join the project. Their attorneys cited discrimination laws, human rights precedents—they really scraped the barrel."

"Yes," Anahi said, "I do remember. I felt sorry for them."

"Me too, until I met Frederick Aparicio." Cariad turned to the interface and Strongquist. "After they'd run out of appeals and the final judgment was given, Aparicio contacted me. He wanted to speak to me in person, he said. I was insanely busy, of course. We all were. But I agreed. Like Anahi, I pitied him. The litigants had spent millions fighting to join the Project and lost it all. I think they had to pay our defense costs too. I should have wondered then where a systems engineer got all that money, but I was overwhelmed with work and other concerns."

"Wait," Strongquist said, "I have to echo Anahi. Are you sure you're thinking of the right person? We have records of that court case. If Frederick Aparicio was involved, his name would have come up in our searches."

"I'm sure. I also don't know why his name isn't on your records, but I remember him coming into my office as clearly as if it were yesterday. He was pissed as anything. In fact, he was so angry, I was a little scared and considered calling security. I got him to sit down and I tried to explain the importance of optimum fertility in the candidates, which turned out to be a very bad move. He took it as an insult to his masculinity. So I tried a different tactic. I told him about the strict limitation on the numbers of the First Generation, and that all the supplies and the life support systems had been calculated based on that number, so we couldn't add even one extra person. I emphasized that if we added him it would mean someone else would lose their place.

"Nothing I said convinced him or even calmed him down. Finally, he accepted that a face-to-face meeting with one of the project organizers wasn't going to help him. He stormed out. That was the last I saw of him. When I think about the encounter now, I'm surprised it took me so long to remember him. It was only when I was talking to a colleague about the decisions around what gametes to bring along that I finally slotted him into place."

Strongquist said, "I'm sorry but I have to ask you again, are you absolutely certain the person you remember was Frederick Aparicio? The human mind can play tricks, inserting memories where there are none and seeing patterns that don't exist. Could it be that you're mixing up your visitor with someone else?"

"What can I say?" Cariad asked. "I'm as sure as I can be. Do you have my work records from that time? I would have made a note about the meeting."

"I'll look into it," said Strongquist. "All we've found on our suspect so far are his affiliation with the Natural Movement, public data on him, and the recordings you saw. We haven't traced a single direct connection with the *Nova Fortuna* Project. If he was an applicant that should have been immediately apparent. That he was one of the twenty litigants in the... " He paused. "I have an idea. I need to do some further research. I'll contact you again if I need to ask you anything else."

Anahi said, "Strongquist, before you go, I want to

speak to you about the current situation."

"Yes?"

"This latest catastrophe has put everything on a new footing. People are panicking."

"That isn't surprising," Strongquist said. "What do you want to say to me? We'll do everything we can to catch the perpetrator of this crime, if that's what it is."

"I understand that," Anahi said, "and I appreciate the Guardians' efforts. But I wanted to know if you can help with the situation here."

Cariad stared at Anahi. "What situation?"

Ignoring her, Anahi continued to Strongquist, "I'm concerned that things might get out of hand aboard ship. We don't have any security here, and with feelings running so high, I'm worried someone might get hurt."

"You want Guardians aboard *Nova Fortuna*?" Cariad exclaimed. "You want your bully squad to control Woken too? Is that what things have come to?"

Strongquist was looking uncomfortable. "Do you believe your life or other lives are under threat?"

"No," Cariad interrupted. "No one's life is under threat. Anahi, we do not need or want Guardians patrolling the *Nova Fortuna*."

"We're in a state of emergency," Anahi replied. "I just think everyone would feel more comfortable—"

"*You* would feel more comfortable, you mean. Two guards with weapons standing outside your office and protecting you when you fail to do your job would help you relax a little, right? Have you entirely lost your mind?" Cariad found she was shouting. She breathed deeply, in and out, and went on in a quieter tone. "Half of those people in your office are your personal friends. You want to threaten them with guns?"

Before Anahi could answer, Strongquist asked, "How many are aboard *Nova Fortuna* right now?"

"About seventy Woken," Anahi replied, "and roughly fifty Gens helping to run the ship. Some Woken were working planetside when the shuttle exploded."

"Our resources are stretched at the moment," said Strongquist. "We'll have our hands full controlling the situation at the settlement, and we're doing all we can to catch this saboteur—"

"He or she has to be aboard the ship, right?" Cariad interjected. "To have planted the bomb on the shuttle?"

"Not necessarily," Strongquist replied. "The shuttles aren't searched, more's the pity. A bomb could have been planted on one at any time. The bomber might have secreted it somewhere aboard a ship on one trip, then activated it from the surface when the shuttle returned. They would only need to wait until the vessel came within range of their signal."

"Still, it's a possibility the saboteur is among us," said Anahi.

"I don't think it's any more likely than the person living in the settlement," Strongquist said. "Actually, after hearing Cariad's new information, and all other things considered, I think it's very likely that person is a Gen."

"I'm not surprised," Anahi said bitterly.

Cariad said, "Most of the surviving Woken are here, and we won't be taking shuttles to the surface anytime soon. That means the Gens can operate with less oversight and interference."

"Yes," Strongquist said. "The shuttle explosion could have been planned with that intention. With that in mind, I believe the best deployment of our resources will be planetside. The Woken who are currently there are at risk. We have to protect them and return them to *Nova Fortuna* as soon as possible."

"Looks like you're just going to have to deal with all these people up here asking difficult questions yourself," Cariad said to Anahi.

Despite the fact that her blind eyes were hidden behind her visor, Cariad felt Anahi's glare.

"Unless the situation aboard *Nova Fortuna* escalates," Strongquist said, "I would strongly suggest that we devote Guardian resources to more threatening or urgent situations."

Anahi hesitated before saying, "I understand."

Strongquist signed off.

"When will you be restoring comms to the surface?" Cariad asked. "I need to speak to Ethan urgently. I was supposed to be aboard that shuttle. He must be thinking I was killed."

"You nearly took that shuttle? You were lucky. I think ship-to-planet comm can return in a couple of hours. I'm waiting on confirmation of the deaths so I can put out an official notice, and for things to calm down."

Two hours would have to do. When Ethan saw her name wasn't on the notice of the deaths, he would know she was okay. Cariad's comm button chirped. It was Alasdair.

There was only one reason the medic would contact her. Aubriot must have regained consciousness, but Cariad didn't want Anahi to know. She wanted to be the first Woken to speak to him. "I have to go," she said to Anahi. "Good luck with your little gathering."

As she was about to leave, however, Anahi's interface signaled an incoming comm. It was Strongquist again. When Anahi opened the screen, the Guardian's face was grave.

"Have you received a message from the surface?" he asked.

Anahi replied that they hadn't.

Strongquist said, "The Gens must have decided to allow the information to filter through. We just heard from one of the teams planetside that the Gens are refusing our instructions to remain inside while we collect the debris from the crash. They're stating that any attempts to control their movements will be resisted with extreme force."

CHAPTER TWENTY

"I'm not going anywhere," Ethan said.

The Guardian was outside his flitter, about to move on after issuing her command. His response halted her mid-step. She turned back. "It wasn't a suggestion. All Gens must return to their dwellings immediately."

Grief and despair gnawed at Ethan. Cariad was gone. The one person he felt close to. First Dr. Crowley, then Lauren, and now Cariad. And it wasn't only that he would miss her so badly. Cariad had been the only friendly Woken he'd known apart from Dr. Crowley. She'd given him hope of a future when Gens and Woken would see eye-to-eye. Her death had killed that hope.

"I said," he replied through his teeth. "I'm not going anywhere."

The Guardians didn't want anyone interfering with the evidence from the shuttle explosion, of course. That was why they wanted to get the Gens off the streets. But the command turned his stomach, even if he understood the rationale. He imagined the rest of the Gens would have the same reaction. It was like they were all under suspicion. But Gens had died on that shuttle too. The pilots and cabin crew at a minimum, and there had probably been one or two more returning home after working on the ship.

The Guardian hesitated.

"The wreckage from the explosion must be spread over kilometers," said Ethan. "Gens can find those pieces. We want to help. Why won't you let us help you?" As he spoke, a sudden dread seized him. What if he came across Cariad's remains? But his point stood.

"I'm afraid that isn't possible," said the Guardian. "We can't have hundreds of people tramping all over the crash site and contaminating the evidence. If you really want the person who caused the explosion brought to justice, you need to go home and let us do our job."

Ethan said, "Right. Because you've been doing well so far, haven't you? How many people died in the First Night Attack? How many died in the stadium bombing? And now this. For all your technology, for all your superiority, you're useless. All you're fit for is walking around waving your guns."

"Look," the woman said impatiently, "I'm not the one who gave the order, and I don't have time to stand around arguing with you. Return to your residence. Now." She rested her hand on the butt of her weapon.

Ethan clenched his jaw. There it was again—the threat of force. It was galling, but there was nothing he could do about it. Not right then and not alone, anyway.

He kicked open the flitter door. The Guardian backed quickly away, her eyes widening in alarm. Ethan slammed the door closed and stumped off across the lot.

He didn't go home. He went to Garwin's house. Twyla opened the door. She too took a step back at the sight of Ethan's glower.

"Garwin isn't here."

"Where is he?"

"He went to collect his credits from the cash office."

The cash office was a simple bank where Gens could

receive vouchers representing credits in return for labor they had performed for the benefit of the colony. They could use the vouchers to buy more luxurious items than the basic food and essentials they were all guaranteed. It was a stop-gap measure until the planetside data systems went live.

When Ethan arrived, Garwin wasn't in the cash office. The room was empty and the transactions window was closed and locked. Ethan had a good idea of where Garwin would be, however. He went through to the back. As he'd predicted, he found Garwin, along with Cherry, Misha, Phy, a few more farmers, and other Gens who had joined the subversive faction.

"Ethan," Garwin said as he saw him come in. "I thought we might see you before too long. Cheer up, man. We aren't going to take this lying down. Here." He picked up a small device from a pile on a table and handed it over. "One of our engineers put them together. It goes in your ear. Planetside comm, Gens only. There's nothing in the Manual that says we can't have our own comm, but I'm betting the Guardians and Woken won't like it, so do your best to hide yours, okay? Pull your hair forward over your ear."

Ethan took the device and looked at it lying in his palm. He lifted his gaze to Garwin's eyes. "Cariad's dead," he said leadenly.

Garwin's cheerful smile faded.

"She was on the shuttle," Ethan went on. "We'd arranged to meet. I was waiting for her."

"I didn't know," said Garwin. Ethan had always found Garwin hard to read, but the man looked genuinely stricken at the news. "I'm sorry to hear it. I didn't know her, but she seemed like a good person, and she was a great asset to the colony."

"She was."

The gathered women and men murmured their sympathies.

"I'm sorry, Ethan," said Cherry.

He nodded his thanks. "So we're here to discuss the latest violation of our rights?"

"Naturally," Garwin replied. "It's outrageous. They're treating us like criminals, and it isn't to be tolerated."

"I agree," said Ethan. "What are we going to do about it?"

"Resist," exclaimed Cherry. "Refuse to do what they tell us. Confront them."

"But is this the right time?" Misha asked. "Maybe we shouldn't draw too much attention to ourselves. It might make the Guardians watch us more closely. They could discover our side project." The new settlement at the caves was already under construction. It had been given the name "side project" to reduce the risk of eavesdroppers discovering what they were doing. The original settlement was alive with "projects," and a reference to one more wouldn't stand out.

"I thought about that," said Garwin, "but some conflict could work as a useful distraction. If the Guardians are on guard against our violent resistance, they're less likely to notice other activity, like transporting stores and equipment out of the settlement."

"I'd love a chance to show them what we're made of," said Ethan. "I'm sick of taking everything lying down."

"We didn't let them take away our weapons," Cherry pointed out. "We stuck up for ourselves then."

"Right," Ethan said. "And it's time we did it again." A rage was rising up in him. He didn't know if it was in response to the Guardians' oppression or his grief at Cariad's death. The events of the last time they'd been alone together, after the incident at the storage shed, kept playing in his head. He'd been cold and argumentative, yet Cariad had been the one who had made the Guardians stand down. She'd possibly saved his and the other farmers' lives.

He'd hoped he could smooth the difficulties between them when she visited. Now it was too late, and there was nowhere for his regret and sorrow to go. "I say we ignore the Guardians. We leave the explosion debris alone, but we go about our business as usual."

"Exactly my thoughts," said Garwin. "Are we agreed?" His question drew nods from all those assembled.

"I'll spread the word," Cherry said. "But people are going to ask what they should do if a Guardian orders them point blank to go inside. What should I tell them?"

Garwin said. "Tell them to notify us and we'll send someone who can give armed support."

"If we have one-on-one gun battles in the street," said Ethan, "Guardians aren't the only ones who are going to get hurt. We should give them a warning. Tell them we're ignoring their command, and if they try to force us, then we'll respond with violence. That might make them think twice before trying anything. Strongquist said at the meeting on the ship that they wanted to avoid hurting us. Let's see if that's true."

"That makes sense," Garwin said. "Cherry, find a Guardian and tell them personally. Say that it's a consensus decision and you're only the messenger. I would do it myself, but I want to maintain the impression that I'm neutral in this power struggle."

Cherry said, "I'll do it now." She hopped down from the table top where she'd been sitting and went out.

Ethan told Garwin that he would be available if armed backup were needed before also leaving. His capacity for being around others was at its limit and there didn't seem much more to be said. As he went, he pushed the comm into his ear. The device immediately activated. Random conversations and messages were passing between the Gens. No one had yet set up protocols for using the new system.

Ethan walked back to the farmer's dorm where he kept his weapon. It was in the ceiling above his bed behind removable tiles. But when he arrived he didn't retrieve the gun. He lay on his bed in the empty dorm with his hands behind his head. Conversations between Gens chattered through his ear comm as he thought about Cariad.

He recalled the first time they'd spoken, when Lauren was attacked by the predatory organism. Cariad had arrived, flaming brands of vegetation in each hand, telling him to burn the creature.

Gens always gave him the credit for saving lives on the First Night Attack. The truth was, Cariad had saved many more people than he had. But Gens didn't like to admit it. She was—had been—a Woken. They wouldn't admit anything that didn't fit with their prejudice that all the Woken were against them.

Ethan turned on his side. The loss of Cariad to the colony was great, but the loss to himself was greater. He wished he'd had the opportunity to tell her how he felt. Exhausted by the turmoil of his emotions, he drifted to sleep.

"Ethan, Ethan, can you hear me?" It was Cherry, calling him through his ear comm.

He sat up. "Yes, I'm here. What is it?"

"A confrontation with two Guardians is going down. Can you help out?" Cherry gave him the location. "I'm going there too but I'm on the other side of town. I'll try to get over as soon as I can."

"I'll be there in two minutes." Ethan stood up on his bed and pushed against the ceiling tiles. He took down his weapon and checked it over.

After leaving the farmers' dorm, he jogged toward the corner Cherry had named. Four figures stood there: two Guardians, a Gen woman, and a child. One of the Guardians was trying to take something from the child, but the small boy held the object behind his back. The woman, who seemed to be the child's mother, moved between them and pushed the Guardian away. The other Guardian's hands moved to his weapon.

"What's the problem?" Ethan asked as he ran up.

"Your boy could be holding vital evidence," the Guardian who was trying to retrieve the item said to the woman, ignoring Ethan. "I demand that you hand it over immediately. It's already been contaminated. Don't make things worse."

"Ethan," the Gen woman said. "Please help. These two want my son to give them this piece of my husband's shirt."

"What?" Ethan said. "Why...?"

The woman's expression was wracked with pain. "He was on the shuttle."

Ethan looked at the little boy, whose grimy face was tracked with tears. The child brought the torn rag from behind his back and clutched it to his chest. It was covered in dried blood.

"He's been searching for his father ever since he saw the explosion," the woman said. "I couldn't stop him. If I tried, he became hysterical. I'm thankful this is all he found."

Ethan turned to the Guardians. "Do you really need the cloth? It might be the only thing the kid has left of his father."

"We do need it," the male Guardian said. "We need everything. Any piece of debris could be the single thing that holds the evidence that will lead us to the bomber. The child must hand it over now. If he doesn't, I'll have to force him."

"You're not laying a finger on my son," the woman exclaimed.

"Then make him hand over the cloth."

"Wait," said Ethan. "What if we put the cloth inside something to protect it, and just let the little boy hang onto it for a day or two? It's going to take you a while to examine all the evidence you find. I'm sure he'll promise not to touch it. The kid's lost his father. Don't you have any sympathy?"

"We can't afford the luxury of sympathy," the Guardian said. He turned to his colleague. "Take it." He raised his weapon and pointed it at the woman.

Ethan pulled his own gun from his shoulder and also raised it. He fixed the muzzle at the armed Guardian. "Leave."

The other Guardian was unarmed. She looked between her colleague and Ethan.

"Ethan, what's happening?" Cherry asked through his comm.

He couldn't reply without revealing to the Guardians the fact that he had an ear comm. He said to them, "Leave now." To the woman he said, "Take your boy and go."

"No," the male Guardian said. "Do not leave with that evidence. If you disobey, I'll be forced to shoot."

"You better shoot me first, then," said Ethan. He adjusted his grip. His finger was a millimeter from the trigger.

A taut pause stretched almost to breaking point. The woman and child didn't move. The little boy held tightly onto the piece of cloth and watched with round eyes. The male Guardian made his decision. He took a breath and moved a fraction, ready to shoot—

"Hey," a voice shouted. Cherry had arrived. The two Guardians, the Gen woman, and the child switched their focus to the street behind Ethan. He didn't want to take his eyes off the armed Guardian.

"Guardian, put down your weapon," Cherry yelled. "Go back to your ship. You're not welcome here."

For a moment, the male Guardian didn't react, then he reluctantly lowered his gun. Ethan risked a glance over his shoulder. It wasn't only Cherry who had arrived to back him up. Two more farmers walked on either side of her. All three were armed.

Ethan returned his gaze to the Guardians. "I'd do as she says if I were you. She's more dangerous than she looks."

The female Guardian said to her colleague, "Let's go. We'll log this incident and return for the evidence later." They departed.

Cherry came up by Ethan's side. "What was that you said about me?"

"Nothing," he replied. To the Gen widow he said, "They were right when they said your son could have found important evidence. Could you put it in a bag to prevent it from being contaminated?"

"I will," the woman replied. "And I'll hand it in soon. I just couldn't bear to take it from my son right away. The Guardians wouldn't listen when I tried to explain."

"I understand," said Ethan. "This could all have been avoided with a little more compassion and respect. I'm so sorry for your loss."

"Thanks for helping us," said the woman. She took her son's hand and walked away with him.

"Ethan," said Cherry, "did you hear the list of the shuttle passengers?"

"No. I'd stopped listening to the messages. I was asleep until I heard you call me."

"I don't want to get your hopes up, but Cariad's name wasn't on it."

CHAPTER TWENTY-ONE

"I must say," Alasdair said when Cariad arrived at the revival center, "he's quite a specimen."

Aubriot lay under a sheet, unconscious, but alive.

"The finest genetic engineering money could buy," Cariad said.

Alasdair reported that Aubriot's vital signs were all normal and that he'd opened his eyes but then quickly lapsed back into unconsciousness again. A standard reaction after a successful revival. Cariad could vaguely remember the phase. At that time, she hadn't been able to distinguish between dreams and waking. It had been a few hours before she understood that her cryonic suspension had come to an end and she'd survived.

Aubriot didn't look too bad after his one hundred and eighty-four years of freezing. His skin was fresh and peeling, which was an effect of the drugs he'd been treated with. They would speed up cell renewal for the first few months after revival to replace the many cells that had died during suspension.

All of Aubriot's hair had fallen out, as was also standard. His large, aquiline skull was perfectly smooth. His sizable, well-muscled body was outlined by the thin sheet. His large feet poked out at the bottom.

The sight of the man's face, even asleep, caused Cariad's stomach to knot with tension. As a person he was definitely preferable in his current state.

"He didn't seem very angry," Alasdair offered, "when he came round."

"What do you mean?"

"You said he'd be pissed that he wasn't the first to be revived."

"I thought he would. What did you tell him?"

"I told him his revival was going well, and he'd soon be able to meet the other Woken."

"And how did he react?"

"He just seemed to take in the information. Then he slipped away again. He's probably not understanding much yet."

"Perhaps he didn't understand who you meant when you mentioned Woken. You Gens only began calling us that a few months after you began reviving us, as I recall."

"Oh yes," said Alasdair. "Maybe that's it."

"He'll soon realize what's happened when he sees me. Though I'm not sure if I want to be there for that revelation."

"Why? You asked me to tell you."

"I know, but... I told you who he is, didn't I? He financed the majority of the *Nova Fortuna* Project."

"Yeah," Alasdair replied. "You said he sunk his life's fortune into it."

"Not just his life's fortune. It was his grandmother who made the family's trillions. His father and he only added to the family's wealth. So, yes, it was understandable that he would want that pain-in-the-ass close oversight I mentioned. But imagine, Alasdair, what it was like for him being brought up with the kind of privilege his family had. The Global Government couldn't touch them, for instance. They were beyond the law. They could do exactly as they wanted to whomever they pleased, and no one could do a thing."

"I'm beginning to see what you mean."

"The family made no secret of how much they spoiled him," Cariad said, "and he was the only child. Whatever Aubriot wanted, he received, maybe even before he conceived the wish. He had servants waiting on his every whim and desire from before he emerged from his mother's womb. Fulfilling his needs to perfection, anticipating his wants. As a child, he must never once have experienced disappointment, and then under his father's stewardship he took over the business. With the disposal of more money than you or I could imagine, he crafted the most advantageous deals and met with great success. Until one day, I guess, Earth wasn't big enough for him. The Solar System wasn't big enough. Aubriot wanted the stars, and what Aubriot wanted, he got."

"How eloquent, Cariad," said the figure lying on the bed. Aubriot opened his eyes. "I couldn't have put it better myself."

Cariad swallowed. "You're awake."

"I've been awake for a little while. I just didn't want to interrupt your wonderful tribute to my achievements."

He hadn't changed. Only Aubriot could have interpreted her words as a tribute.

"Welcome back," said Alasdair. "How are you feeling?" He was reading the scan results on the screen beside the bed.

"I feel... " Aubriot sat up. The sheet fell to his waist, revealing a brawny, hairless chest. He stretched, triggering ripples beneath his skin. "I feel bloody marvelous. That four trillion extra credits I invested in the cryo system paid off, hey, Cariad?" He looked at her from head to toe.

"We had some failures, actually," Cariad said. "Sadly, some didn't survive the revival process, and some suffered irreversible physical damage." *And some, like Anahi, might have suffered psychological damage too,* she added to herself. She hoped that wasn't the case with Aubriot, who was, in her opinion, already bordering insanity.

"Is that so?" Aubriot asked. "Interesting." No sadness tinged his statement. No pity. He stretched again. "I seem to feel fine." He threw back the sheet and stood up, entirely naked.

"Careful there," said Alasdair, running to his side. "Take it easy. Those legs haven't borne weight for nearly two centuries."

Aubriot wobbled, and the medic eased him down to a sitting position. He tried to cover Aubriot with the sheet, but the man waved him aside.

"So when were *you* revived?" he asked Cariad, his eyes narrowing.

"Two years before Arrival, as planned."

"Which was...?"

"Two years and three months ago."

"You mean we've arrived?"

"Yes."

Aubriot rose to his feet once more, eyes blazing. When Alasdair went to support him, he pushed the man aside so violently he hit the floor. "And why the FUCK wasn't I revived first?"

***

After some time, Cariad managed to calm Aubriot down. She explained that after the failures, they'd wanted to perfect the revival process to ensure he didn't come to any harm when it was his turn. The white lie mollified him. If there was one thing Aubriot understood, it was his own importance.

Having gained this small victory, Cariad went on to press her advantage. She told him about the rift that had opened between Gens and Woken, and how the Gens only wanted some autonomy and responsibility.

They wanted to help run the colony they had been bred to take part in, she explained, but Anahi and other Woken had seized the reins and wouldn't let go.

"Makes sense," Aubriot replied. Alasdair had finally persuaded him to put on some clothes. He was sitting on the edge of the bed. "You scientists had your faults," he said, "but you did seem to know what you were doing most of the time. These Gens, as they call themselves, they're the seed corn, right? The seed doesn't get to decide where it's planted or how it's going to grow."

Cariad pursed her lips, biting back a retort. Speaking with Aubriot was like walking a tightrope over a pit of vipers. If she wanted to steer the *Nova Fortuna* Project financier to her point of view, she needed to tread carefully. "We engineered the Gens, it's true, but we didn't remove their humanity. They're people, the same as you and I."

Aubriot raised his eyebrows.

"The same as me anyway," Cariad corrected. "Their desire to be in control of their own destinies is entirely natural. The more independence we take from them, and the more control we exert, the more they're going to rebel. I don't know why Anahi doesn't understand that."

Yawning, Aubriot gestured to Alasdair, who brought over the wheelchair that he'd demanded. "I'm going to see the planet now."

Alasdair gave Cariad a look of panic. Aubriot was having his usual effect.

"There's more that you need to know," said Cariad. "While you were being revived, one of the shuttles exploded en route planetside. We think it was a bomb."

"What?!" Aubriot looked as incensed as if the bomb had been intended for him.

Cariad told him about the First Night Attack, the arrival of the Guardians, the bomb in the stadium, and the shuttle explosion. As she went on, Aubriot turned red, then white, his eyes staring and his jaw clenching. Alasdair watched the readings on the scanner screen with concern.

"The Natural Movement? The fucking Natural Movement?" Aubriot went on to curse loudly while he vented his fury. Then he suddenly sagged. His strong features turned haggard.

"Maybe you should lie down," Alasdair said.

Aubriot flopped to his side and collapsed on the bed.

"It's been too much for him," Alasdair said. "He's still weak. You should go."

Cariad stood to leave.

"Wait," Aubriot said. His eyes remained on fire in his pale, tired face. "I want to meet these Guardians, then I'm going down to the planet. You all fucked up, and I expect you to put it right. You're going to get this project back on track. I'm holding you personally responsible, Cariad."

Great.

CHAPTER TWENTY-TWO

Ethan hit his head twice on the protruding rock before he decided to chip it away. Plenty more people would be entering and leaving the storage cave and the stony spur would have more victims if he didn't do something about it. As he worked away with a hammer and chisel, the ocean view spread out in front of him, Ethan ruminated.

Cariad quickly entered his thoughts, as always. He hadn't spoken to her for weeks, not since the moment the ship-to-ground comm had been reopened and they'd contacted each other simultaneously.

"It's good to hear your voice," Ethan had said. "For hours, I thought you were dead, until I saw you weren't on the list of fatalities. Thank the stars you weren't on the shuttle."

"Yes," Cariad replied. "I was incredibly lucky. It's good to finally talk to you again, Ethan."

Then they'd both paused, uncertain what to say. Ethan spoke first. "I wanted to tell you I'm sorry I got angry at you after the fight at the equipment shed. That was why I invited you down to visit. I wanted to apologize, face to face. The argument we had has been on my mind ever since. When the shuttle exploded, I hated the idea that we'd parted on bad terms."

"Me too," said Cariad. "I mean, even before the disaster, I regretted some of the things I said. And I really do understand how you and the rest of the Gens feel. I'm doing everything I can up here to make things better."

"I know you are, and I appreciate it. Now I've got the chance, I wanted to say, we shouldn't ever argue like that again. We have something special. There aren't many friendships between Gens and Woken. We have to try to preserve what we have."

"I know," said Cariad. "I agree."

A silence followed. There was more to Ethan's words than he'd stated, but he was struggling to express himself and didn't know if he should try.

"Do you know when the shuttle runs are going to start up again?" he asked.

"No. No one knows. I don't think Anahi has any idea what she's doing. She's out of her depth and too proud to admit it. She was requesting Guardians as an armed presence on the ship."

"On *Nova Fortuna*? The Woken need protecting from each other now?"

"No, we don't," said Cariad. "That's the problem. She's paranoid. And she's insisted on reviving another nutcase—Aubriot, the financier. Between the two of them, who knows what's going to happen up here. I wish I was planetside with you."

"I wish you were here too." That was how they'd left it. They'd mended their rift, but Ethan felt the weight of things unsaid. The timing wasn't right and he didn't know if it ever would be.

Since then, he'd avoided Cariad's comms. The subversive Gen group had made their plans known to the wider population and found they were welcomed. The process of slowly fitting out the cliff caves to make them suitable for human habitation was well under way. Equipment and supplies were being transferred surreptitiously, piece by piece. Ethan knew that his silence had to hurt Cariad and he was sorry for it, but he was worried that he might let slip a reference to what the Gens were doing. If she guessed or discovered the secret, it would put her in a difficult position. He didn't think it was fair of him to do that to her.

One day, within a few weeks or months, she would know the reason for his silence. He hoped she would understand and forgive him.

The caves were dry and a little warmer than their surroundings, except for when the wind was blowing in from the sea. Sanitation had been the biggest concern at first. At the original settlement, the sewage treatment plant had been one of the first facilities that had been built. The Manual had laid out all the plans and instructions, so the Gens had an intellectual understanding of such things but no practical experience in creating their own facility from scratch in a different setting.

Luckily, the proximity of the caves to the ocean provided somewhat of an answer. They had a never-ending supply of water and the rocks below were regularly washed by waves. It wasn't the perfect solution. At some point they would have to figure out a way to treat the waste, but it would do for the moment. The new settlement's first latrines were built.

Garwin had devised a solar- and wind-powered pump that kept the latrine storage tanks supplied with seawater, and another engineer set to work on building rainwater storage facilities. Then, after the basic plans for storage, private, and communal caves had been decided, the Gens had begun the preparations for transferring the population.

Sneaking supplies, machinery, and tools out from under the noses of the Guardians turned out to be even easier than anyone had guessed. Guardians didn't involve themselves in the day-to-day running of the settlement, and they rarely stayed planetside overnight. No Woken remained on the planet surface either. After the shuttle explosion, they had all returned to the ship in an emergency evacuation, so the Gens had avoided their prying eyes too.

Day by day, little by little, the original settlement slowly emptied as the Gens transported everything they needed a two-hour flitter ride away to their new home. When the first crops were ready to harvest, they would transport them over too.

The effect on the general mood was almost palpable. An air of hope permeated Gen society. Complaints and worries were rarely voiced. Everyone seemed constantly energized and happy. Ethan felt the same. He missed Cariad a lot, but not a single other Woken nor his time aboard the *Nova Fortuna*. Living in the new settlement was hard and promised to become harder still, but he felt more alive than ever. He was finally living his own life in his own way, not an existence that had been dictated to him by others and the accident of his birth.

Then the day had come when regular Gens could begin giving up their homes in the original settlement and going to live permanently in the caves. One of the first to make the move was Twyla, Garwin's wife. She was a kindergarten teacher, and she arrived to help set up the first small school, ready for the families who would transfer soon. The parents needed somewhere for their children to go while they worked on fitting out their caves.

Cherry had also been heavily involved in the moving-in process. Ethan wondered how she felt about seeing Twyla so often. Did it make things awkward for Garwin? Did Twyla know about her husband's affair or wasn't she even aware of his reputation as a philanderer?

Ethan paused at chipping away at the rock to wipe

dust out of his eyes and rest his arms.

It had seemed to him that people had become more serious about their relationships over the few months since Arrival. Couples had grown less casual about exclusivity. Extra-marital affairs were more frowned upon. Even if Twyla had chosen to ignore Garwin's frequent dalliances in the past, she might have changed her mind. She could be young enough to still be able to have children, and she had to like them, going by her chosen profession. Now that procreation was actively encouraged, that might throw a whole different light on things for her.

Ethan inspected the dent he'd made in the protruding rock, which had turned out to be extremely hard. Considering that he'd been chipping at it for about half an hour he hadn't made much progress.

He didn't mind the delay too much. The view over the ocean never ceased to enchant him. He didn't think he would ever tire of it.

One of the other farmers, a man by the name of Seaberg, arrived. He'd lowered a box on the pulley system to the cave entrance, descended himself and retrieved the box from the platform. When he reached Ethan, he stopped and put it down. Appraising Ethan's effort, he remarked, "It's tough stuff, isn't it?"

"The rock? Yeah. I'm going to be here a while yet." He lifted his hammer and chisel to resume chipping.

"You know, we could just blow that piece off."

"Huh?" Ethan lowered his tools.

"We could drill a hole, about here." Seaberg pointed to a spot above the dent Ethan had made. "Pop in a little bit of explosive. Boom. It would blow most of that lump away, I'm guessing."

"Really?"

"I've been talking to Garwin about opening up some of the passages at the rear of the caves in the same way," Seaberg went on. "Widening the tunnels to make more room, you know? Before people begin to arrive in large numbers. It would be better to do it now. Safer."

"You know how to do that?"

"Pretty much. So do you, don't you? You studied farming too, right? We had a course on clearing vegetation with a subsection on blowing out tree stumps."

"Yeah, that's right. I'd forgotten."

"Well it's all explosives, isn't it? The same principles apply to rock. I was talking to an engineer about it and she agreed. She said they'd studied using explosives for demolitions, though they hadn't gone into the subject in any depth. Demolitions aren't a priority in a new colony. But anyway, we could begin with small projects like this."

"You said you were talking to Garwin about it. What did he say?"

"He said to talk to you."

"Right." Ethan didn't mind the extra responsibility, but he didn't know much about explosives. He would have to do some research. But something else was bothering him. "I'll think about it. Thanks for the suggestion."

"No problem," Seaberg said. He picked up his box and carried it into the back of the cave.

Ethan lifted his hammer and chisel and recommenced chipping at the rock.

Seaberg passed Ethan again on his way out. He gave a nod and disappeared out of the cave front. He would climb the ladder to the top of the cliff, from where he would lower another box. The transportation method was cumbersome but it conserved the finite power of the flitters and overcame the previously awkward attempts to transfer boxes into caves that were too small for the flitters to fit.

Ethan mulled over Seaberg's words. He'd known the man all his life, though they had never been close friends. They'd been through school and then farmers' training together. He'd never liked or disliked Seaberg, but he thought that he knew him pretty well. Now he wasn't so sure.

He knew his suspicion was unfair, based on an apparently innocent conversation, but the actions of the Natural Movement had changed his attitudes to others. Someone from the movement had taken Lauren and Dr. Crowley from him via First Night Attack. And a Natural Movement follower had nearly killed Cariad, twice.

More than anything, Ethan wanted that person or those people caught and prevented from hurting anyone else. Seaberg's casual mention of explosives had sparked alarm. The context and the conversation had been normal and natural, but Ethan couldn't help making the connection. Was Seaberg the Natural Movement bomber?

CHAPTER TWENTY-THREE

Cariad's careful maneuvering to be the first Woken Aubriot spoke to as soon as he was revived had also brought her excessively under the man's scrutiny. On balance, however, she didn't regret her move. It meant that when he demanded to be taken planetside, she could go too. Anahi didn't dare try to prevent Aubriot from doing exactly whatever he wanted, so when Cariad told her that Aubriot was traveling to the surface and she was going along, she didn't protest.

Aubriot's initial energetic recovery after his revival had been short-lived. Extreme weakness soon assailed him and had plagued the man for weeks. He had undergone intensive rehabilitation, as if he'd been in a serious accident. Re-learning gross and fine motor skills had taken up much of his time. Yet all the while, the man's mind had been as active as ever. The two factors combined led to many outbursts of frustration and fury, mostly directed at Alasdair, who had helped the ungrateful patient through his treatment.

Eventually the day had come when Aubriot decided he was strong enough to go down to the planet that he had sacrificed his fortune to see. There was no question that Dr. Montfort would agree, mainly because Montfort's opinion wasn't sought, which didn't mean the doctor would escape blame if the trip proved too tiring.

Aubriot believed himself to be a prime target for Natural Movement resentment. Cariad privately concurred, though for reasons that were probably different from Aubriot's. He undoubtedly thought he was a target because he was so important, but Cariad thought that, as the primary financier of the *Nova Fortuna* Project, he could easily be seen as the one most to blame for diverting humankind from its "natural" destiny.

Woken who understood the complexities of explosives were screening a shuttle for bombs. They ran scanners over every inch of the vehicle before also visually inspecting it, and the crew were similarly scanned and body searched before being allowed aboard.

Under the informal title of Person Responsible For Getting the *Nova Fortuna* Project Back on Track, Cariad's natural inclusion in Aubriot's entourage meant that she should undergo the same procedure. At this, however, she drew a line. She yearned to go planetside. She wanted to see what was happening in the settlement, and she wanted to walk on soil and feel the sun on her face again. Most of all, she wanted to see Ethan, who had been silent for weeks. She hadn't even been able to contact him to tell him she would probably be arriving soon.

But then again, maybe she wouldn't be. She wasn't going to let Aubriot treat her like his slave and undergo the indignity of a body search. When her turn came, she said loudly, "No. I'm not doing it."

By this time, Aubriot was halfway up the shuttle ramp. "What?"

"I'm not going behind those screens to have people

poke and prod me. I'll be scanned if you insist on it, but I'm not undergoing a body search. It's undignified and unnecessary."

"The scanners don't pick up every known explosive," Aubriot said. "You have to be searched."

"Look," said Cariad, "do you really think I'm the bomber? You know how hard I worked on this project. Do you think I'd do all that and say goodbye to my family and Earth forever, just so I could come here and sabotage the colonization? I nearly died in the stadium bombing. Do you think I did that to myself?"

"Hmph," Aubriot said, his lip curling beneath his aquiline nose. "I guess not. Whatever." He waved dismissively. "Get aboard then."

Cariad exhaled. Standing up to Aubriot was always risky but occasionally his capricious temperament allowed some wiggle room.

As the shuttle flew down to the surface, Aubriot nodded to himself every so often as if carrying out a private conversation in his head. The shuttle made its final approach and the settlement was plain to see—a neat block of civilization in a sea of wild vegetation. Aubriot's nods became more vigorous, like he was giving his approval.

"Not bad," he murmured. "Not bad." He turned to Cariad. "Looks all right so far. I was expecting worse from what Anahi told me."

"She's exaggerated the problems we've been having with the Gens," Cariad said. "For the most part, they've been following the Manual. It's only been in a few areas that they wanted to do things their way. You can see that the houses and roads follow the original plan, and they've begun farming according to the schedule."

"Yeah. Those are fields out there, right?"

"That's right. And don't forget, no Woken has been down to the surface for weeks. As far as I know, there haven't been any disasters. Everything's going as it should. In a few months they'll start harvesting the first crops, and in time they'll begin mining for iron and other minerals. Complete self-sufficiency should be achieved in around three years, just as we predicted. The only obstacle to that is the Natural Movement infiltrator, and that's hardly the Gens' fault. It was our security that failed back on Earth and allowed that to happen. Anahi's overreacting when she says we can't trust the Gens. Look at what they've managed to do, mostly by themselves. They were bred for it. We should let them get on with it. These are their lives. It's their planet."

Aubriot had been gazing out of the window while Cariad gave her speech, but at her final sentence he turned to her with a deep frown. "If anyone *owns* this planet it's me. Fuck knows, I paid enough for it."

Cariad regretted her bold statement. Now was not the time to antagonize the man. He'd already granted her one concession. She couldn't expect another anytime soon. "Well, the ownership of the planet isn't in question," she said, hoping her ambivalent statement would mollify him.

It seemed to do the trick. Aubriot returned his gaze to the shuttle window as the vessel landed. "What did you name the place in the end?"

"We didn't, actually. The previous Leader was about to announce the results of the voting when the stadium bomb went off. Since then, things have been in such disarray, the question of the planet's name has been put aside. I think we may have another vote when we've finally put the Natural Movement problem to rest."

"What about Aubriot's World?" Aubriot said. "It has a ring to it, don't you think?"

Cariad couldn't tell if he was joking.

***

Cariad couldn't help but notice, as she left the shuttle field and walked the streets of the settlement, that the place seemed unusually quiet. Though she hadn't been planetside for weeks, she was sure that there used to be many more people out and about. She guessed the Gens were all busy at their jobs, working hard to get the colony on its feet. Ethan was probably at his farm. He had no reason to be in town during the daytime.

Alasdair, whom Aubriot had appropriated as his personal medic, formed part of his retinue. An agricultural scientist—not Anahi, who hadn't wanted to come down—an ecologist and a meteorologist had also come along. Aubriot insisted on leading the way.

They first visited the machine works, where the kits for vehicles, agricultural machinery, and the massive roadmakers were assembled. Garwin was there, covered in grease, his smile wide, white and gleaming in his oil-besmirched face. "Pleased to meet you, sir," he said as soon as Aubriot entered the workroom.

The news of the financier's revival had spread planetside, and Garwin hadn't taken more than a second to understand who was paying a visit. He rubbed his palm on his dirty overalls, looked at it and smiled again apologetically. "I would shake your hand, but... "

"Don't worry about it," Aubriot said, expansive in his generosity. Uninvited, he went to look around the place. Garwin raised his eyebrows as Cariad then followed him. Aubriot went over to a half-finished solar-powered, wheeled electric vehicle, intended for traveling paved roads.

"You in charge around here?" Aubriot asked Garwin. Then without waiting for an answer, "Got any of these working yet?"

"Yes. We've finished five, but only in order to check that we could. These aren't a priority at the moment. The settlement's still small enough to walk from one side to the other. This one here is the final one for now. We're concentrating on the harvesters, to get ahead of the demand, if you see what I mean."

"I do. Makes sense."

Garwin shrugged. "Just following the Manual."

"Any problems?" Aubriot asked.

"Not anything major. Occasionally a kit will be missing a small part, or the tool will be the wrong size for the job. Not anything we can't work around."

"On schedule?"

"Ahead of it."

Aubriot narrowed his eyes. "Garwin, isn't it?"

"That's right."

"I heard about you."

Garwin looked as though he was about to make a flippant reply but checked himself. He had the measure of Aubriot already. "I try to speak for the Gens when I can."

"Someone's got to speak for them, right?" Aubriot joked.

Garwin laughed good-naturedly, though Cariad detected a hint of well-suppressed ire. "Is there anything else you'd like to see?" he asked Aubriot. "You've caught us a little unprepared. We haven't had visitors from the ship in quite a while. If I'd known you were coming, I would have organized some demonstrations for you."

"No," Aubriot said. "I don't want to see demonstrations. Bad idea. I want to see things as they really are. No point in giving notice. Might as well not bother going."

Cariad remembered Aubriot's impromptu visits to the genetics center well. Catching people unawares and attempting to wrong-foot them was his style.

"Is there anything in particular you're interested in around the settlement then?" Garwin asked. "I'd be happy to show you around. The hospital's nearly finished, the school's already open, and we've started up the credits-for-labor exchange scheme. We've got people working on residential building projects at the edge of town. The construction program's on track to supply everyone with a private dwelling by the end of next year."

"Hmm," Aubriot said. "I don't often say this, but I'm impressed. I got a whole different idea of what was happening down here. I'm going to have a look around by myself. In fact... " He turned to Cariad and the rest of his companions. "You can all wait here."

He strode out of the building. After a short pause as everyone adjusted to his abrupt departure, Alasdair said, "Do you think he meant we have to stay here until he comes back?"

"Probably," said the agricultural scientist sardonically. "Not that it means we have to. I mean, who does he think he is? What gives him the right to order us around? He might have been the richest man who's ever lived, but that was on Earth. Here, he's just another Woken, except he doesn't have any useful skills. Unless we *need* the ability to wheel and deal in the colony's economy."

Cariad smiled. The scientist had only just met Aubriot. He'd been an external applicant for a cryo preservation spot and not part of the original team. The man would find out soon enough that Aubriot was a force to be reckoned with.

"Whatever he meant, I'm not staying here to wait for him," Cariad said. "Do you know where Ethan is?" she asked Garwin.

"No, but he's out on his farm, I expect. That's where he is most of the time these days." He said to the others, "I have to get back to work, but you're all welcome to wait here for your new Leader to return."

The agricultural scientist huffed. "Aubriot isn't the new Leader. What gave you that idea?"

"Isn't he?" Garwin asked, picking up a tool before bending over a machine.

Cariad left the machine shop, wondering if she could use a flitter to go out to Ethan's farm and visit him there. Then she recalled that it wouldn't be an "authorized use." She was thinking like a Gen. Or was she only thinking as was natural and normal? Anahi loved to categorize the Gens' behavior as deliberately defiant, but they were only doing what seemed to work best in the situation they'd been placed in. What if the Gens weren't disobeying the Manual because they wanted to do things their way, but because they actually had the best idea of what was the appropriate way?

It was she and other Woken who had bred the Gens to be well-fitted to the task of establishing the colony, and they'd created their education to teach them all the skills they needed. Ethan had pointed that out to her one time. By not trusting the Gens, the Woken weren't trusting their own ability to create the best people for the project.

The idea excited Cariad. Not only was her reasoning sound, it would appeal to the Woken's way of thinking. She could argue if they didn't believe in the Gens, they were doubting their own ability to create the best-suited colonists.

She went through the quiet streets to the flitter shed, hoping to find one not in use. The shed was empty, however. Even the person in charge of it wasn't there. Cariad paused, looking around the quiet, cool space. It was odd that every single flitter was gone. She didn't think the Gens needed them so badly. They were only useful for traveling outside the settlement, and Garwin hadn't mentioned any particular events going on that would require flitters.

Cariad went out again. If she couldn't take a flitter to Ethan's farm, she would go to the farmers' dorm on the slim chance that he might be there. The place was ten minutes' walk from the flitter shed. All the way there, she didn't see a single other person.

At the farmers' dorm, no one was in the lobby area, so Cariad went through it to the living area, which was also empty. She poked her head into the communal sleeping room. Only one person was inside, and it wasn't Ethan. Cariad was about to leave until she heard what the man was saying. His words made her halt. The man was in the middle of a conversation via the room's interface and he hadn't noticed Cariad at first. When he did finally see her, he abruptly stopped talking and turned red.

"I was looking for Ethan," Cariad said. "I guess he isn't here."

"No, er," the man stammered. "He's working out on his farm today, I'm pretty sure."

"Okay. Thanks." Cariad left and went directly back to the machinery workroom.

No one else seemed to have gone out while she was away. Aubriot wasn't there. The others were standing around, not talking, looking bored and frustrated. The agricultural scientist who had been so verbally defiant of Aubriot had apparently stayed in the workshop.

Cariad walked over to the group. Garwin was close by, though he was under a large machine, his legs protruding.

"Did any of you go and have a look around?" she asked.

"No," Alasdair replied. "We've been here all this time. Why?"

Before Cariad could reply, however, Aubriot showed up.

"There's something fishy going on here," he announced angrily as he came inside. "Something isn't right, and I'm going to find out what it is."

Cariad couldn't help but agree. When she'd gone into the farmers' dorm, she'd heard the man say, *Right. I'll try to act normal. Do you think they suspect anything?*

CHAPTER TWENTY-FOUR

Ethan had known the day would come, of course. Everyone had. Somehow, that didn't make anyone less jittery when it arrived. The Woken knew that something was up. It was only a matter of time until they discovered exactly what the Gens had done. What wasn't so clear was what the scientists and their oppressive Guardians would do about it.

A party was down from the ship, including someone newly Woken—a bigwig of some kind. Cariad was there too, Ethan had heard. He would have liked to have gone to see her. On the other hand, he feared her realization that he'd kept something important from her for so long and he would have found her inevitable questions hard to answer.

The Woken were asking plenty of them. Why was the settlement almost empty? Where had everyone gone? As agreed, every Gen there was giving the same answers: *Sorry, I don't know. I have no idea. Maybe they're working somewhere else today. Yes, it is strange, but I'm sorry, I can't help you.*

Ethan wondered how many were managing to sound convincing in their answers. Not that it really mattered. Only an idiot would believe them, and the Woken were no idiots. What was remarkable was that the Guardians hadn't noticed the increasing absences for so long.

However, the next question the Gens had to answer was, what were they going to do now?

The new settlement at the caves wasn't anywhere near finished. The habitable caves remained little more than holes in the cliff with sanitation. The storage caves were full, stuffed with as many of the supplies from the original settlement that would fit inside them, but the supplies themselves were in a terrible mess. No single person had overseen the transfer, and everyone who had helped had organized the boxes and crates according to their personal idea of how everything should be stored. Certain essential items, like disinfectant and salt, had gone missing. No one thought they'd been stolen. The containers had to be somewhere among the randomly stacked jumble. It was just that no one knew where.

The discussion to decide how to respond to this latest turn of the screw tightening the tension between the Gens and the Woken took place on the top of the cliffs above the caves. No cave was large enough to hold everyone who wanted to take part, which was some three or four hundred Gens.

Some young children remained at the original settlement, and many parents were nervous that they would be separated from their offspring. They wanted to go to retrieve them. Others argued that it would look suspicious if lots of people suddenly appeared on flitters, racing into town, especially those who could give no good reason for being away.

Wait until we think up an excuse, the objectors argued. Only no one could think of anything that made any sense. Others wanted to tell the Woken and Guardians exactly what the Gens were doing and defy them to put a stop to it.

Ethan didn't know the right answer, and without Garwin there to lead the discussion, it had descended into chaos. Loud arguments between individuals had broken out, while others were shouting themselves hoarse asking for quiet. The debate was going nowhere and Ethan needed some peace. He left the group and climbed down the network of ladders that led to his personal cave.

He'd felt a little guilty at taking a cave all to himself, but others had urged that he deserved it, considering his service to the colony. That argument hadn't made a lot of sense to him. He'd only done what seemed right and what anyone else would have done in his position. But the cave was tiny, too small even for a couple, so he'd decided it wouldn't hurt to accept it.

Ethan was nearly down to the level of his cave when a rung on the ladder gave way as he put his weight on it. He let out a cry of surprise and gripped the sides of the ladder while seeking blindly with his foot to find the next rung. He looked down at the beach, thirty meters or more below him, and the waves that pounded it. He'd come close to having his entire involvement in the Gens/Woken problem solved for him.

Climbing down further, he reached the defective rung. It had slipped out from its hole in the side of the ladder. The nut that held it there had become loose. Ethan sighed. The ladder system was pure Gen construction. Whenever they made something of their own, they never seemed to do it as well as when they followed the Manual. It was an ingrained problem they faced. The Gens had been brought up to follow instructions, not to be creative or innovative.

Ethan stepped sideways into his cave and nearly moved backward and off the cliff. Twyla was there. She was near the entrance, lifting a bag over her shoulder, as if she'd been about to leave.

"Ethan," she said, moving out of his way. "Sorry. I had to come inside. Having no doors makes it hard to knock. I was looking for you."

It was a poor excuse. She could have easily called out and left when he didn't answer. Ethan casually glanced around. He didn't have much in the way of personal possessions, and nothing seemed to have been disturbed. The likelihood of Twyla wanting to steal from him was remote, but he couldn't think of another explanation for her presence. "Can I help you with something?"

Twyla looked at her feet, then out across the ocean. For an older woman, she suddenly seemed young and vulnerable. "You're angry with me for waiting for you here, aren't you? I'm sorry to invade your privacy, but I need to talk to you alone about something that's bothering me. It's kind of embarrassing. I'm not sure I know how to put it."

Ethan's suspicions fell away. He had a horrible presentiment of what Twyla wanted to speak to him about. He began to grow uncomfortable.

"It's weird," Twyla went on. "I had it all clear in my mind what I would say before I came here. Now I can't remember a word."

"Do you want to sit down?" Ethan asked. If he was right about what Twyla wanted to talk about, he didn't relish the prospect of the conversation they were about to have, but he felt sorry for her. He would have hated to be in her position.

She looked for a place to sit. Ethan pulled a storage box out into the floor space and wiped off the fine dust that permeated everything in the caves. He sat down on his mattress.

Twyla put her hands on her bony knees. "I wanted to ask you something. I hope it's okay. You're the only person I can ask. I don't trust the others to tell me the truth. You're honest. That's what people say, anyway. You have a lot of integrity. Only..." She swallowed. "Now that it comes to it, I don't know if I want to ask you. I don't know if I want to know the answer."

The situation was becoming extremely awkward, but what Ethan felt most was sympathy and sorrow. He almost opened the subject for her but stopped himself. If his guess was wrong, it would be extremely embarrassing for them both and potentially disastrous for Twyla's marriage.

"On the other hand," Twyla went on, "I got up the courage to come here, so I guess I should go through with it." All the time she'd been speaking, she hadn't met Ethan's gaze. Now she looked him directly in the eye. "Ethan, you spend a lot of time with Garwin, right?"

He nodded.

"Do you know... Have you noticed anything?" She stopped, closed her eyes, and took a breath. She opened her eyes. "Ethan, is my husband having an affair?"

For some reason, Ethan felt almost as bad as if *he* was the one who was being unfaithful to his wife. Twyla looked fragile, like a breath of wind would break her in two. Ethan didn't want his words to be that breath, but what could he do? He couldn't bring himself to lie to the woman. She'd been lied to enough already.

Yet the words were difficult to say. Instead, he nodded. "I'm sorry."

He'd expected Twyla to burst into tears or begin an angry rant, but instead she only looked defeated. Her shoulders sagged and her head hung down like something inside her had been crushed. "I should have known. The signs were all there. I just didn't want to see them. Do you know how long it's been going on?"

"I'm afraid I don't."

"Or who the woman is?"

Ethan hesitated. He thought he'd been right to tell Twyla the truth about her husband's affair, but was Cherry's personal business his to tell? Was she doing anything wrong? *She* hadn't broken any vows.

"No. Don't tell me," said Twyla. "It doesn't matter,

whoever it is." She abruptly stood up. "I think I'll go. Thanks for being honest, Ethan. I appreciate it."

"I wish I had a different answer for you."

"Me too. I wonder how long he's been at it. I've suspected him for a long time."

Ethan said again, "I'm sorry."

Twyla went to the cave entrance as if to leave, but she had another question for him. "Do many people know?"

"I don't know how many people know about it," Ethan replied. It was the truth, though a more accurate statement would have been, *I think everyone knows.* But he couldn't bring himself to add to her anguish. The woman had enough to deal with at that moment.

Twyla said, "No one else even gave me a hint. You were the only one to tell me and only when I asked you about it directly."

Ethan struggled to find an answer. Should he have told her? No. He hardly knew her. Luckily, Twyla left before he could think of a response. He stuck his head out of the cave and warned her about the broken rung, but she didn't reply and carried on climbing up the cliff.

He sat down heavily. Big and small, the problems for the settlement were compounding. His revelation to Twyla could have a wider impact than it should. If Garwin was affected by the breakdown of his marriage, he might not be able to continue on as he had, leading the Gens to their freedom and independence while playing a double game with the Woken. The chaotic meeting going on at the top of the cliffs was evidence of how much the Gens needed the man.

Out over the ocean, clouds were building up on the horizon. A storm was coming. Ethan got up and began moving his belongings deeper inside the cave, where the bone-dry sand indicated that rain never reached it. He thought he should go up to the cliff top and draw others' attention to the impending downpour but he didn't have the motivation. He sat on a box and watched the gathering clouds.

It wasn't right that Garwin was repeatedly unfaithful to Twyla. She wasn't a bad person, and Garwin had wanted to marry her after all. It also seemed unfair to Ethan. Garwin had the opportunity of a happy relationship with someone he loved, or at least someone he *had* loved at some point, while Ethan's first love had been murdered, and... He avoided the train of thought. It would be a long time before he could be with someone else. Perhaps that might never happen, especially if whoever he chose didn't choose him.

His thoughts strayed to safer ground. While he felt sorry for Twyla, he was also bemused at her ignorance about her husband's affairs. Garwin was notorious among the Gens for his numerous flings. He had confidence and charisma that few single and even married women seemed able to resist. It hardly seemed credible that the first news Twyla had heard of Garwin's dalliances had come from Ethan's lips. Garwin wasn't careful about hiding what he was doing, as his behavior that day they spent exploring the caves attested. Could Twyla really be that naive? He guessed she had to be. Perhaps the old saying he'd read in Earth literature was correct—the partner was always the last to know.

A creaking from outside told him someone was approaching. Ethan jumped up and went to the cave entrance. "Watch out for a broken rung," he called before he could see who it was.

He was looking up at Cherry's legs and bottom as she climbed down the ladder.

"Where is it?" she asked, calling down to him.

"The third one below where your left foot is now."

"Okay. Thanks."

A moment later, she jumped into the cave. "These ladders aren't very safe, are they?"

"No," Ethan replied. "Someone needs to go over

them and double check all the connections. And we need to install a safety system, something like a harness that we clip onto the struts. Eventually we're going to have to cut stairs into the cliff and wall them in."

"That's a great idea," said Cherry, "but it'll take forever."

"Maybe not. Someone was saying we might be able to use controlled explosions to break away areas of rock. That would speed up the process quite a bit."

"Ethan," said Cherry, "what would we do without you?"

"I don't know. Find another dumb farmer?"

"Don't run yourself down like that. When are you going to understand how important you are to this colony?"

"Thanks, but you're exaggerating. So, is there something you need me for?"

"Something I need you for? What kind of a question is that? Why did you go off when we were discussing what to do? It's anarchy up there. You have to come up and help us decide how to respond to the Woken sniffing around the settlement. We need your opinion, Ethan. People will listen to you."

He was in no mood for the meandering, confused discussions and arguments he'd just slipped away from, but he said, "Okay. I'll come up. But there's a storm coming. Can you see? We have to move everything away from the cave entrances."

"All right. I'll organize that. There are plenty of people avoiding the debate just like you. You go and talk some sense into those Gens up top."

***

When Ethan returned to the clifftop meeting, it didn't seem to have moved on from where it had been when he left. The same people were repeating the same arguments. No side was willing to back down or even listen to anyone else. The only difference was that the mood had grown even more argumentative. If things were to continue in the same way, the debate could soon turn into a brawl.

"Hey," he shouted, raising his hands. "Hey!" He jumped up and down, waving the crowd to silence.

The Gens turned to him and gradually the noisy discussions subsided.

"Have we heard any more news on what the Woken have said or done?" Ethan asked.

"They haven't done anything yet," someone replied. "Least ways, that we know of. Just been asking awkward questions."

"And the people in the settlement have been offering no explanation, like we agreed?" Ethan asked. "Just saying they don't know?"

"That's right," someone said.

"Then it seems to me the best thing for us to do," said Ethan, "is nothing."

He paused to let his statement sink in. "Look at it this way: Why should we answer the Woken's questions? We're not their slaves. We don't owe them our compliance, and even if we did, we've done nothing wrong. We have *nothing* to be ashamed of. Even if we believe we should follow the Manual, which, by the way, I don't, there's nothing in there that states we can't do what we're doing, and nothing that states we have to keep the Woken informed."

The immediate reaction to his statement was silence.

"That's right," someone said in the tone of receiving a revelation. "In fact, the Manual states that we *should* move out of the original settlement and start new ones. We've only brought the schedule forward."

"Whether we're following the Manual or not," said Ethan, "makes no difference. So what if the Woken have noticed the settlement's half empty? This is our planet. We can do what we like. We don't answer to them unless we choose to. So we do nothing. Right?"

Someone said, "I guess it makes sense. So, we just carry on?"

"Yes," said Ethan. "Just carry on as we have been, making our new home habitable, and moving *our* supplies here."

No one had any further comments to make, so Ethan said, "Glad we've sorted that out, because we've got more important things to deal with. It's going to start raining soon. We need to get everything we can into the back of the caves."

The crowd began to dissolve.

"But take care on the ladders," Ethan added. "Some of the rungs are coming loose." The Gens moved away, forming lines as they waited to descend to their various locations within the cave system.

Ethan wondered if he'd said something different, whether the Gens would have gone along with that too. It was like they were only waiting for someone to take charge and tell them what to do. They had far to go to begin behaving like autonomous human beings. Their conditioning had made them into sheep or children, which is exactly what Cariad had accused them of being. It was partly a problem of confidence, he realized. The Gens needed to think more independently, it was true, but in order to achieve that they needed to believe in themselves.

He joined the back of a line. As he waited his turn on a ladder, another realization hit him. What he'd been thinking about his fellow Gens also applied to himself.

CHAPTER TWENTY-FIVE

Aubriot was in a rage and he'd gathered all the Woken together to witness it. He'd even demanded that representatives from the Guardians attend his rant. Strongquist and Faina sat at the back of the large meeting room aboard the *Nova Fortuna*. Strongquist's arms were folded and his legs outstretched and crossed at the ankle. Faina sat erect, her hands together in her lap. The female Guardian's eyes were bright and alert, while Strongquist's were hooded, as if he was mentally a great distance from the event.

Aubriot's weakness following his revival had entirely disappeared. To Cariad, while he lectured and threatened everyone about the situation planetside, where most of the Gens seemed to have left the settlement, he appeared as athletic and dynamic as he'd been on Earth. "This is unacceptable," the man thundered for the third or fourth time. "This situation is entirely out of hand, and it's your fault." He jabbed an index finger at the seated Woken, who were as meek as sheep. "What the hell were you thinking of, leaving them alone down there, unsupervised? I mean... " He put his hands on his hips. "What did you *think* was going to happen? *Of course* they were going to get away from you. *Of course* they were going to do their own thing. They aren't robots. They're human beings. Of course they're going to want to be independent."

Cariad rolled her eyes as Aubriot echoed her words like they were his own.

He paused and glared before going on, "Since you've all proven yourselves incapable of handling the situation, I'm going to take control. What's going to happen is this: none of you are to do anything—*nothing*, do you hear?—either with or to those people on the planet without my express say-so. Seeing as you've proved your incompetence, I'm going to have to sort this situation out and get the Gens back where they're supposed to be—on that settlement, and doing exactly what they're supposed to be doing."

Anahi stood up. All the gazes in the room swiveled to her, Cariad's included. *This ought to be interesting.*

"I protest," she announced, though rather weakly. "I'm Leader of this colony and I—"

"You're relieved of duty," Aubriot snapped without even looking at her.

"You can't do that," exclaimed Anahi. "It doesn't even make any sense. My duties are my work. Leader is an... Leader is an official position."

She'd been about to say, an *elected* position, Cariad was certain.

Anahi swallowed and continued, "It's the highest position in the colony. You're welcome to offer suggestions and advice... That was why I gave the order for you to be revived. I recognized that we would benefit from your expertise in managing people, but I'm the one who has the final decision on how to address any problems with the Gens, not you."

Cariad was impressed at the woman's bravery. Though her ploy to revive Aubriot was severely backfiring, she wasn't giving up easily. Cariad didn't agree with what she'd done, but she couldn't help but feel a small measure of admiration. Anahi was aware she was playing with fire. Aubriot could be utterly ruthless in getting whatever he wanted.

"Listen," Aubriot said, finally gracing Anahi with his eye contact. "In my business, on *my* ship, people only get to do what they're good at. You're a shit Leader. If you hadn't screwed up, we wouldn't be down around fifteen hundred people. So you're out. Understand? I don't give a fuck what rules you've laid down. I'm the one running this place now. I've heard you might be a bit sick in the head too. So if you know what's good for you, you'll trot along to the medical center and stop interfering in things you don't understand."

The anger that emanated from Anahi at Aubriot's words was almost palpable. The woman was rigid and her hands clenched and unclenched at her sides. She couldn't seem to find the words to reply, however, for she stalked from the room, clinging to what little dignity she had left.

Before she had even exited, Aubriot appeared to have forgotten her. He returned his attention to the assembled Woken. "Right. Stop all your other work. You need to fix this problem and fix it now. How many of you are there? About seventy and some more in the freezer. Think you're going to make it on your own? When the supplies run out, do you think you're going to survive by yourselves down there? Forget it. You need those two thousand people you've managed to piss off. *We* need them.

"Organize yourselves into teams of five. First, find out where the Gens have gone. Next, bring them back to the settlement. I don't care how. I heard the Guardians have guns. Use them. Finally, make the Gens bloody well do what they're told. We need to get this colonization back on track and we need to do it now."

Aubriot glared at the assembled Woken. He put his

hands on his hips and leaned forward before barking, "Move!"

The scientists, who had been frozen in shock and awe, jumped out of their seats. They scurried toward the exits. Cariad's stomach was in knots. Aubriot was going to make everything worse. If they forced the Gens back to the settlement, they would have a war on their hands. Ethan had threatened as much at the meeting after the incident at the equipment shed.

"You," yelled Aubriot over the noise of the departing Woken. He was pointing at Strongquist and Faina. "I wanna talk to you."

The two Guardians stood as Aubriot strode across the room, Woken scattering before him like fish at the approach of a shark. Cariad sidled across to Strongquist and Faina, hoping to be privy to the conversation that promised to follow.

"I've been hearing a lot about you Guardians," was Aubriot's opening sentence. "I wanna hear more. What are you doing here? What's your remit? What have you found out about the shuttle bombing? And I wanna see your ship."

"Well, your final request is easy enough to fulfill," Faina replied evenly. "Would you like to see the *Mistral* now? You could return with us. Then perhaps we can answer your other questions on the way."

Strongquist only watched Aubriot from beneath his brows.

Cariad was surprised at the Guardians' ready acquiescence to Aubriot's demand to see the *Mistral*. As far as she knew, she remained the only person who had been invited to it. Yet, unlike the Woken, their attitude to Aubriot didn't seem to be fearful. Their demeanor indicated they weren't remotely cowed by the overbearing, abrasive man. And in truth there was nothing to stop them refusing him and walking calmly away while he ranted and raved. Clearly, being on

Aubriot's right side suited their plans. Not that the man had a right side.

As no one told her she couldn't come too, Cariad tagged along. She had to do something to stop the conflict that threatened the colony, though she had no idea what.

They took the Guardians' shuttle to the *Mistral*. As they swiftly crossed the intervening space and drew near their destination, Aubriot closely studied the Guardians' ship.

"Is that weaponry you've got there?" he asked.

Cariad's ears pricked up. Weaponry? The Guardians hadn't mentioned their ship was equipped with weapons.

From the look on Faina's face, the Guardians hadn't expected Aubriot or anyone else to recognize them. However, she didn't prevaricate. "Well spotted. We have pulse cannons fore and aft, rail guns on mounted turrets, and—"

"Rail guns?" Cariad interrupted, peering out. "I thought those things were some kind of scanner."

"The *Mistral* has scanners too, of course," said Strongquist. He said to Aubriot, "I'm impressed that you knew what they were."

"Had some dealings in the arms trade," Aubriot explained. "I think I'd recognize a weapon when I saw one. It doesn't look like the designs have changed much."

"Are they for space warfare?" Cariad asked, hoping the Guardians' arms weren't intended to be used on the planet. "I don't understand. We barely had the technology to build the *Nova Fortuna* when we left Earth. Don't tell me we were already developing weapons to fight battles in space."

"Always pays to be ahead of the game," said Aubriot. "Especially when it comes to war. Offense is the best defense, like they say."

"But who would we have been fighting?" Cariad asked, aghast. "We had the Global Government. No more wars, remember?" When Cariad had been a girl, the Asian, Euro-Asian, African, Latin, and Pacific federations had finally come to the table to join with the Western Alliance to form a single world governing body. Each superstate had been vying for power over the others, political tensions increasing, until finally the wisest heads had prevailed and a catastrophic conflict had been narrowly avoided. Cariad remembered it as a time of great relief and optimism.

Sadly, the prevailing vision of the future at that time had turned out to be grossly inaccurate. The single government had been no better at solving the problems of exhausted resources and a burgeoning population than the smaller governments had been. Cariad had grown up during a time of increasing concern and fear over the future of civilization. It was one of the factors that had led to interest in the possibility of leaving the Solar System entirely and seeking out a new path for humankind in deep space. Conversely, the fear had also given rise to the Natural Movement as people blamed reliance on technology and science for the problems.

"Could have had a breakaway federation on the Moon or Mars," Aubriot replied. "Might have needed to quell that. And that's not even counting the possibility of an alien attack. Yeah," he ruminated, "if ten-foot alien predators tried to invade, there wouldn't have been many calls for peace and disarmament then. Talking of which," he went on, "I take it there haven't been any signs of an alien presence around here. You would have said if there was, right?"

Cariad didn't know if he was talking to her or the Guardians. She hadn't thought about the possible existence of aliens in the sector for a long while. "We haven't seen any signs of sentience on the planet, if that's what you mean," she said. "There are two predatory life forms but I don't believe the xenozoologists have found anything else other than plant life and microorganisms in the area of the settlement."

"And the *Nova Fortuna* didn't pick up on anything on the way over?" Aubriot asked.

"I don't think so," Cariad replied. "I'm not responsible for going over the records. But as far as I know, the scanners didn't sense anything indicating intelligent life." Cariad's thoughts returned to Aubriot's earlier remarks. She asked, "So was the weapons development you were involved in legal?"

Aubriot gave her a look that told her he neither knew nor cared. He said to Faina, "So, are these weapons standard now on Earth starships?"

The Guardians told Aubriot the story that they'd repeated ever since they arrived—that the *Mistral* was unique, the only FTL starship ever constructed, and that it had been built specifically to catch up to *Nova Fortuna* and protect the new colony. They explained that the weapons had been only precautionary. They hadn't known what they might encounter on the way over or when they arrived.

As she listened to the story again, Cariad found that it rang hollow. There was something about the tale the Guardians told that didn't ring true, though she couldn't put her finger on it. Aubriot was watching the two of them like a hawk. Cariad was sure he didn't believe them either.

***

As she stepped from the shuttle into the Guardians' ship, Cariad experienced the same sensation of stepping into the future she'd had before. The sleek, spotless appearance of the interior of the *Mistral* and purity of its atmosphere made the place seem sterile. She wondered if the Guardians enjoyed living aboard their ship or if they missed the organic scents and untidiness of Earth.

She would have loved to ask them, but she'd never achieved the kind of casual friendliness with them that would allow such a question. Although the Guardians were always polite and civil, none of them had ever given the impression of wanting to be friends, not even Strongquist, who she'd spent the most time with. The Guardians also never talked about Earth unless they were directly asked, and they never spoke a word about their personal lives or each other.

The more Cariad thought about it, the odder their behavior seemed. She would have expected a softening of relations by then. She resolved again to do her best to find out more about the enigmatic group, or at the very least she wanted to discover the reason for their standoffishness. Perhaps it was only a feature of human culture that had developed in the centuries since she'd left.

The group went to the ship's bridge first. Faina explained the functions of the consoles to Aubriot. They were the same as on the *Nova Fortuna*, like comms, scan reports, navigation. Though Cariad didn't recognize the consoles, she wasn't familiar with the *Fortuna's* bridge either. Aubriot also seemed much less familiar with these than he'd been with the *Mistral's* weapons. He didn't say anything to indicate that, however, probably choosing to mask his ignorance with silence.

They went to the engine room next, where Strongquist once more explained the working principle of the drive.

Aubriot said, "I knew we'd get there in the end. Didn't realize it would take so long. Lucky we didn't wait around, eh Cariad?" He winked at her. "Would've been nice to avoid traveling as an ice cube for nearly two centuries, though." He put his hands on his hips as he surveyed the engine. "Yeah. Beautiful. Beautiful.

Almost makes me want to go back to Earth and build another one. Not that I could afford it. All out of cash. But maybe I could raise the money."

"The Guardians have said that Earth and the Solar Settlements are full to bursting," Cariad said. "It doesn't sound like it would be a good idea to go back."

"Is that right?" Aubriot asked Strongquist and Faina. "But what if I wanted to? What if I wanted to go back on your ship?"

"That wouldn't be possible," Faina replied firmly. "We are here to support the settlers and the founding of the colony. You said earlier that you wished to know our remit, and that is it, put simply. Returning individuals to Earth is out of the question."

Aubriot didn't reply at first. He was trying to out stare Faina. The woman didn't buckle. In fact, she betrayed not the slightest sign of any tension as Aubriot gazed down at her, unblinking. Finally, he laughed and turned to Cariad, saying, "Well, you don't know unless you ask, do you?"

It was a pride-saving move. Aubriot was clearly simmering as his massive ego tried to deal with his failure to intimidate the Guardian.

"We'll show you the medical center next," said Strongquist. "If you're interested, that is."

"*I* am," said Cariad. "I didn't get to see it when I was here before."

"This isn't your first time?" Aubriot asked. "I heard the Guardians didn't allow people on their ship."

So that was why he'd particularly wanted to see it. He'd wanted to exercise his self-perceived privilege.

"Cariad was helping us with our investigation into the Natural Movement saboteur," said Strongquist. "I invited her over to view some records."

"Hmph," said Aubriot. "Got your fingers in lots of pies, haven't you, Cariad? I'll have to keep an eye on you."

They walked to the medical center, which was empty. The place was large and full of pristine equipment. Strongquist took the lead in showing them each item and explaining its function. Most interesting of all to Cariad was the gene therapy equipment. The Guardian explained that it engineered the patient's genes to correct developmental abnormalities.

Cariad's excitement grew as Strongquist spoke. "You mean we finally cured genetic conditions retroactively?" she asked when he paused.

"Absolutely," he replied.

"This is marvelous," Cariad said. "This will help enormously to keep the colony healthy. I weeded out genetic conditions as far as I was able, but I can't prevent mutations further down the line. So is this available on Earth too?"

"Only within a limited area," Faina said. "Most of human civilization has no access to advanced technologies such as these."

Aubriot was looking bored. Two more Guardians had appeared. They were dressed in medical scrubs. Cariad wondered what they were doing there as the center currently had no patients. One of the medics activated a self-powered gurney. He brought it over, presumably to show them, though Cariad didn't think the design had altered much from her time.

"Cariad," said Strongquist. "Perhaps you'd like to see the immuno-manipulator?"

"I'd love to," she replied.

"I'd like to take a look at your weapons systems," said Aubriot. "Medical treatment isn't really my thing."

Strongquist led Cariad away from the main group and over to another item of equipment.

"I've seen as much as I want to in here," said Aubriot.

Cariad was inspecting the immuno-manipulator when she realized she hadn't heard a reply to Aubriot's comment, yet she also hadn't heard him and the other Guardians leave. She glanced over her shoulder out of curiosity and gave a squeak of surprise. The large man was collapsing and the medics were catching him.

"Oh no," Cariad exclaimed as she rushed over. The medics were supporting Aubriot's considerable weight and placing him on the gurney. His color was normal. "What happened? Did he faint?"

Faina grimaced as if in distaste. "No. Don't be alarmed. Would you please move out of the way?"

Cariad stepped backward to give the medics more room, bumping into Strongquist, who had come up behind her.

"Perhaps it's a delayed effect of the revival process," said Cariad. "I thought he'd recovered. This is terrible. I need to get him back to the *Nova Fortuna* as soon as possible."

"I think Aubriot will be better off here," said Strongquist. "As you've seen, our medical facilities are superior."

"That's true, but... " She looked at Faina, who was as unperturbed as ever, as were all the Guardians. "You said he didn't faint. How do you know? Why aren't you checking his pulse and airway and pupils? He could be seriously ill."

"We know what's wrong with him," said Faina. "We injected him with a sedative."

"You *what?!*"

The medics were strapping Aubriot onto the gurney, restraining his flopping limbs. He was deeply unconscious. His mouth lolled open.

"You sedated him?" Cariad exclaimed. "Why?"

"It was necessary, unfortunately," said Strongquist. "As we've explained, we are here to support the foundation of a healthy, thriving colony. We assessed Aubriot's personality based on his behavior since he was revived and we checked into his background. We've come to the conclusion that this man's influence would be detrimental to the colony. Therefore we will keep him sedated until such time as he is no longer a threat."

"You... you..." Cariad was so outraged she couldn't speak.

"I understand this will be something of a shock to you," said Strongquist. "But please try not to be alarmed. This isn't something we undertake lightly. Aubriot will come to no harm, his absence will be temporary, and it is for the overall good of the colony. We have all the necessary equipment and treatments to maintain him in an unconscious state until the *Nova Fortuna* Project returns to stability. I'm sure you'll agree that its health is fragile at the moment."

Outrage finally broke through Cariad's shock. She shouted at the Guardians over Aubriot's prone figure. "You can't do this! You can't just knock people out if you think they're going to do something bad. This is barbaric! Who do you think you are? You aren't even a part of this project. No one invited you along. You've turned up out of nowhere." Frenzied possibilities rushed through her mind. It was impossible to verify the Guardians' story. "You could be anyone. Maybe it's you who turned off the electric fence in the First Night Attack. Was it you who planted the bombs in the stadium and on the shuttle? It was, wasn't it? No Guardian has ever been hurt. Not ever. It's only ever been Gens or Woken."

As the words tumbled out, Cariad was backing away from the Guardians, who regarded her impassively. She reached a corner and she could go no farther. She was the only non-Guardian on the ship and entirely at the mercy of these people—people who thought it was okay to sedate someone indefinitely because of something they thought he *might* do.

"Who are you?" she whispered.

CHAPTER TWENTY-SIX

Since the Woken had discovered the absence of significant numbers of Gens at the settlement, tension had grown at the caves. What had been a happy mood of optimism as they fitted out their new homes had turned to a quiet, constant sense of anxiety for some, and for some, plain fear. There was talk of setting up armed defensive positions and a watch to constantly check for signs of an impending attack.

If such an attack were to come, Ethan speculated, they could easily be trapped. The only exit he, Garwin, and Cherry had discovered that time they had explored the caves was narrow and difficult to navigate. The Gens would only be able to pass through slowly, one at a time. They'd hoped that more escape routes would be discovered later when people arrived and began to investigate the site, but none had turned up.

As Ethan pondered the problem again one day, stealing some precious moments of solitude in his cave, he decided it was time to look again. They'd already found one route from the rear of the caves to the surface. There had to be others. The cave walls all bore the signs of being worn by water, and what appeared to be a dry river bed ran along the route to the coast. Ethan was no expert on such matters, but everything he saw pointed to the fact that, at some point in the history of the area, the river water had sunk into the ground and drained out from the cliff through the caves, as well as pouring over the edge in the now dried-up waterfall.

Even if he found a tunnel that was too narrow to climb through, maybe they could blast them wider with explosives, as Seaberg had suggested. They needed all the escape routes they could get.

Ethan filled a canister from his water container, grabbed a helmet that held a headlight, and climbed out of his cave and up the ladder on the cliff face, heading for one of the larger storage caves. He'd remembered that at the back of it was a tunnel that hadn't been deeply explored yet. It could lead to just the passage they needed.

As he climbed, he noticed Garwin coming down above him. Garwin had rarely been at the caves in recent weeks. He'd taken the responsibility of remaining in the settlement for the time being, helping to keep up the appearance of activity in the place. Also, his workshop was there. He had to finish off putting together the kits to create the remaining machinery and vehicles the Gens needed.

Ethan called out a greeting. Garwin looked down.

"Ethan," he replied. "I was just coming to see you. I wanted to catch up on how things have been going here."

After Ethan briefly explained what he planned on doing Garwin said, "That's a great idea. I'll come with you. You can tell me about the progress here while we explore. I'll just tell Twyla where I'm going, then I'll meet you there."

Twyla had recently arrived to set up a school for the younger children and she and Garwin were sharing one of the larger caves with several other childless couples.

Ethan continued climbing up to the storage cave. The place was more orderly than it had been the last time he'd seen it, and the areas were clearly labeled with signs that hung from the rock overhead. Garwin soon joined him. However, Twyla had also come along.

She gave no sign to Ethan of their earlier conversation. Had she told Garwin she knew about his affair? It didn't appear so. Garwin was as relaxed and easy as he'd ever been. His arm was around his wife's waist as they came over to Ethan at the back of the cave.

"I brought this," Twyla said. She held up a thick yellow crayon. "I'll write on the wall so that people will know where we've gone, and we can mark the walls as we go along so we don't get lost."

"Good thinking," said Ethan. He'd been concerned about that possibility.

"That's my wife," Garwin said affectionately.

Ethan felt sick. The man's duplicity nauseated him.

"It's this way," he said after Twyla had written her message, walking into the opening at the back of the cave, turning sideways to squeeze through the gap. Garwin and Twyla followed him. "Unless we find something better, we need to make the current escape route safer. It's too cramped and uneven."

"Yes it is," said Twyla. "I had a look at it. The younger children won't deal with that floor very well. We'd have to carry them. The whole place needs to be safer, in fact. The caves themselves don't need much work—only smoothing out some walls and erecting barriers to prevent kids from accidentally falling out— but we have to find a better way of getting around than those ladders. I don't even like the idea of adults using them. It's really dangerous. People are getting lazy. If two people meet, instead of one of them backing up to a safe place, they go around each other. I'm surprised no one's fallen off already."

Ethan explained his ideas of safety lines attached to the ladders and eventually constructing walled-in stairs in the cliffs.

Garwin said, "Those are great solutions."

They'd gone deeper into the cliff where the tunnel widened out and sloped upward. Very little light made it in from the cave, and all Ethan could see was within the narrow beam of his headlight. The smooth, water-worn rock was ridged, which helped his feet maintain purchase on the sloping floor. A black entrance loomed to the right, narrower than the main tunnel.

"What do you say we try this side route?" he asked. "I think others have been down the main route already."

Garwin and Twyla agreed. Twyla marked the entrance with a yellow arrow pointing in the direction of the way out, and they went in. This route was markedly steeper than the first, and Ethan had to use his hands as well as his feet to move along it. The atmosphere was moist and clammy, and he soon found himself wet with sweat. The moistness of his palms made the going even harder.

He was just about to suggest that they return and try a different passage when the tunnel evened out and split into two. This time, they took the easier passage, bypassing the crack in the wall that was barely as wide as Ethan's shoulders. Twyla marked the direction of the exit again in yellow crayon.

Silence fell as they conserved their breath for the effort of navigating the passage. Ethan wondered how far they'd come, but he'd lost track of the distance. Without landmarks for guidance it was impossible to tell. They also seemed to have gone farther vertically than horizontally. He guessed they'd been going for around half an hour.

Another split in the passage appeared. They had a choice of three directions this time. Once more, they chose the easiest of the three, which was really the only possible choice. The other two were so steep they were impossible to climb without ropes.

Water began to drip from the ceiling, and a fat drop landed on Ethan's helmet. As the cold water fell onto his shirt and trickled down his back, a thought occurred to him. "Hey," he said to the other two, who were a short way behind him. He paused as they caught up. "Do you think it's possible that the river isn't totally dried up? What if it still runs here, just underground?"

"I don't think it does," Garwin replied. "It would have to come out somewhere, wouldn't it? I haven't noticed any sign of water exiting the cliffs."

"No," Ethan replied. "But... Maybe it comes out below ground, in the ocean." He looked upward. His headlight reflected wetly on the bumpy surface of the ceiling. Thick drops of water seeped through here and there, hanging heavily before they fell. Small stalactites were forming. "Or what if there isn't a river as such, just a lot of water? If we have a massive storm, the water might run through the caves again."

Twyla said, "I hope not. That would be a disaster."

"Do you think it's a possibility?" Garwin asked.

"No," Ethan replied after a moment's consideration. "The caves directly inside the cliffs are extremely dry. No plants or anything else lives in them. It's like they haven't seen water for decades or centuries."

"I never considered the cave settlement our long-term home anyway," said Garwin. "Their advantage is that we aren't out in the open if the Woken or Guardians decide to attack us and force us back. But when things settle down, we should look to creating a proper town somewhere where we don't have to climb to go from one place to another. Maybe we could look at the area on the other side of the farming district. We'll need those crops when they're ready to harvest."

They walked on, panting a little with exertion in the humid darkness. Apart from the noise of their breathing and the drip of water, the tunnel was absolutely silent, and they could only see whatever the beams of their headlights illuminated.

The passage suddenly dipped downward and Ethan lost his footing, falling hard on his rear. He slid down the wet, slimy slope, grabbing vainly at the tunnel sides, but his hands slipped off any bumps he found.

Garwin and Twyla had suffered a similar fate. They were coming down behind him. The beam from Ethan's headlight bounced around as he went along, wondering when he would reach the bottom.

Then empty space yawned wide beneath him. A hole in the floor of the tunnel. Ethan grabbed wildly. His hands encountered a lump of rock that he gripped with all his strength. He just had time to blurt, "Watch out," before Garwin also arrived at the opening.

Holding tight to the rock, Ethan hauled himself out of the hole and onto the floor of the slope. There was a cry that sounded like Twyla. He swung his headlamp around to find out what had happened.

Garwin was half in, half out of the hole, barely holding onto a rough, lumpy area of the floor, and Twyla was in the hole, holding onto Garwin. Her knuckles were white as she dug her hands into his shirt and her face was panic-stricken. Garwin's expression was tortured as he tried to prevent his wife and himself from plummeting down the hole.

Garwin gasped, "Get Twyla."

Ethan slid quickly closer. Lying flat on his stomach, he reached down and grabbed Twyla's arms. Garwin gasped and slipped toward the hole. Twyla cried out and dug her hands deeper into her husband's back.

"I've got you," said Ethan. He squirmed backward, tugging on the woman's arms. Now that Ethan was taking a lot of her weight, Garwin also pulled himself upward, grunting with effort. Ethan tugged harder, eventually lifting Twyla's upper half over the edge. She didn't let go of Garwin until he was entirely out of the hole and she was three-quarters out.

All three lay on the tunnel floor, panting. Ethan sat up and looked along at the passage they had slipped down. They seemed to have come a long way. He couldn't see the top.

"Are you okay?" Garwin asked.

Ethan turned his gaze to the couple and saw that Garwin was talking to Twyla. They had sat up too and were hugging.

"Yes, I'm okay," Twyla replied, though her voice sounded teary.

Garwin hugged her closer. "Thank the stars. That was close." His voice was emotional too and his face was white with shock and fear. He stroked his wife's hair and looked into her eyes. "Are you sure you're all right?"

"I'm fine," she said. "Really."

The look that passed between the two was so intimate, Ethan looked away, embarrassed to intrude on the moment. Their deep love for each other was clear. Ethan couldn't understand why Garwin had affairs if his relationship with his wife was so strong, or why Twyla was so unaffected by the revelation of his cheating.

"I don't know if we'll be able to get out the way we came down," he said. "The slope's too steep."

"Can we get around the hole?" Twyla asked.

When Ethan looked toward the couple again, they'd broken their embrace and Garwin was peering over the edge of the hole. He ran his hands over the ground as if searching for something. "Anyone see a pebble? I wonder how deep this is."

They looked but the tunnel was bare of any loose rock. Instead, Twyla broke her crayon in half and handed one piece to Garwin. He reached out and dropped it in the hole. A *plop* signaled that there was water at the bottom, quite far down. When Ethan leaned over carefully and shone his headlight into the darkness, the light reflected on a wet surface.

"It's probably fresh water," Twyla said, "from the old river. Unless we've come down to sea level, which I don't think we have."

"If it is fresh, that'll save us a lot of trouble with desalinating the sea water," Garwin said.

Ethan had been exploring the other side of the hole and found that the rock was wide enough to allow them safe passage. They went on. The slope had evened out and they were on a flat stretch. No one mentioned the fact that it was now imperative that they find another exit. Returning the way they had come could prove impossible. It was clear that the passage was useless as an escape route too. Their new focus was on their own escape.

The tunnel began to climb, which Ethan chose to look upon as a good sign. They had to have been traveling for at least an hour, he guessed. Their lights would last another hour or so. If they couldn't get out, they could last quite a while down there, though it would be in total darkness. Though no one had brought any food along, they could lick the water from the cave walls. However, lasting weeks could be a good or a bad thing.

Ethan was also worried by the thought that a rescue party might follow the markings Twyla had made and fall down the steep slope that led to the hole. They might not be as lucky as they had been. Anyone landing in the water could drown.

Ethan gave a shiver and pushed the thought from his mind. He needed to concentrate on escaping the cave, not on what would happen if they couldn't. He worked upward, clutching the slippery rocks, the sound of Garwin's and Twyla's heavy breathing joining his own. In spite of the heat of his exertion, he was chilled from the water that had dripped onto him, soaking his clothes.

A gap opened in the wall to his right. Ethan poked his head through it, illuminating the view with his head lamp. The passage looked a little drier than their current tunnel, though it was even steeper.

"This looks promising," he said. "What do you say we go this way?"

"It's as good as any other," said Twyla. Both she and Garwin were sweaty and grimy and their haggard expressions told of their exhaustion. Ethan imagined he probably didn't look much better.

Without any more discussion, they took the route he'd suggested. It wasn't long before the signs indicated it had been a good choice. The tunnel walls and the air turned noticeably drier. Ethan panted heavily as he climbed higher. He grew warm again and his sweat began to dry on his skin.

A change in the darkness made him stop. "Hold on a second," he said to the others. "Turn off your lamps." He turned off his own too. Faint rays of light were piercing the black. Farther along the tunnel a ragged hole in the rock ceiling was faintly outlined by light.

"Thank the stars," Twyla breathed. "We must be near the surface."

The prospect of escape from the cave system invigorated them all. Ethan climbed quicker, heading toward the tantalizing glimmer of light. His head struck rock. The blow was so hard, if he hadn't been wearing a helmet he would have suffered a serious injury. As it was, he was only a little dazed.

"What was that?" Garwin asked in response to the sound.

Ethan explained that the ceiling had lowered and told them to be careful. He was forced to crawl. The space was barely high enough to avoid slithering on his belly. But he didn't mind. Daylight was clearly visible ahead, green-hued but bright.

In a few moments, he had pushed his way out

through vegetation that overhung the exit. The sunlight blinded him and he had to put his hands over his eyes. Behind him, Twyla and Garwin also emerged and exclaimed in relief.

When Ethan's eyes had somewhat adjusted to the light, he opened them wider and squinted at their surroundings. They were low down on the dried up river bed, the valley walls rising on each side. The route that he, Twyla, and Garwin had discovered would be useless for escape, but it didn't matter. He was glad they'd made it out alive.

CHAPTER TWENTY-SEVEN

Cariad demanded that the Guardians reverse Aubriot's sedation, but they absolutely refused to wake him up, emphasizing the threat he presented to the success of the colony. Their words were little more than a meaningless jumble to Cariad. She was terrified that they might do the same to her. The horror of a potentially never-ending sleep, like returning to cryo, rose up before her.

Both Strongquist and Faina continued to try to persuade her of the necessity the sedation. Cariad couldn't get through to them, and, fearing for her own safety, she insisted on being returned to the *Nova Fortuna*. She wanted nothing more than to put as much distance between herself and the Guardians as possible.

"Take me back, then." She repeated, "Just take me back."

She had to tell the other Woken what the Guardians had done. If she couldn't persuade them that their behavior was unacceptable, maybe others could, or Anahi might. The Guardians had said they would follow the Leader's instructions. She had to speak to Anahi. Whatever happened, even if they complied with Anahi's command, the Guardians' act had changed the nature of their relationship with all the colonists irrevocably.

Eventually, Strongquist and Faina acceded to her demand. Cariad sat in stony silence, her hands trembling, the entire shuttle flight back to the colony ship. When she disembarked onto the *Nova Fortuna*, she left the Guardians without a parting word and went directly to Anahi at the Leader's quarters.

The outer door to what had once been the public office was locked.

"Let me in," Cariad demanded through the door comm when Anahi answered. "I have to talk to you."

"What about?" Anahi asked cautiously.

Cariad blurted the news of Aubriot's sedation. At first, Anahi seemed to not believe her, her expression suspicious.

"Do you really think I would make this up?" Cariad asked. "Open the door and let me in. We have to figure out a way to fix this."

The door slid to one side and Cariad strode inside. Anahi was standing behind the desk in the lobby. Cariad put her hands on the desktop and leaned toward the older woman. "They just gave him a shot and knocked him out," she exclaimed. "I only turned away for a minute, and when I turned back, they were laying him out. Just like that. Like it was the most normal thing in the world."

"What did they say?" Anahi asked.

Cariad related the tense conversation she'd had with the Guardians, finishing with, "I thought they were going to do the same to me. It was insane. They were so calm about it. Not acting guilty at all. I can still hardly believe it. I feel like I should pinch myself."

"Are you sure he wasn't being violent?" Anahi asked. "Did he take a swing at them?"

"No. He was just being Aubriot. You know what he's like. I don't know what you were thinking when you wanted to wake him up. But there was no reason to knock him out. I mean, even if they were right that he's a threat to the colony, they can't just take him out of the equation. What if they decide to do it to someone else? If they do it to a Gen, we'll have a revolution on our hands."

"All right," Anahi said. "Sit down."

Cariad slumped into a seat, some of her tension and fear finally dissipating.

Anahi's expression was grave. "I'll speak to them. We'll see what they say." She opened her desk interface and sent a comm request.

Cariad couldn't see the screen from where she was sitting, but she recognized Strongquist's voice immediately.

"Leader," he said. "I thought I might hear from you. I'm guessing you want to speak to us about the unfortunate decision we had to make."

"I do want to speak to you about your unlawful assault on a colonist, yes."

Cariad admired Anahi's strong stance, but she doubted it would do any good. The Guardians held all the cards. They wouldn't have gone ahead with the sedation if they thought they could be forced to back down.

"As we explained to Cariad," Strongquist said, "Aubriot's attitude and behavior threatened the future of the colony, and so—"

"You have no authority to act in this way," Anahi said. "None at all. You aren't even members of the *Nova Fortuna* Project. I demand that you return Aubriot to our ship immediately."

"It is with great regret that I must refuse your request," Strongquist replied. He did actually sound regretful.

"But you have to do as I say," Anahi exclaimed. "You have to obey the Leader."

"That isn't quite correct. We have to ensure the future of the colony, at any cost. In most cases, that means we bow to the Leader's judgment. Aubriot's case is extreme, however, and we have no choice but to deny your request at this time. When the colony is more stable—"

Anahi closed the connection. She looked suddenly older, and very tired. After a pause she asked, "What have I done, Cariad? I never meant for things to turn out like this. I was only trying to keep us all safe."

The long-time colleague Cariad remembered seemed to have returned. Though she wasn't sure Anahi's understanding of her motivations was accurate, she pitied her. She reached out and touched the woman's hand. "You didn't bring the Guardians here. They're the ones we need to be dealing with right now."

Anahi said, "But what can we do? They're armed and only the Gens have weapons."

"I don't know yet, but we have to figure out a way. We can't let the Guardians walk all over us."

Anahi shook her head. "Their technology is far superior to ours. If we refuse to allow them aboard the ship, they can force their way on. And we can't stop them from interfering on the planet. They can come and go as they please. They could take over the entire colony if they wanted to. If they start giving the Gens orders, there's nothing we can do about it."

"The Gens have already broken away," Cariad replied. "If the Guardians decide they want to take over the colony, they'll have their work cut out for them. There are lots more Gens than us and the Guardians don't even know where most of them are. Thinking about it, it's we Woken I'm more concerned about. What if the Guardians decide *we're* getting in the way of the success of the colony? There are only a few of us."

"Do you really think it'll come to that?" Anahi asked. "They've left us alone up until now. It's only been

Aubriot they objected to. They've been generally supportive, and they have tried to catch the Natural Movement saboteur."

"Have they?" Cariad asked. "Or were they only making a show of it? Don't you think it's too much of coincidence that they turned up at exactly the right moment? What if they're responsible for everything that's happened? We only have their word about the Natural Movement plot to destroy the colony. Has anyone actually seen any evidence of it? After what I witnessed just now, I don't feel like I know the Guardians at all. It was so cold-blooded. I don't feel like we're even the same species, as if humanity underwent some fundamental change after we left."

"Interesting, but it doesn't really help us."

"No," Cariad agreed.

"The fact is, the Guardians are armed and we aren't. And it isn't like the Gens are just going to kindly hand their weapons back if we ask. We found that out already."

Cariad bit back the retort that popped into her mind regarding Anahi's handling of that situation. "That isn't to say we can't make our own. We have plenty of scientists who could figure out how, I'm sure. We have printers we can program to make the parts. There has to be something we can do."

"Yes," Anahi said. "We have to do something to protect ourselves."

"First off, we have to tell the Guardians they're no longer welcome aboard the *Nova Fortuna*. And we have to continue to demand they wake up Aubriot."

Anahi took a breath. "He's going to be so mad."

Cariad smiled. She preferred Anahi without her megalomaniacal streak. "I'm glad we agree about something." She wasn't going to let Anahi's conciliatory mood go to waste. "What's happened has made me realize more than ever that we need a change of attitude. We've been seeing the Gens as a problem that we need to fix. We've been imagining that we have all the answers, but both us and the Gens are alike—unfamiliar with the new world and without any experience of building a colony. We should work with the Gens, not try to control them. They aren't our adversaries. The Natural Movement is what's really out to make this colony fail, and now we have another enemy: the Guardians."

CHAPTER TWENTY-EIGHT

Ethan was piloting a flitter along the dry river bed that led to the caves, the vehicle piled high with supplies he was bringing over from the original settlement, when he saw Twyla. She passed him on another flitter going the other way, flying quickly. He lifted a hand to acknowledge her but she didn't seem to notice him. He continued his journey, mulling over the impending issues the Gens would soon face.

Though the Gens had already transported so many containers that they'd nearly filled the caves designated as storage areas, they only had in their possession around a tenth of what had been brought down from the ship. It was a big problem. If they wanted to entirely cut ties with the Woken and the Guardians and go it alone, they couldn't keep returning to collect more food, equipment, and other essentials. If they wanted to be independent, they had to wean themselves from their milk mother. Yet they didn't have enough room to store everything they might need.

Ethan was also beginning to worry about the constant use of the flitters. The Manual warning that the flitters' power supplies were finite was suddenly becoming more real. Once the flitters' energy ran out the fledgling colony would not have the technology to replenish them.

Independence was bringing the Gens constraints and pressures as well as benefits.

Another concern on Ethan's mind was his farm. He hadn't been back there in a long while after Cherry had sown his crop of soy beans. He had no idea how the plants were doing. He hadn't fertilized as he was supposed to or irrigated when the weather was dry. The work he was doing to found the new settlement was important, but was it more important than growing the food that would feed them when the ship's supplies ran out?

He arrived at the top of the cliffs and began unloading the boxes from the flitter onto the rocky ground. Next came the job of strapping each box to a platform and lowering it to the storage cave where someone would be waiting to haul it inside. Before beginning the task, he went and sat at the edge of the cliff to take a few minutes' break. Dangling his legs over the precipitous drop, he watched the ocean. The sky was cloudy and the water gray and foamy as it churned.

A crazy scheme took shape in Ethan's mind. He would leave the problems of colonization behind and build a boat. Ancient vessels on Earth used the wind for power, catching it in enormous pieces of cloth called sails. He would harness the power of the wind and travel by boat across the ocean. There was another continent beyond the one chosen for the first settlement. He wanted to see it. He wanted to travel across the entire globe, visiting all the landmasses. There was a whole world out there to discover.

Ethan sighed. Maybe one day he would do it. Maybe. He already had a lifetime's work ahead just helping to provide a reliable supply of food. He got to his feet to return to the supply boxes.

As he stood, he heard a dull thud and a shock radiated up from the ground. It was an odd sensation, unlike anything he'd ever experienced. Was it an earthquake? He'd learned about them in school. He waited to see if anything else was going to happen but nothing did so he walked over to the boxes and lifted one, ready to carry it to the platform.

A shout came from the caves, followed by a scream. Ethan returned to the cliff edge and peered over. People were climbing the ladders that led up from the caves. They were moving fast, but he couldn't see why, or not at first. Then the cause of the disturbance became clear: water was pouring from some of the caves. They were escaping a flood.

Frozen in surprise, Ethan gaped at the sudden deluge of water. Loose, light items like clothes and packaging were being carried out and falling into the ocean below.

More waterfalls appeared. Ethan tried to figure out what was happening. Where was the water coming from? It hadn't rained heavily recently and the river bed was as dry as ever.

"Help," a voice cried. The sound galvanized him into action. He ran to the nearest ladder but it was full of people climbing up. He spotted another farther away that was empty, sped over to it, and began to climb down. If the caves were flooding, people would have to get out fast or risk being swept away. Even if they survived the drop into the ocean, no one could swim.

He raced down the ladder.

Another cry sounded out. Over to one side of the cliff face, the ladders were filling up rapidly. People were trying to leave the caves but the ladders didn't have the capacity to hold all of them at once. Ethan worried that if people overwhelmed them, the structures might break free and send hundreds to their deaths. At one cave entrance people crowded, jostling and shouting as they waited their turn to get onto a ladder.

"Stay calm," Ethan shouted across to them. "Wait your turn."

They either didn't hear or ignored him. The jostling grew rougher. "Hurry up," someone shouted. "I can hardly stand up." Ethan was amazed that any of them could stand in the torrent that swirled around their legs and poured down the cliff. Ethan could only hear the arguing voices faintly because the noise of falling water was turning into a roar.

"Help me," a woman's voice called. "Someone. Please!"

In the opposite direction Ethan saw a woman teetering on a cave edge, holding the hand of a toddler. A barrier had been erected at the front of their cave but it was hanging askew and water rushed through the gap. As Ethan climbed across the network of ladders toward her, the barrier swung wide and broke off entirely before spinning and tumbling down to the waiting waves. The woman lifted the child into her arms and balanced it on one hip, gripping the cave wall with the other hand. Her legs were spread out, bracing herself against the water's current.

She couldn't both hold the child and climb out onto a ladder. Whatever carrier she had for carrying the toddler on her back must have been swept away. "Give him to me," he said as he reached the woman. She was soaked through and her features were pale and frightened. She hesitated, gripping the child tighter, gazing down at the waves, her eyes round.

"It's okay," Ethan said. "I can help you."

A shriek sounded out. Someone was falling from the crowd Ethan had seen at one cave opening. The figure hit the water so hard the sound reverberated up the cliff over the noise of plunging water. The person quickly sank out of sight.

"Give him to me," Ethan yelled. "Hurry up."

Another cry came as someone else fell. Ethan turned around. Were people pushing in their fear and haste to get onto the ladders? Or had the current grown so strong it was sweeping them away?

The woman thrust the toddler at him. He grabbed the child and held him with one arm while using the other to grip the ladder. "Now you."

A rumbling crash and roar came from deep within the caves and the cliff face shook. The mother screamed as a wave of water poured out, carrying her with it. She grabbed Ethan just in time, but his feet slipped from the rungs and he almost fell. For a frantic second the woman dangled below him, her legs windmilling. Ethan's other arm gripped a ladder rung, bearing his weight and the weight of the woman and the child. Then one of his feet found a rung. He heaved upward. His other foot slid onto a rung. The woman also managed to climb onto the ladder.

Ethan's gaze swept the cliff face in horror. The cave entrances that had been crowded were now empty. The second flood of water had swept countless more people to their deaths. Only the people on the ladders had survived, and possibly some others who remained within the caves, holding on against the rush of water.

Ethan climbed quickly to the clifftop. As he was putting the little boy on the ground, his mother arrived.

"Thank you," she gasped as she grabbed her child, but Ethan was already climbing down again. There had to be more people who needed help. The entire cliff face could break away soon in the deluge.

As he was speeding down, he wondered what had happened. He'd guessed where the water had come from. It had to be from the aquifer he'd discovered on his most recent exploration. But why had it suddenly burst? The caves had all been dust-dry. No water had flowed through them for a very long time. There was no reason for its sudden appearance except that something catastrophic had caused it.

The implications of his line of thought began to pile up in Ethan's head but he pushed them to one side. Figuring out the why and how of what had happened would have to come later. For now, he had to help the people remaining in the caves.

He reached the first entrance and peered inside. The dark interior was empty save for the water running through it, pale and frothing with dust. Ethan made his way over to the next cave. Inside this one a handful of people were clustered. They were huddled tightly together at the back, where the floor was higher.

Cherry was among them.

"Ethan," she said when she saw him. He couldn't hear her over the rush of water, but he read her lips. She smiled bravely but her face betrayed her fear. Little Cherry. She was the smallest of them all. To get out of the cave, the people would have to withstand the force of current in the deeper water at the front. Deep water that was growing deeper. If they stayed where they were, eventually the water could rise high enough to sweep them away.

"You have to get out," Ethan shouted at them. He beckoned. "I'll help you." Holding on firmly with one hand and balancing on one foot, he leaned out into the cave and beckoned again. A young man stepped tentatively out. His body pressed against the wall, he inched over to the cave entrance. As soon as he reached Ethan's outstretched hand, Ethan grabbed him and gripped tightly. "Hold onto me and climb around me onto the ladder."

The youngster did as Ethan had instructed, grasping onto his body until he finally reached the safety of the ladder. A woman and another man did the same. Then only Cherry was left. She was hugging the wall, fighting the current and watching the rushing water.

"Cherry," Ethan shouted. "You have to come out.

Come on. It'll be okay." He didn't think she could hear him. She seemed mesmerized by the fast-flowing water. Ethan bellowed at her, "Cherry. Now. Hurry up."

Her eyes lifted and met his gaze. She shifted a tentative step toward him. The strain of staying upright showed on her face. The water was up to her thighs. Ethan wondered if he should go into the cave and grab her, but then neither of them would have a firm hold of anything and if he fell he would take her with him.

She moved another step, and another. Her progress was painfully slow, and the water visibly rising. How much of it had been hidden underground? It seemed an impossible amount. Cherry moved closer. He could almost reach her. He strained with his might to close the distance between them.

Her gaze fixed on his, the fear on her face seemed to fade a little. She stretched out to him. Her fingertips brushed his hand, but then she lost her footing. She toppled backward into the water, sending up a splash as she hit. Her head was above the surface and her arms were flailing as she slid past on her back. Ethan made a wild grab for her. His fingers touched her shirt.

Then she was gone.

Cherry was gone. Ethan's gaze desperately searched the cascade of water that was falling into the ocean. He couldn't see her. Shock froze him, clinging one-handed to the ladder. He watched the boiling water below, which mixed with waves coming in from the ocean. Some supply boxes and other items that had been washed from the caves bobbed in the tumult. There was no sign of any people.

Cherry was down there. Smart, funny, sparky Cherry, losing her fight with the water. Ethan pressed his forehead against the cold, wet rock of the cliff face. He gripped the ladder like a vice, afraid that he would jump into the water to save her. He couldn't swim. He would drown too, and there had to be more trapped people who needed his help.

Exerting every ounce of willpower he had, Ethan forced himself to move. He climbed across and up and down the cliff, checking the caves. Others were doing the same. Ethan found several more people and helped them to safety.

The water continued to rise. Just as Ethan was estimating that all the caves had been checked and that anyone who could be saved had been saved, an immense boom thundered up from below. Ethan's ladder juddered. He looked downward in time to see part of the cliff break away. A lakeful of water spewed out as the rocks crashed into the ocean, sending out a massive wave.

Ethan flew up his ladder, his hands and feet a blur of motion. When he reached the top of the cliff he launched himself onto the flat ground. People were hanging around near the edge. "Get back! Run," he shouted. He urged them to run toward the hills that bordered the dried-up river where other survivors were gathering.

"Move," he yelled. "The cliff could collapse any second." Finally they took notice and began to move. Running with the others, Ethan reached and then climbed the hill slopes, slipping on loose stones and dirt. When he thought they'd gone far enough to be out of danger, he halted. Gasping, he threw himself to the ground. As he panted, the image of Cherry tumbling over in the cave and being swept out into the torrent played again and again in his mind.

A lump rose in his throat. He couldn't believe he hadn't been able to save her. She'd been so near. He'd touched her. If he'd only managed to reach just another couple of centimeters, he would have caught her for sure. Just a couple of centimeters had meant the difference between her life and her death.

When Ethan had caught his breath he sat up. The

surviving Gens were dazed and weeping. Some were going from group to group, trying to find lost loved ones. As the tragedy of Cherry's death gripped him, other thoughts crowded in. Why had the aquifer burst?

The suspicion that he'd pushed aside in his rush to help resurfaced. As far as he knew, only he, Garwin, and Twyla were aware of the existence of the aquifer. Now that he replayed the memory of the sound he'd heard and the sensation he'd felt just prior to the flooding, he realized that they could have been caused by a bomb exploding. Had someone deliberately cracked the aquifer walls and caused the disaster? Tens if not hundreds of people had died.

His grief and guilt over Cherry's death churned up inside him. Anger and fury took their place. He was sure he knew what had happened and who was responsible. He would make them pay.

Ethan ran down the hillside, passing through the clumps of survivors. Already people were organizing help for the injured. It was a very different scene than the reaction after the stadium bombing when the Gens had been a mess of confusion and inaction.

The flitter remained where he'd left it, close to the cliff edge. The cliff hadn't collapsed as he'd feared it might, or not just yet. Ethan sped over to the vehicle and jumped inside. He would head back to the settlement. He needed to confront Garwin and Twyla.

CHAPTER TWENTY-NINE

When the news of the disaster at the Gens' new settlement filtered through to the *Nova Fortuna,* Cariad's first impulse was to go planetside and help. It turned out that the Gens had set up home at a cave system next to the ocean and that the entire place had flooded. The rest of the Woken also wanted to help with the rescue effort, but Anahi was reluctant. She cautioned against using the shuttles.

Everyone, including the shipboard Gens, had assembled at the shuttle bay.

"What if they're booby trapped?" Anahi said.

"The Guardians went over them all with a fine-toothed comb," said Cariad's soil biologist friend, Rene. "And no one except that party that Aubriot took down has been near them since. No one's been allowed. They must be safe."

"We have to go and help," Cariad said. "What will the Gens think if we stay up here all safe and sound and leave them to deal with this alone? If they ever needed us, it's now. And what better opportunity to try to heal the rift?"

Anahi tried to voice another protest, but others were

already arguing with her. Cariad desperately wanted to go down to the planet, and not only to offer what help she could. She needed to see Ethan. She'd heard that he'd been there at the time of the disaster, but nothing more than that. She wanted to be sure he was okay.

"Wait," she said suddenly. "Why am I even listening to you?" She'd realized that Anahi could do nothing to stop her or anyone else if they wanted to go planetside. Ignoring the Leader's reply, she said loudly over the discussion, "Well, I'm going down. Is there a pilot here willing to fly me?"

Anahi's mouth dropped open as Cariad walked right past her into the shuttle bay.

"I'll do it," called one of the Gen pilots. She also strode past Anahi, and several Woken followed her. Soon, everyone who had been waiting and arguing with Anahi was in the bay and boarding the shuttles.

Cariad was on tenterhooks all the way down. The shuttle flight had never seemed so long. As soon as the ship landed, she was first to disembark. She ran to the passenger processing area and asked the clerk if she knew what had happened to Ethan. The woman said he'd been seen in the settlement, but she didn't know where he was. Cariad sped to the farmers' dorms, not really expecting to find Ethan there, but she hoped she might find someone who knew where he was. She was in luck. A man in the lobby told her that he thought Ethan was with Garwin, and he gave her directions to Garwin's house. Cariad raced over and impatiently rang the door chime. When no one answered she rang it several times again, wondering if maybe Ethan wasn't there after all.

After ten or twelve rings, a tall, bony woman answered, looking deeply agitated or perhaps harassed. She seemed more agitated than was reasonable due to someone aggressively ringing her doorbell. Cariad didn't know the woman but assumed she was Garwin's wife. "I'm looking for Ethan. I was told he was here."

"Oh, he's here all right," the woman said.

Ethan appeared behind her in the hall. "Cariad!" He pushed past Garwin's wife and grabbed Cariad, hugging her so tightly he lifted her feet from the ground. He stepped away but held onto her upper arms. "What are you doing here?"

"We heard about the disaster. We've come down to help, of course. A lot of Woken are on their way out there now, but I heard you were here. I wanted to make sure you were okay."

Another figure appeared behind Ethan. Garwin had come into the hall too. Ignoring Cariad, he told Ethan, "I think it's best that you leave."

Ethan turned away from Cariad to face Garwin and said, "You might be able to make me go away for now, but what I've said remains the truth. I'm not going to let it rest." He faced Garwin's wife. "I know what you did. You're not going to get away with it. I'm not going to let you hurt anyone else."

"Ethan?" said Cariad. "What's this about?"

He shot another look at the woman before saying to Cariad, "I'll tell you all about it."

"Not here, you won't," Garwin said. "Don't come back. I don't want to see you here again. Come on, Twyla." He disappeared into the darkness of the hall.

Ethan was taking Cariad's arm to leave with her when Twyla leaned toward him and hissed, "I should have put an end to your interference while I had the chance."

Her expression was so full of hate and evil, Cariad stepped backward. The door slammed. As they went along the narrow pathway to the street, Cariad said, "What was that about? You sure pissed them off."

"That's nothing to how they'll feel when I prove that I'm right." Ethan looked puzzled. "I'm not sure what Twyla meant by that last remark, though."

"Right about what?" asked Cariad as they walked down the street.

"Twyla—Garwin's wife—she's a Natural Movement follower, and maybe he is too. I'm not sure about that part."

"What?! How do you know?"

"The flood at the caves was caused by an aquifer bursting. Only two people knew where that reservoir was apart from me, and that was Garwin and Twyla. We were together exploring the caves when we accidentally stumbled across it. It was difficult and dangerous to reach, and I'm certain no one else has gone that way after us. Twyla almost fell into it. Things might have turned out better for everyone else if she had." He halted, his expression shifting from anger to sorrow. He hung his head. "A friend of mine died, Cariad. I nearly saved her, but she got swept away. She drowned in the ocean, like who knows how many more. And Twyla's responsible. I'm sure of it. Just before the flooding, I saw her speeding away from the cave site."

"Oh Ethan," Cariad touched his arm. "I'm so sorry. So you came back here to confront them? What did they say?"

"What do you think? They denied everything of course. Dammit. I went about it the wrong way. I shouldn't have said anything. Now they know they're under suspicion so they'll cover their tracks even more carefully. They're gonna wipe every trace of their possible connection with the disaster more thoroughly than they already have.

"When I told them I'd seen Twyla race away from the caves just before the aquifer broke, Garwin stood by her like a hero. He wouldn't hear a word I said against her. Thought up every excuse he could as to why she couldn't possibly have anything to do with it." Ethan shook his head. "I'm not sure that Garwin's involved. I don't think even he is that two-faced. But her... I had a weird feeling about her the moment I met her. And their relationship is very strange. She's odd. Nervy. Garwin doesn't seem to see it. He's in love with her."

"Well, she is his wife."

"Yeah, well... their relationship's complicated."

They'd resumed walking as they talked and wandered over to the shuttle field. It was full of *Nova Fortuna* shuttles.

"What are so many shuttles doing here?" Ethan asked. Only two or three would have been enough to transport all the Woken.

"We didn't know how many Gens had been injured," Cariad replied. "We thought we might need to take them up to the ship's medical facilities. No one knew if the hospital here was fully operational. And, Ethan, we thought some of you might want to return to the ship anyway. It's safer for you up there. All the bombings and disasters have taken place on or near the surface."

"It's a good thought," Ethan said. "Plenty of us will appreciate it, I'm sure. But though I can't speak for the others, I don't think I'll ever be returning to the *Nova Fortuna*. This is my home now. I don't want to abandon it. I want to put right what's wrong here, not give up on it."

Cariad was about to reply when the sight of an approaching shuttle distracted her. "Uh oh."

"What's wrong?" Ethan asked.

"It's the Guardians."

"You didn't expect them to show up?"

"I should have," Cariad replied. "I just didn't think about it. Ethan, what have the Guardians been doing around here the last few weeks?"

"I don't know exactly. I haven't been around the settlement much myself. I was at the caves most of the time."

Cariad nodded and was quiet for a few moments. "I guess that's why you haven't spoken to me for weeks."

"That's right. I didn't want to lie to you, and... Well, I'm sorry."

She touched his arm. "It's okay. I understand. Ethan, I have to ask you about the Guardians. Have they taken anyone away or hurt anyone?"

"No. I'm sure I would have heard about it if they had. Why?"

Cariad explained what the Guardians had done to Aubriot. After his initial surprise, Ethan laughed wryly.

"What's funny about it?" Cariad asked. "They had no right to sedate the man. He hadn't done anything. They were shutting him down because of what they thought he might do."

"Kinda like what you Woken wanted to do to us?"

Cariad winced.

Ethan said, "That wasn't fair. I know you were trying to fight it."

"I was. Maybe I should have tried harder."

The Guardians' shuttle had landed. The ramp was down and a group containing two especially familiar figures were heading toward Ethan and Cariad across the shuttle field.

"What do you think they want?" Ethan asked as Strongquist, Faina, and other Guardians drew nearer.

"They'll say they want to help," Cariad replied.

"Then I think they'll find their help isn't needed or welcome. Especially not after word gets out about what they did to that guy. If the other Woken are telling Gens about it that might be the final... what is it? Stick?"

"Huh?"

"The final thing needed to send someone over the edge. It's a saying."

"Oh. Straw. The final straw that broke the camel's back. Do you think the Gens will be hostile toward the Woken?"

"Probably not. You aren't armed. The Guardians are already hated down here."

Although neither Strongquist nor Faina were carrying weapons, others were, and they were behaving like guards, flanking the unarmed Guardians. They were acting as though they expected to be attacked, which, given the tensions in the colony and the high feelings after yet another disaster, wasn't unlikely.

"Cariad," said Strongquist. "I'm glad to see you. We're here to help with the disaster response, but I also have some news. I've had another breakthrough in our investigation into the Natural Movement saboteurs."

If she hadn't been there to witness it, Cariad doubted she would have believed the nonchalance with which the man and other Guardians were behaving in the face of their outrageous actions.

"Fantastic," said Ethan. "Why don't you tell that to the bodies floating in the ocean? I'm sure they'll feel much better about being dead. Knowing you've *nearly* caught the person who killed them."

Strongquist was nonplussed by Ethan's sarcastic response. "The flooding was caused by a Natural Movement saboteur?" he asked.

"Possibly saboteurs," Ethan replied. He said to Cariad, "Garwin was here the whole time as far as I can tell. I doubt he planted the bomb. But he had no explanation for Twyla's behavior and neither did she."

"It was a bomb?" asked Faina. "We heard it was a natural disaster. From the sound of it, the caves were unsafe from the outset. It was unwise to attempt to create a new settlement in such an area. There was always a risk of something like this happening."

"The caves were safe," Ethan said angrily. "They were bone dry. No water had flowed through them in decades, if not hundreds or thousands of years. This was a deliberate act, designed to kill as many people as possible. Designed to..." He paused. His hands were clenched into fists and he was leaning toward Faina. One of the armed Guardians had gripped his weapon.

Ethan turned his face away. "Go back to your ship. You helped us in the First Night Attack, but since then you've done nothing but interfere and make things worse. Leave us alone. We can deal with this ourselves."

"I think we'll be the judge of whether our help is needed," Faina said. "We've identified the site of the disaster, and we'll be flying the shuttle there."

She walked back to their ship and the other Guardians went with her. Cariad wondered why they'd come to the settlement at all if they intended taking their shuttle to the caves. Unless they had only just discovered where the caves were? Faina hadn't received any comm that Cariad had seen.

"I just wanted to tell you," Strongquist said to Cariad, "we found that Frederick Aparicio somehow managed to get aboard the *Nova Fortuna* as one of the First Generation. We cross-matched our vids of him from Earth with the vids from the first decades of the voyage. We had no access to the ship's recordings until we downloaded them from the archive. The appearance match was one hundred percent accurate. There's no doubt that it was him aboard the ship after it departed Earth."

"How the hell did he manage that?" Cariad asked.

"We don't know for sure, yet if the Natural Movement had operatives who could manipulate and falsify court records and newspaper reports about the legal appeal, perhaps they were able to do the same with data about the First Generation."

"But he must have taken someone else's place," Cariad protested. "And whoever was bumped off the list wouldn't have kept quiet about it."

"Perhaps the Natural Movement paid for their silence," said Strongquist. "Successful candidates were offered millions to sell their places, according to the records."

"I know, but that was strictly prohibited. The

candidates had been selected with extreme care. Their genetic codes were verified before they were allowed aboard and no twins were allowed. You couldn't get tighter security."

"I don't have the answer to that," said Strongquist. "What we do know without any doubt is that Frederick Aparicio lived and died aboard the *Nova Fortuna*."

"And he passed on the Natural Movement philosophy to a group of young Gens," Ethan said. "Indoctrinating them from a young age. And when they grew up, they passed it on to other young children down the generations right up until Arrival Day."

"But I don't see how," Cariad said. "Maybe if the Gens lived in families, I could see it happening. Back on Earth, parents usually brought up their kids to follow their own beliefs. But the controls we put in place on reproduction prevented that. Children were brought up in small groups with caregivers, not in families."

"I know how they did it," said Ethan. "This guy, Aparicio. He was a kindergarten teacher, wasn't he?"

"Yes," said Strongquist. "How did you know?"

"Because that's Twyla's job."

CHAPTER THIRTY

After the Guardians left, Ethan returned to the caves with Cariad on a flitter. The Guardians' shuttle was much faster than their vehicle and by the time they arrived at the site of the disaster a stand off was already in progress.

On one side, their backs to the cliff edge, stood assembled Gens and Woken. The two groups had banded together and were facing the small party of Guardians, who stood with their backs to Ethan and Cariad as they walked across from the parked flitter. The wind was high, gusting along gray-black clouds that threatened rain.

Shouts could be heard from each side as they approached, but Ethan couldn't make them out until they got nearer.

The first voice he recognized was Strongquist's. "I repeat, we only want to help," the Guardian shouted.

"Yeah, right," a faint voice from the crowd replied. "Is that what you told Aubriot?"

"That was an entirely different matter," came Faina's high, crisp voice over the noise of the wind. "Sometimes it's necessary to remove elements that threaten the success of the colony."

"He isn't an element," replied the same voice from the Gen and Woken side. "He's a human being."

"An asshole human being," another voice said, which brought a tense burst of laughter, "but that doesn't give you the right to knock him out."

"I assure you," Strongquist said, "as soon as the colony is thriving and able to withstand the repercussions that derive from the presence of extreme personalities, we will bring Aubriot out of sedation."

"How nice of you," another voice piped sarcastically. "We'll look forward to it." This drew some more chuckles, but the expressions of the Gens and Woken were soon hard and confrontational again.

"This is wasting precious time," said Faina. "There may be people trapped in the caves. We want to prevent any further structural collapse and then conduct a thorough search. Let us through immediately."

"For the last time," someone shouted, "go away. Your *help* isn't needed or wanted. We've already searched the caves thoroughly. We got everyone out. We can manage this ourselves. We *will* manage this ourselves. We don't trust you and we don't want any more of your interference. Do you understand? Leave. This is our colony. Not yours. Go back to whatever's left of Earth, or go find another colony to poke your noses into. You're not welcome here."

"Yeah," another voice yelled. "But give us back Aubriot before you go."

As Ethan and Cariad arrived behind the Guardians, they stopped talking, as if wondering what to do. Ethan also wondered what he and Cariad should do next. Should they cross the space to stand with the Gens and Woken? Cariad put a hand on his arm. They both halted and waited. As far as Ethan knew the Guardians were unaware of their presence.

He wondered how they would respond to the refusal

of their offer of help. The news of Aubriot's sedation had spread as fast as a comm. Surely they would have to give up now. The assembled Gens and Woken were too hostile and the situation too strained. They couldn't possibly do any good by remaining.

The Guardians had gone too far. Gens already hated and feared them due to their armed control, and now the Woken understood they might also be subjected to Guardian control, they detested them too. It would take drastic action to redeem themselves and earn the colonists' forgiveness. A good first step would be to apologize. Then they should go. Even Ethan, who wasn't any kind of politician, knew that.

Except for the rush of the wind and the sigh of waves on the beach below, all was silent. The Gens and Woken stood defiant, their arms crossed, waiting for the Guardians to back down. The Guardians watched them, not speaking.

The tension stretched thin and taut. There was no way the Gens or Woken were going to allow the Guardians to help. They either had to leave or force their way through.

They made the wrong choice.

Guardian weapons were lifted. Gasps came from the crowd of Gens and Woken.

"This is your final warning," said Faina. "We demand that you let us pass. We must search for trapped settlers."

But some Gens had thought ahead and were ready for the escalation. They stepped forward, weapons at their shoulders. Cariad grabbed Ethan's arm. "This is insane," she whispered. "We have to do something before someone gets hurt."

"Wait," Ethan called out to the Guardians. "Let's talk about this."

They swung around to him, which meant that he and Cariad were looking down the muzzles of Guardian weapons. Whether the gun-bearing Guardians intended to aim at him, Ethan didn't know, but the threat was enough. The Gens fired. Pulses flew from their weapons, hitting Strongquist and Faina as well as the armed Guardians. The group took pulse hits on their torsos, heads, and limbs.

None had any effect.

Almost before the shock of this fact could register, the Guardians swung back to face the Gens who were firing on them. They returned fire, felling the weapon-bearing Gens and others in the crowd.

"Stop," shouted Cariad.

Ethan ran at an armed Guardian, knocking him from his feet. Other Gens and Woken were also running over. The remaining armed Guardian began picking them off. Ethan fought with the Guardian, trying to grab his weapon. The man was exceptionally strong. As they wrestled, others were fighting around them. The Gens and Woken who had reached the Guardians were attacking the group, hitting them with their fists and tools they'd been carrying.

Ethan was losing his battle with the Guardian. The man was just too powerful. As they tussled on the ground, the Guardian beneath Ethan, the man wrenched his weapon from Ethan's slipping grasp and turned the muzzle to face him. Ethan managed to push it away as a pulse round flew out. He grabbed the gun again, but the man was forcing it relentlessly upward toward Ethan's chest.

A cry of effort sounded from above. A rifle butt pounded down onto the Guardian's skull. The man's skin split, revealing... Ethan sucked in a gulp of air. He let go of his hold on like the man was contaminated with poison. He leapt up and stared at the prone figure.

Where the weapon butt had struck the Guardian's forehead, there was no blood. And what was that under the man's skin?

It was Cariad who had struck him. She too was gaping at the wound she'd inflicted. Where there should have been blood, tissue, and bone, there was only a pale gray, non-organic surface. Ethan couldn't tell if it was plastic or metal, but whatever it was, it wasn't something that should exist inside a human being.

What was more, the Guardian was only mildly affected by Cariad's devastating blow. He should have been knocked out, but he only blinked a few times. He grasped his weapon close with one hand and reached up to feel the loose, skin-like material that was hanging from his head with the other.

The sounds and sight of his surroundings had faded away. Ethan could only see the artificial interior of the Guardian's head. Then he heard Cariad shouting. "What are you? You aren't people. You aren't human!"

Around them, Gens and Woken were still fighting. Three had overwhelmed the second armed Guardian and managed to wrest her gun from her. More had targeted Strongquist and Faina. A group had lifted up Faina and were carrying her, as she writhed and struggled, toward the Guardian shuttle. The ones who had attacked Strongquist had him on the ground and were raining blows down on him.

But Cariad's shouts penetrated the perceptions of the fighters and as her words were heard and understood, the violence quickly ceased. Woken and Gens alike got up and backed away from their victims, eyeing them warily. Faina was lowered—almost dropped—to the ground. Strongquist rose to his feet, looking none the worse for his ordeal, though his expression was grave.

"I always knew there was something wrong about you," said Cariad, her voice trembling.

Ethan said, "What are you? And why are you here? You lied to us. You've lied to us all along."

"We're here to help you," Strongquist replied. "That's always been our intention. Yes, at times we've been forced to lie, but that was only when we had to, when telling you the truth would have been dangerous to you."

"Answer the question," Ethan demanded. "What the hell are you?"

"They must be some kind of android," said Cariad. "That was why the pulse rounds had no effect on them."

"Yes," said Faina. "We are what you would call androids. We are complex machines designed to look human."

"Designed to fool us," Ethan spat.

"Designed to help you," said Strongquist.

"You call this help?" a voice asked incredulously.

"However," Faina went on, "in a sense we are human. Our consciousness is an amalgamation of data from thousands of stored human minds. In the last years of human civilization, the remaining survivors uploaded their minds to storage systems. The technology to upload distinct personalities had never been perfected, but the information from thousands of memories and facets of personality is sufficient to form a new, human-like mind."

The Guardian who had been struck by Cariad got to his feet, holding his torn skin to his forehead. Without any communication taking place between them, he and the other armed Guardian left, heading toward their shuttle.

"The last days of human civilization?" Cariad echoed.

"Yes," said Strongquist. "I am afraid to say that was one of the points on which we weren't entirely honest. We judged that to reveal the actual state of humankind would be too shocking and would exert too much pressure on the settlers when the colony was in a fragile state. Also, we couldn't reveal the truth without raising questions among you about our identity. Now that our true natures have been inadvertently revealed, we have decided to follow through with an accurate and complete explanation of why we're here."

The remaining Gens and Woken who hadn't taken part in the fight had walked over from the cliff top. They crowded around, leaning in and remaining silent as they listened to the Guardian's words.

Strongquist went on, "We've only withheld information on certain things. Everything we told you about the finding of archaeological evidence that revealed the Natural Movement plot to sabotage the colony is true. And we did come after you in the *Mistral* to avert the plot's success."

He looked at Faina as if listening to her, then turned again to the crowd. "I will begin with what we know about the collapse of civilization. After the departure of the *Nova Fortuna*, environmental degradation and resource depletion increased. This was despite the fact that the Natural Movement's philosophy, intended to prevent these things, had predominated. As far as we can tell, research on how to solve the problems had entirely ceased. The difficulties worsened until the physical and societal infrastructures that supported civilization began to break down.

"When fledgling colonies on Mars and the outer moons could no longer be supported with resources from Earth, the colonists who could return did so. Urban centers began to lose their populations as people returned to the land to find and grow their own food. Economies wavered as credit systems disintegrated and people returned to cash and barter economies.

"At that point, human society might have continued at subsistence level or it might have continued to gradually decline. We will never know, because a new, deadly mutation of the flu virus appeared. A pandemic traversed the globe. Its passage was slower than it would have been in the days of massive movements of people, but it was inexorable nonetheless. A few scientists remained who had studied epidemiology in secret, wary of public disapproval, but they lacked the know how and technology to create a vaccine in time to halt the epidemic's progress."

"Toward the end, those who foresaw the destiny of humankind remembered the attempts of earlier scientists to upload their minds to data banks and live on as digital information. The funding for the research had ceased decades previously. It had not been thought natural or fitting to seek to live beyond the natural human lifespan. Thus the technology had never been developed to its full potential, but some saw it as a chance to live on, in a small way. Even if they would not exist as full, complete personalities, a part of them would continue as long as the machines storing their data still functioned.

"Most of those wishing to upload their minds' data were scientists. Despite the prohibitions on research and experimentation, some had continued their work in hiding, teaching and passing on what they knew to others. People who heard of the scheme to save something of human consciousness traveled down empty, pot-holed roads for weeks to reach the site. They removed forbidden renewable energy devices from storage and set them up. When their time came, they uploaded their minds. It was the last gasp of humankind."

"Everyone's dead?" gasped Cariad. "All of humanity has been wiped out?"

"Not all," Strongquist replied. "Some people remain, representatives of the tiny fragment of the population who is naturally immune to the virus. This is why you cannot return to Earth. You do not have any immunity. If you go back, you will all die."

Strongquist paused. No one spoke. The Guardian hadn't yet told them the entire story. He hadn't explained how he and the other Guardians had been created and sent out to the colony, but what he had told them was so momentous, it was taking time to digest. The assembled Gens and Woken remained still, as if the news had robbed them of movement. Ethan himself could hardly believe it, and not only because it was almost too amazing to believe. The Guardians had lied to them before. They had lied to them all along in fact. Who was to say they weren't lying now?

Then a movement he saw from the corner of his eye attracted his attention. He turned to see what it was. Someone was walking toward the group, coming from the plain beyond the hills that led down the as-yet-unexplored coast. The person was walking along the cliff edge. Ethan's heart lurched. He thought he recognized the figure, but he didn't dare believe he was right.

His legs weren't listening to the disbelief of his mind. Before he knew it, he was running. He sped over the ground toward the person approaching them. Yet he'd crossed half the distance to the woman before he could allow himself to believe what he saw. "Cherry," he yelled. "Cherry!"

Cherry raised a weary hand and halted, waiting for him to reach her. When he did, he scooped her up, her feet dangling, and hugged her to his chest, reassuring himself that she was real.

"Yow," she exclaimed. "Glad to see you too, Ethan, but you're crushing me."

He set her down carefully. She had a large graze running across her face and her clothes were torn, but she seemed okay.

"What happened to you?" Ethan asked. "I thought you were dead. I was *sure* you were dead!"

"I thought so too," said Cherry. "I thought exactly that all the way down from the cave. I thought it when I hit the water, and I thought it the whole time I was trying to get to the surface. The falling water kept pushing me down. That was the only way I knew which way was up. But I got out from under it in the end, and when I made it up to the light, a storage box was floating on the surface. A sealed one. I grabbed it and held onto it for dear life. I didn't know what else to do. I got carried away from the cliffs by the current, a long way along the coast, but then the waves pushed me to the shore. I arrived at a beach kilometers away."

"You've been walking back all this time?" Ethan asked.

"Yes, and I'm freezing," Cherry said.

Ethan immediately pulled off his shirt and put it over her. The hem hung down around her knees. By this time, Cariad and some others had arrived, including Strongquist.

"Let's get you something to eat," said Ethan. "You must be exhausted. Here, I'll carry you."

"It's okay," Cherry said. "I can walk a bit farther."

"Please come to our shuttle," urged Strongquist. "We have medical facilities aboard."

"No," said Cariad. "Don't. Ethan and I will take you to the settlement hospital on a flitter."

Cherry hesitated.

"You seem in good health despite your ordeal," said Strongquist. "I'm sure that the treatment you receive at the hospital will be perfectly adequate for your needs."

At last, thought Ethan. The Guardian seemed to have begun to understand how severely they had breached the colonists' trust.

Ethan put an arm around Cherry and began to guide her to where he and Cariad had left the flitter. Faina ran up carrying a blanket of thin material. She wrapped it around Cherry, saying, "This will conserve your body heat. I have some oral rehydration solution and nutritional supplements too." She handed the packages to Cariad, who broke one open to give to Cherry.

After some expressions of relief to Cherry over her safety, the crowd of Woken and Gens began to break up. They returned to the task of assessing the safety of the cliffs and salvaging what supplies they could. By the time Ethan reached the flitter with Cherry, only Cariad, Strongquist, and Faina remained.

Ethan helped Cherry aboard. She lay down across the back seat. As he got in the driver's side, Cariad said to Strongquist, "You didn't explain what happened after. Where did your ship come from? Where did *you* come from?"

"What individual minds couldn't achieve separately they could accomplish en masse," he replied. "Without cultural boundaries and clumsy languages preventing the passage of ideas, the uploaded minds began to work together. The surviving, living scientists worked with them, trying to find a way for human civilization to continue to exist. Not in the degraded environment of Earth, but out here, in a pristine, untouched world. I understand that you might find it difficult to believe, given everything that's happened—we have made some mistakes. We see that now—but we really are here to help the colony to survive. You are all that's left. If the *Nova Fortuna* Project fails, human civilization fails with it, perhaps never to rise again."

"No pressure then," Cherry said from the back of the flitter.

CHAPTER THIRTY-ONE

While the doctor checked Cherry over at the settlement hospital, Cariad sat in the waiting room with Ethan, her thoughts spinning almost out of control. She could hardly believe what Strongquist had told them. She couldn't imagine an Earth almost entirely empty of human beings. The previous story the Guardians had told them, that resources were stretched to the limit and humanity was struggling to survive, had been hard to hear, but she'd believed it. In fact, it seemed that the conditions they'd spoken of had existed, but they had occurred much earlier in time, long before the Guardians had left the planet on their rescue mission. The second part of their story about Earth scientists working together to save the *Nova Fortuna* Project was harder for her to swallow.

Ethan was quiet. His hands were on his knees and his head was bowed.

"Do you believe the Guardians' story?" Cariad asked him.

He looked up as if coming out of a dream, or a nightmare. "I don't know. I'm not sure I can believe anything they say. But does it matter? Whatever happened on Earth, the result is the same. We're here, and we have to do the best we can to survive while avoiding killing each other in the process. I only hope the Guardians will leave us alone now."

"I guess you're right, but I can't wrap my head around the fact that Earth's a wasteland, and from now on, we're it. Humanity's best hope. After thousands of years of civilization, it's come down to us to carry the torch."

Ethan shrugged. "It's different for me. From my perspective, Earth was only ever a picture or a vid or an ancient book. It's never been real. Not like this place, anyhow. I mean, I believed it. I just never really cared."

Cariad hadn't thought about it in that way, but Ethan had just defined one of the gulfs that separated the Gens and the Woken. The Gens already thought of the planet as their home. It was a place they could finally live as themselves and not as someone else's idea of what they should be. To the Woken, the colony was a project that they wanted to succeed according to the plan they'd set out. Maybe the difference in perspective was one of the causes of the problems between the two sides.

"I'm glad your friend didn't drown," she said to Ethan.

He leaned back and closed his eyes. "So am I. I've seen so many deaths, Cariad. People I loved and cared for."

She took his hand and held it in her own. She had lost people too. Or rather, she had chosen to leave them, breaking their hearts and hers. She didn't think she would ever get over the guilt of what she'd done. They sat together like that for some time, quietly waiting.

The doctor came into see them. "I'm happy to report that Cherry's going to be fine. Secondary drowning is a possibility in cases like this. We checked her lungs for water, but they were clear. She has some bumps and scratches, but no broken bones or any other serious injuries. I would say you could go and see her, however she's sleeping right now. We're going to keep her here overnight as a precaution, but I'm sure she can leave tomorrow."

"Great," said Cariad. She was impressed that the doctor knew about secondary drowning. None of the Gens had been near large bodies of water until coming to the planet so he would have had no experience of treating drowning victims. Then Cariad realized what she was doing. She'd slipped into a patronizing attitude toward the Gen doctor, just like a typical Woken.

"Thank the stars," Ethan said, visibly relaxing as if suddenly relieved of a heavy weight. He rubbed his face before getting to his feet.

"We'll leave her in your capable hands then," Cariad said to the doctor.

As they left the hospital and went out into the settlement, Cariad noticed that Ethan's expression had darkened.

"What's wrong?" she asked, touching his arm.

"Garwin wasn't there. He should have been there."

A flitter arriving came down the street toward them, heading for the hospital. Cariad and Ethan moved out of its way.

"You mean he should have come to the hospital to support the disaster victims?" Cariad asked.

"I mean to see Cherry. He doesn't even know how she is."

"Oh. Are they good friends?"

"They're lovers. Garwin was having an affair with her. You'd think he cared about her, wouldn't you? But instead he's at home protecting his traitorous, murdering wife."

Cariad took a moment to digest this new information. "If he's been at home all this time, maybe he doesn't know that Cherry survived and she's at the hospital."

"Oh, he knows all right," said Ethan. He reached up to his ear and removed something from it. He held out his hand, palm upward. A tiny electronic device rested in the center.

"Is that a comm?" Cariad asked, incredulous. She'd seen similar devices on Earth but none had been brought along on the *Nova Fortuna*. "You have your own comms?"

"Yes. It's separate from the Network and encrypted. We needed a way to talk with each other without Woken or Guardians snooping on us. I've been listening in on the conversations ever since the disaster. For a while, Garwin was fielding questions about Twyla. I'd told others what I suspected. Then he went silent. But that was after Cherry came back. He knows that she barely survived the flood and that we took her to the hospital. He knows all about it. He just doesn't care."

"Hmm... I agree that he's an ass for abandoning Cherry," Cariad said, "but maybe he doesn't dare to leave Twyla. He might be thinking that people could take the law into their own hands. Maybe he's staying home for self-preservation and to protect his wife in case something happens."

Ethan didn't answer. His brow remained furrowed in anger, but then his eyebrows shot up and he halted.

"What's wrong?" Cariad asked.

"That's what she meant," Ethan exclaimed.

"What? Who meant what?"

"Twyla. When she said she should have put an end to me when she had the chance. One day a few weeks ago, I caught her in my cave. There was a big argument going on among the Gens and I left to get some peace and quiet. She must have thought I wouldn't be back for a while."

"What was she doing in your cave?"

"Well, she told me she was there to talk to me in

private. She asked me if Garwin was having an affair."

"She did? What did you tell her?"

"What could I tell her? I told her the truth. I wasn't going to lie to her. But it was strange. Garwin has a terrible reputation in that regard. I was amazed she didn't know."

"Oh no. How did she take it?"

"That's not the point. I think she did know. She knew all along. She was covering up for her being there. It was all a big lie. She had me completely fooled."

"Huh? So why was she there if not to ask you about Garwin's affairs?"

"She had a bag with her. I think she was there to plant a bomb in my cave. She wanted to get rid of me."

"Oh, Ethan." Cariad felt like bursting into tears. She'd come so close to losing him.

The settlement was bustling. Cariad guessed it was for the first time in weeks. She and Ethan were wandering with no particular direction in mind, but the majority of the crowd appeared to be heading in the direction of the stadium. It made sense. After the disaster at the caves and the Guardians' revelation, there were decisions that had to be made. The future of the *Nova Fortuna* Project hung in the balance. Things could not continue as they were, and the implications of the true nature of the Guardians had to be discussed.

They turned in the direction of the stadium too. When they arrived and Cariad saw the size of the crowd, her heart plummeted. Even allowing for people who couldn't attend because they were injured, or helping to care for the injured, the number of people in the stadium was pitifully small. She recalled the first time the stadium had been used, which had been at the announcement of the results of the vote to name the planet. Then, the place had been two-thirds full. Now the crowd filled less than half the available space. The First Night Attack, the stadium bombing, the shuttle explosion, and the flooding of the caves had drastically reduced the population.

It was a painful realization, but even if they eliminated the Natural Movement threat tomorrow and the colony experienced no further unexpected deaths, in its current state the *Nova Fortuna* Project was doomed to fail.

Cariad and Ethan took seats at the lowest tier, where they looked up into the dignitaries' box. Strongquist and Faina sat there, presumably in order to explain who, or rather what, they were to the gathered crowd. No other Guardians were present. As Cariad watched, another figure appeared in the box. Anahi's black visual aid gazed out across the stadium. She seemed to be looking for something or someone. Though Cariad was somewhat distant from the older woman, she detected weariness and stress etched on her face.

The black strip turned in Cariad's direction and stopped. Anahi beckoned. Did she mean for Cariad to go up to the box? The Woken lifted her lapel to her lips. Her voice came over the loudspeakers. "Cariad, Ethan. Come up here."

After exchanging a look, they rose and made their way along their row then through the stadium seating to join Anahi and the Guardians. When they arrived, the square space seemed empty with just the five of them there. Garwin was conspicuous by his absence.

The crowd was already mostly quiet. It didn't take more than a few words from Anahi to entirely silence them. "Gens, Woken," she said, "I'm sorry." She paused for her words to take effect. "I'm only going to speak for a short time before I hand you over to wiser and more compassionate people. I confess that I've been foolish and impatient, and if I'm honest I've been scared. I acted too hastily in assuming control of this project. I feared for its success and by extension, my own survival.

"Since I declared myself Leader, people have died. I feel that I bear some responsibility for those deaths and that is something I shall regret to my dying day. It took the egregious behavior of the Guardians and the disaster at the caves to shock me out of my delusion and pride. I only wish I had seen sense earlier. But I can't reverse time and take back the stupid decisions I made. All I can do is try to make amends for my mistakes, and my first attempt is to step down as Leader.

"Before doing that, however, I am making one last amendment to the Manual, and that is to revert the election of Leader to its former process. Leaders may only be elected from among the Gens by majority vote as before. I only have one final thing to say: I nominate this man to stand for election." She pointed at Ethan, who was leaning forward in his seat, his head bowed. At Anahi's final statement he looked up to see who she was indicating. When he saw it was him, he shook his head.

A cheer of approval rose from the crowd, but still Ethan looked unhappy and embarrassed.

Cariad stood and turned her comm to general broadcast, to be picked up and transmitted by the stadium's speakers. "Admitting that you made a mistake is a hard thing to do, Anahi. You have my respect, and I'm glad to see the return of the scientist I admired and looked up to for all the years that we worked together."

Anahi nodded in acknowledgment of Cariad's words and went to the rear of the box to sit down next to Strongquist and Faina. Ethan was staring at the floor. Cariad suddenly found herself the only person remaining to address the crowd. She struggled to think of what to say. The gathered folk were waiting for someone to address their fears and show them the path to a viable future, but she wasn't sure she was capable of either.

All she could do was explain how things stood as she saw them. "I wish I could stand here and tell you that everything will be okay—that we've got everything figured out. But it just isn't true. I'm a geneticist, as some of you already know. I can tell you now, we've lost too many people for this colony to survive as it is. Our genetic diversity is too low. Within five to seven generations, we're going to start to see noticeable effects of inbreeding. So I've decided to restart the reproduction process aboard the *Nova Fortuna*. We have gametes stored that will add variety to the gene pool."

She became aware of a presence at her side. Ethan had joined her.

"Give me your comm," he said.

She unpinned it and handed it over.

"The time for fighting among ourselves is over," Ethan said. His voice echoed around the half-empty stadium. "I don't know about you, but I've seen enough of fighting and death to last me a lifetime. That isn't why any of us are here. I've been listening to the exchanges between the Gens while I've been sitting here, and I want to set you straight on the rumors that have been flying around."

"First, the rumor that the Guardians aren't human is true. We saw it at the fight at the caves, and they've told us so themselves." Ethan went on to relate to the crowd everything that Strongquist and Faina had told them about the situation on Earth. "I don't know if I believe everything they said," he went on. "They've told us plenty of half-truths and outright lies, all in the name of trying to ensure our survival. I don't know what the facts are about them, and I doubt we'll ever know for sure. They saved us in the First Night Attack, so we saw them as our saviors and protectors. They occupied a position of trust and reliance in the early days, but that quickly changed and they became a force to control Gens.

"What they're planning on doing now, what role they

intend to take up, I don't know. What I do know is, their presence has harmed our colony. Anahi used the Guardians as a tool to assert her power over us Gens. If the Guardians hadn't been around, she wouldn't have been able to take over. And the fact that the Woken had an armed force to control us only deepened our resentment and desire to break away. For all the times they've said they're here to help us, the Guardians have done nothing but make things harder.

"I'm no Leader, and I don't want to be, but if I were, the first thing I'd do is order the Guardians to leave. We don't need them and their tech. Everything we need we brought on the *Nova Fortuna*, and that includes each other. We need to trust each other and work together to survive, without interference from the Guardians."

During the latter part of Ethan's speech, Strongquist had come up to Ethan. "If I might speak? I have a proposal to make."

Ethan looked distrustful but gave a small nod.

"We Guardians are in agreement with Ethan. Our presence has not had the desired effect. Though we have carried out our mandate to the letter, the *Nova Fortuna* Project does not seem to have experienced a net benefit and in fact it seems reasonable to conclude that our actions have been detrimental. However, if we were to leave, we would be depriving the colony of the advanced technology aboard our ship. Therefore, we would like to propose that we place ourselves in suspension. Facilities in the *Mistral's* storage areas allow for this. Then, if at some future time the *Nova Fortuna* colonists require our services, you may reactivate us."

Ethan turned to Cariad. She raised her eyebrows then shrugged. If the Guardians were like the more rudimentary androids she'd been familiar with on Earth, they could be turned off or turn themselves off. Whether the Guardians could reactivate themselves at will was another question. Perhaps it would be possible to bar their exit from the storage area Strongquist mentioned to prevent any surprise awakenings. Strongquist's proposal might work, but the Gens and Woken had a lot to consider. The Guardian was right when he said they could benefit from their ship's tech.

Ethan asked the crowd, "Who agrees that the Guardians should deactivate?"

The stadium was set up for voting. At each seat an interface allowed the participants to record their responses and the totals were relayed to the stadium's screen. The response was clear. Most of those present wanted the Guardians to deactivate themselves and leave the Gens and Woken alone to run the colony.

Strongquist nodded and turned to Ethan and Cariad. "We will conduct training in the operation of the *Mistral* before handing it over. I also have some key information to impart before entering deactivation."

"You also have to bring Aubriot out of sedation," said Cariad.

The Guardian's face expressed reservations, but he nodded again. "If you insist."

"We do," said Ethan. He addressed the stadium again. "We have plenty of work to do, but if we stop fighting and hindering each other, we can do it. We don't have a choice. We have to do it."

A voice floated up from the crowd. "What about the Natural Movement?"

"We're on it," said Ethan. "I'm not saying any more than that. But we're closer than we've ever been to rooting them all out."

Cariad realized the truth of his words. Ethan's reasoning on the evidence strongly implicated Twyla and possibly Garwin too. They also had the records of all the children Twyla had cared for over the years. Natural Movement followers were among them, and others who had been in her class would remember things she had done and said that would give them more clues.

"Voting for a new Leader starts tomorrow," said Ethan. "Like I said, I'm not standing. There are plenty among you who can do a better job than me. But there's another vote I want to hold. We need to name this planet! It's our home. Let's give it a name that shows it belongs to all of us. We need a name to unite us. Input your suggestions to your screens. In five minutes, we vote. Then it's done. The past will be over, our new lives begun."

Cariad had sat down while Ethan spoke. As she watched him talk to the crowd, she didn't think she'd ever seen a more natural leader. If only he would realize it.

"That's a good idea," she said as he sat down beside her. "We need something to unite us. Oh, I've thought of a name." She quickly typed her idea for a name for the planet into her interface.

When Ethan read what she'd written, he said, "What does it mean?"

"It's a play on a word that means agreement."

"I like it. You've got my vote."

More suggestions appeared on Cariad's screen along with the option to vote for them in order of preference. The countdown began and they both waited while the system collected the votes. The winner would appear on the stadium screen when the time was up.

While she waited, Cariad looked at the back of the box. Anahi had gone, but Strongquist and Faina remained, sitting impassively while the voting took place. Cariad could still hardly believe that the Guardians weren't human. The tech that had created them and their ship was so advanced, it didn't seem credible that the remaining Earth-dwelling humans had devoted all their skill and energy to trying to save the colony rather than themselves.

If the Guardians carried out their promise and deactivated themselves, Cariad would try to find out the whole truth about them.

"Voting's up," said Ethan, nudging her.

Cariad looked up at the screen to see the result. The name she'd suggested had won. The crowd was cheering. For the first time in a long while, Cariad laughed.

"Welcome to Concordia, your new home," she said to Ethan. Then as she gazed out at the crowd of mixed Gens and Woken, Concordia's colonists, a realization hit her. Through the painful days of struggle and conflict, she'd come to see them not as two separate groups, but as one group of people—a group of people to whom she belonged. The family she'd left behind on Earth, the sorrow and sense of loss at parting from them had been real, but it was in the past. If what the Guardians said about what had happened on Earth was true, it was likely that even her family's descendants were long gone. The people of Concordia were her people now.

CHAPTER THIRTY-TWO

Two Gen farmers, after hearing Ethan's suspicions about Garwin and Twyla, had volunteered to guard Garwin's home and prevent his or Twyla's escape. As soon as the applause and general celebration at the stadium over the naming of the planet had begun to die down and the crowd began to break up, Ethan left to head straight for the house. He wasn't sure what he would do when he arrived. He didn't have any authority to take the two suspected Natural Movement followers into custody—that would be the decision of whoever was elected Leader the next day—but he could keep them under supervision until then.

Cariad had come along with him, as had Strongquist. Faina had excused herself, saying she would return to the *Mistral* to begin organizing the hand over. Evening was falling as they walked through the streets.

"Anything happen?" Ethan asked Misha and Phy when they arrived. The farmers were standing outside the gate that led to the small home.

"Not heard a peep from them," Phy replied. "We aren't even sure they're home. No one has come out while we've been standing here and we haven't heard a sound from the place."

Damn. Had Garwin and Twyla already left? Ethan wondered if they'd fled to the home of another Natural Movement follower who would hide them. He should have asked for someone to guard them as soon as he left the place.

He pushed open the gate and walked up to the door of the dark-windowed, silent house. The couple had almost certainly left. It was unlike Garwin to sit passively at home when his wife had been accused of a horrendous crime. The man had to have heard everything that had happened and what Ethan had said at the stadium via his ear comm. He would know that Ethan was about to draw a net around them and that they were at risk of meeting the same fate as the First Night Attack saboteur.

Ethan shivered at his recollection of that fateful moment when the saboteur had been executed. He'd felt as though the long daydream of Arrival was over and he'd been jolted into the harsh reality of life in the new colony.

The door was locked. He shouted Garwin's name. "Open up. I have some more questions for you and Twyla." Silence was the only answer. The bad feeling in the pit of Ethan's stomach grew. He didn't waste any more time on exhorting Garwin to let them in. The house had to be empty, but he wanted to know for sure.

"Stand back," he told Cariad and Strongquist. Bracing himself by pushing his hands against both sides of the narrow porch, Ethan kicked the door with his heel two or three times until the lock broke. The door banged against the wall and bounced back. Ethan caught it and went into the hall.

"Be careful," said Cariad, who was behind him.

No voice or sound of any movement came from the unlit home. Ethan turned on the hall light and went into the living room. It was empty, but a sound was coming from the open doorway that led to the kitchen. Someone was home after all. The sound was a human voice, moaning softly, full of despair. The hairs stood up on the back of his neck and the knot in Ethan's stomach tightened. He went toward the noise, dreading what he might be about to see.

"Maybe you should stay back," he said to Cariad, but she came with him anyway. Strongquist heeded his advice.

Ethan stepped into the kitchen.

Garwin was sitting on the floor with Twyla in his arms. A wide pool of darkening blood surrounded them. The woman was dead. Her skin was devoid of color and deep gashes marked both her wrists. Garwin was rocking his dead wife like she was a baby while moans escaped his lips.

As the man slowly became aware that two people had arrived, he looked up. He was also ashy pale. "I was too late. She only said she would make some tea. Didn't utter a sound when she did it. When I came to check on her, she was already gone."

Ethan didn't know what to say. Pity stirred his heart. Twyla's suicide seemed to be an admission of her guilt, but he wasn't sure that Garwin had known what she'd done. The man seemed to have loved her deeply, in spite of his infidelities.

"She should never have married me," said Garwin. "I think she thought she'd made a mistake. When things became difficult between us after a while, she rejected me. I don't think she ever stopped loving me, but she didn't want me near her. As if to make up for her coldness, she made it clear she'd overlook any dalliances. I don't believe she was a Natural Movement follower, but if she was I don't care. I would have stood by her." He pulled the dead woman closer, burying his face in her hair.

Strongquist came into the kitchen, his gaze cold as

he quickly appraised the scene. The Guardian's face betrayed no sense of disturbance. It was at that moment that the Guardians' inhumanity struck Ethan the most forcefully. Their desire to help the colony in their misguided fashion was not an emotion. It was a function in their machine minds.

"We may be able to discover some useful information from the suspect's remains," Strongquist said. "I would like to retain the body for an autopsy."

Ethan concurred with the Guardian's idea. If she had used explosives, perhaps some traces might remain on her skin. Then they would know for sure that they'd caught one of the saboteurs. At some coaxing from himself and Cariad, Garwin finally released his grip on his dead wife's remains. The man was soaked in her blood but he seemed oblivious.

Ethan called Misha and Phy in to help with Twyla's body. They were both round-eyed when they stepped into the kitchen but were quick to help. They carried the corpse out and Strongquist went with them.

Garwin was almost unrecognizable. His confidence and charm had melted away. He stood, caked in dark red and brown stains, looking like an old man, forsaken and lost.

"We should take him to the *Mistral* too," said Cariad. "He has to be examined as well as Twyla."

They led Garwin out of the house. He came with them without resisting. He appeared almost catatonic, moving mechanically like a sleepy child. The blood on his clothes was already stiffening the fabric. As they walked him through the streets, people stopped and stared. They drew aside, giving the strange procession a wide berth.

Garwin's appearance would have given anyone pause, but the fact that the man had once been well-liked, respected, and often admired, an unofficial leader of the Gens, made the spectacle of his downfall all the more astounding. It was a long walk to the shuttle field.

***

The *Mistral's* shuttle had already departed, so they took another, telling the pilot to fly them up to the Guardian's ship. The *Nova Fortuna's* shuttles traveled at half the speed of the Guardians', so they were still on their way when Strongquist contacted them over the ship's comm to report on his preliminary examination of Twyla's body.

"I would like you to look at something," the Guardian said. The image he sent showed an area of skin bearing a small tattoo.

"This is on Twyla?" Ethan asked. He kept his voice low and glanced at Garwin, but the man didn't appear to be registering anything in his surroundings.

"It is," Strongquist replied.

"Do you recognize it?" Cariad asked Ethan.

"Should I?"

"It's the Natural Movement symbol," she said. "Can you see? It's a stylized N and M."

"Twyla had the Natural Movement symbol tattooed on herself?" said Ethan. "That seems risky. What if someone had seen it and knew what it meant?"

"It *is* risky," Cariad replied. "But I wonder if they needed a way to identify each other and this was it." She leaned closer to the screen. "It would be dangerous to reveal your affiliation unless you were absolutely sure the other person also belonged to the movement. They probably had some kind of ritual when the tattoo was applied. It also explains Twyla's "coldness" toward Garwin. She must have married him thinking she could convert him to the Natural Movement philosophy, then when that didn't work, she was worried he might have discovered what the tattoo meant and expose her."

"He probably wouldn't have. I didn't recognize it."

"Maybe it was still too great a hazard. The Natural Movement wouldn't have survived this long, passing down the ideas from generation to generation, without being extremely careful."

"So now all we have to do is examine everyone and discover who's got the tattoo," Ethan said. "Then we can capture them all."

"Maybe," Cariad replied. "I was thinking, though, by now everyone knows what Twyla did. The Natural Movement members might guess that we would examine her body and find the tattoo. They could remove theirs and pretend the wound is an injury they received when the caves flooded. But I'm still hopeful. It's a step forward. We have plenty to work with."

"Yeah." Ethan had come to a decision. Now was as good a time as any to let Cariad know about it. "But it's work that's going to go on without me."

"What? Why? There's lots you can do to help with the investigation."

"Maybe, but there isn't anything that someone else couldn't do just as well, or even better than me. Besides, someone needs to search the beaches for survivors of the flooding. Cherry's young and fit and she wasn't badly injured. Others could have managed to get to shore but can't go any further. They could be kilometers down the coast. I want to look for them. Then, after that..." He took a breath. "Cariad, someone needs to check for what other dangers there might be out there. We already know about the sluglimpets, but no one has any idea what other predators might live on this continent. We don't know what might attack us at any moment."

Cariad looked troubled, but she nodded. "We've been remiss in that. The planet clearly harbors dangerous life forms that the probes didn't discover. It would be safer if we knew what they were."

"Also," Ethan continued, "I have to get away. I have to be by myself for a while. I've thought about it a lot. I never really got over the First Night Attack and

Lauren's and Dr. Crowley's deaths. I pushed myself to carry on as normal because there was so much that had to be done. Then everything that happened between the Gens and Woken... I wanted to help. I tried, and I did some good, I think. But that's it. I don't have anything left."

"I'm sorry, Ethan," Cariad said. "I didn't know things were so bad for you. If I'd known—"

"It isn't your fault," he interrupted. "It isn't anyone's fault. I didn't know it myself until that moment when I thought Cherry had died. I couldn't stop the scene replaying in my mind. I thought I'd go mad."

"We have treatment for how you're feeling," Cariad said. "With counseling and—"

"I know what I need, and it isn't anything a Woken can offer me. I need to leave and just wander. I don't know for how long, but this planet can heal me. I'm sure of it. I just need some time. I'll explore the continent."

Cariad gave a sigh and said quietly, "If that's what you want."

"It's what I need. Can you take Garwin to the Guardians? I want to return planetside as soon as we arrive and get ready to leave. I want to start searching for survivors as soon as I can."

She held his gaze with her own. "I'll miss you."

Ethan pulled her into a hug. "I'll miss you too. I don't know when I'll be back."

"I have plenty to keep me busy," said Cariad. "The time will pass."

CHAPTER THIRTY-THREE

As Cariad guided the devastated Garwin down the corridors of the *Mistral*, a bone-deep weariness settled over her. Ahead loomed the task of replenishing the colony's gene pool. She would have to look up the genetic codes of the surviving Gens and cross reference the information with that held on gametes aboard the *Nova Fortuna* and the codes of the Woken, revived and in cryo. The genes of every sex cell in storage and every fertile individual would be required to ensure the long-term survival of the colony.

Then she would have to select out the best matches to boost the heterogeneity of the pool while maintaining the optimum physical hardiness, for who knew what trials lay ahead of them? And that was only the beginning. Next would come the task of gestating the fetuses she would create to full term using antiquated equipment.

Strongquist was waiting for her at the entrance to the medical center. Another Guardian who was with him took Garwin away. The man hadn't spoken a word during the entire trip.

"Preparations for our deactivation are well

underway, as well as for handing over possession of our ship," Strongquist said. "The question is, who are we handing it over to?"

"I don't know," Cariad replied, "and to be honest I'm too tired to even think about it right now."

"It's been a long and harrowing day. I understand."

Do you?

They went into the center and to a room where Twyla's body lay on a metal table, looking entirely inhuman. Cariad had seen plenty of corpses during her early days of medical training, yet the sight of this one made her cold and nauseated. The Guardians had cleaned away all the blood but hadn't yet begun an autopsy. The skin was light blue and rubbery-looking, and the gashes on the wrists gaped, empty and dry. The body looked like someone's sick idea of a mannequin.

"The tattoo is here," said Strongquist, indicating a part of the hip that Cariad couldn't see. She went around to the other side of the table. The tattoo was about the size of a fingernail and was placed behind the curve of the protruding hip bone. It was a place only a lover would normally see.

"I regret that we didn't examine the First Night Attack saboteur before or after her execution," Strongquist said. "We incinerated the body. If we hadn't, we might have noticed the incriminating mark and searched for co-conspirators, preventing more deaths."

Cariad nodded. *Regret?* It seemed an odd word for a machine to use. On the other hand, Faina had said their minds were human-like, and though Strongquist's demeanor had always seemed reserved, at times emotions seemed to inflect his speaking tone. "Strongquist, can I ask you something about the Guardians?"

"Of course. Now that you know our true nature, we plan on answering every question you put to us. Until deactivation, that is."

"Do you feel emotion? And if you do, aren't you worried or upset about being deactivated?" Cariad was reminded of her own anxiety before being placed in cryonic suspension, not knowing if she would ever wake up.

"We do feel emotion. It is a natural consequence of intellect and consciousness. But I believe we don't experience extreme emotions as humans do. They would interfere in the execution of our programming. For example, we might be unable to defend a human from a predator if we were terrified of also being attacked and suffering injury or termination."

"That's an interesting example," said Cariad. "You talk about defending us, yet you could also kill a human if it came down to it."

"If it was essential in order to save the lives of more humans, and the death of the aggressor was the only available choice, we could."

"It's odd. We had androids on Earth when I left. They looked fairly human, but they were easy to tell apart from us. Only a small child could have mistaken an android for a person. But they were all fitted with fail safes. None could ever harm a human under any circumstances."

"I can understand the reasoning behind that protocol," said Strongquist, "but if a human were engaged in mass murder, and it was impossible to stop the person without risking their death, it would make little sense to abstain from action and allow more people to die. One death is preferable to several."

"I guess I can't disagree. It's only that during my time it wasn't felt necessary to program androids for such a scenario. Mass murder and war were things of the past."

A Guardian entered the room. "Excuse me," she said as she came around the table. Cariad moved out of her way. "I am about to begin the autopsy. You may wish to leave. The procedure may be disturbing for you to witness."

"No, it's fine," Cariad replied. "I've seen plenty. Go ahead." She said to Strongquist, "I'd like to see the test results when you have them."

"Of course. I'll send them directly to you as soon as they're in."

"There's another thing I wanted to ask you: why didn't the people who made you take the opportunity to escape Earth instead of creating the Guardians to come here and help us? I can understand that they probably didn't want to risk coming here and infecting us with the virus, but then why didn't they build their own colony ship?" However, even as she asked the question, Cariad knew the answer. "They didn't have the resources, did they?"

"That's correct. You are aware of the time and resources that went into building and stocking the *Nova Fortuna*? Mining, refining, industrial processing, manufacturing—these activities no longer occur on Earth. The people who created us and built the *Mistral* had a finite supply of materials. They used up what they had in order to try to save the *Nova Fortuna* colony from the Natural Movement plot."

"They gave their lives for ours?"

"In a sense, though it was also true that no other planet that would support human life had been discovered. If the survivors had used the *Mistral* to escape Earth, they might have been wandering the galaxy until they died. And even if they replaced themselves with their offspring, their descendants would have died out eventually. The *Mistral* isn't a colony ship, designed to support many generations of humans. Besides, it would only have held a fraction of the hundreds who helped to create it and us."

As the Guardian performing the autopsy began to

saw open the body's skull, Cariad imagined those people of an Earth far in the future of her own, toiling to ensure the survival of the *Nova Fortuna* colonists, knowing that they would never personally benefit from their efforts or even see the results. Although Strongquist's explanation made their work slightly less selfless than it had first appeared, they'd had no reason to complete it except for their desire to help strangers. Perhaps they'd seen the colonists as fellow human beings nevertheless, and perhaps they'd dreamed of saving human civilization.

It was a strange twist that the Guardians' creators had worked so hard and with such good intentions, yet they had almost engineered the downfall of humanity's last hope.

"There's something else I don't understand," Cariad said to Strongquist. "Why the big secret about you being androids? Why not tell us the truth from the beginning?"

"I cannot answer that for certain," he replied. "That was never explained to us. If I were to guess, I would say that our creators wished you to accept our superiority and authority and that if you knew we weren't human, you wouldn't do that. They didn't trust that you would accept our advice."

"Ha!"

"Is something amusing?" Strongquist asked.

"That's just like us and the Gens," said Cariad. "We didn't trust them to do the right thing. We didn't respect them or their opinions. Your creators thought they knew best, despite the fact that they weren't even here."

"The exterior of the brain appears typical," commented the Guardian performing the autopsy.

"I think her brain will be entirely normal," Cariad said. "Twyla's problem wasn't a disease, though we'll have to treat it like one."

"I take it you'll be examining all the colonists for the same tattoo?" Strongquist asked.

"Yes, but I don't know what good it's going to do. If the Natural Movement members guess that we might have that clue to identify them, they could remove the tattoos easily enough. It would be painful without anesthetic, but it could be done."

Cariad's tiredness settled deeper. She yawned. "I really need to lie down."

"Of course. I'll arrange a room to be prepared for you." Strongquist didn't speak aloud or go anywhere in order to make the request. Like any machine, he accessed the ship's comm internally. "I'm also arranging that all our data be accessible to you. You may wish to browse the files before we deactivate in case you have any questions. Though you will also have the option to reactivate myself or another Guardian for further information."

"I don't think anyone will be doing that any time soon."

"I understand. However, one item of information that we withheld is very important. We didn't wish to alarm you all, but we have been scanning for signs of life within this galactic sector ever since we arrived, and we have identified several planets that appear to not only bear life, but sentient life. At some point in the future, it may be prudent to reactivate us in order to help protect the colony from hostile alien organisms. I would strongly advise not to hesitate in this scenario."

"Hostile aliens might attack the colony?" Cariad exclaimed. "That's all we need."

"It is only a possibility. As far as we can tell, if there is intelligent life within the local galactic area, it is currently unaware of the colony's existence. And we haven't detected any signs that alien organisms have visited Concordia."

Strongquist's words were not reassuring, but Cariad

didn't have the energy to deal with the new information at that moment. "Fine. Great. Anything else you haven't told us?"

"I'm not aware of anything of equal importance."

"Okay, well, if you think of anything, put it in a comm. I'm going to rest for a while."

As Strongquist escorted her to a room, Cariad felt a pang of envy for Ethan. Exploring the new planet was what he'd always wanted to do, and he would be far away during the long, hard days that lay ahead rebuilding the broken colony. She wished she could go with him but he needed to be alone for a while.

Never mind, Cariad thought. She had new people to grow.

Cariad and Ethan's story continues in...
THE FILA EPIPHANY

Author's note

Thanks for reading *The Concordia Deception!* I hope you enjoyed the story.

In case this is the first of my books that you've read, I'll introduce myself. I'm a British writer who's currently living in Taiwan with my family, which includes a black cat called Black Cat. I've also lived in Australia and Laos so I suppose you could say I'm a bit of a wanderer.

Like most writers, I dreamed of being an author from when I was a child, right from around the time a teacher asked me to read out one of my stories to my classmates. Good teachers make all the difference, don't they? Later on, other teachers and lecturers encouraged me to write, yet for a long time I didn't have the confidence to really try. Then a few years ago when I hit middle age I thought I would give it a go. Better late than never.

The Concordia Deception is book one in *Space Colony One*—Cariad and Ethan's story of living in humanity's first deep space colony. I wanted to write about space colonization from the perspective of someone with recent memories of Earth, and through the eyes of someone who grew up on a starship. I wondered how different their feelings would be and how they might react to life on a new planet. Then I wondered what might happen if a third group of powerful people were thrown into the mix. How would the politics play out and how would everyone react to dangers that faced the settlement? There are so many ideas to explore, I think the *Space Colony One* series is going to be at least three or four books.

I think Cariad's character is a little bit based on myself. I love science and would love to have been a scientist, but words are more my thing. And, like her, I would miss my friends and family a lot during my time in deep space. Ethan, on the other hand, isn't one particular person. He represents all the people I've met who have shown me that book smarts aren't all that we need in this world. Yet he also feels the stigma people sometimes exeprience when they don't meet the standards of rigid education systems.

Space Colony One explores how we might go about colonizing an Earth-like planet and how people might act in that situation. How would we set up the buildings, start up farming, and so on? Practicality is vital but basic human nature is going to figure strongly too. Power struggles are probably inevitable when the colonists are far from Earth and higher authorities. Hopefully if humankind ever attempts such a feat—I wish I could be around to see it—we would be able to weed out colonists with psychopathic or megalomaniac tendencies, though you never know.

I based the number of Gens on the theory that humanity went through a genetic bottleneck about 70,000 years ago. Some kind of catastrophe occurred and only a few thousand humans survived. With Cariad's amazing knowledge of genetics, she manages to whittle the minimum number required for genetic heterogeneity down to two thousand, with additional donated eggs and sperm stored on the ship.

I deliberately kept the colonization equipment fairly low tech and set finite shelf lives on the high tech the colonists bring with them, simply because that's what seems most realistic to me. While we would be able to re-supply the Moon and Mars with tech from Earth, we won't have that luxury on a deep space colony. The only way for a colony to survive in the long term will be to rely on what they bring or build on-site. Until mining, refining, and manufacturing are up and running, high tech equipment won't be available.

Extra-terrestrial species are always a fun factor in space colonization novels. I didn't get into them much in this book but I'm going to make up for that in the sequels. The local life forms feature quite heavily in book two, *The Fila Epiphany*.

In *The Concordia Deception* the characters refer to an event they call the First Night Attack. That story is covered in the prequel novella, *Night of Flames*. You can pick up a free copy of the novella by signing up to my reader group. The link is below. If you don't want to belong to the group, just unsubscribe after you collect your book. I really don't mind.

Want to say hi and meet other JJ Green readers? Come over to my Facebook group, Starship J.J. Green shipmates. I'd love to see you there.

New Taipei City
Taiwan
J.J. Green 2018

Sign up to my reader group for a free ecopy of *Night of Flames*, the prequel to *Space Colony One*, more free books, discounts on new releases, Review Crew invitations and other interesting stuff:

https://jjgreenauthor.com/free-books/

(I won't send spam or pass on your details to a third party.)

ALSO BY J.J. GREEN

STAR MAGE SAGA

SHADOWS OF THE VOID SERIES

*CARRIE HATCHETT, SPACE ADVENTURER
SERIES*

THERE COMES A TIME
A SCIENCE FICTION COLLECTION

LOST TO TOMORROW

DAWN FALCON
A FANTASY COLLECTION